PRAISE FOR ROSEMARY FRIEDMAN

'Delightful and easily read' – *Weekly Scotsman*

'Writes well about human beings' – *Books and Bookmen*

'Accomplished, zestful and invigorating' – *TLS*

'A funny and perceptive book' – *Cosmopolitan*

'A confident, sensitive and marvellously satisfying novel' – *The Times*

'A classic of its kind' – *The Standard*

'Readers will find it as affecting as it is intelligent' – *Financial Times*

'Adroitly and amusingly handled' – *Daily Telegraph*

'An entertaining read' – *Financial Times*

'Highly recommended for the sheer pleasure it gives' – *Literary Review*

'Observant and well composed' – *TLS*

'A pleasing comedy of manners' – *Sunday Telegraph*

'What a story, what a storyteller!' – *Daily Mail*

ABOUT THE AUTHOR

Rosemary Friedman has published 21 novels – which have been widely translated and serialised by the BBC – three works of non-fiction and two children's books. Her short stories have been syndicated worldwide and she has judged many literary prizes. She has written and commissioned screenplays and television scripts in the UK and the US. Her stage plays *Home Truths*, *Change of Heart* and *An Eligible Man* toured major UK venues following their London premières. She lives in London with her husband, psychiatrist and author Dennis Friedman.

THE MAN WHO UNDERSTOOD WOMEN

and other stories

ROSEMARY FRIEDMAN

THE MAN WHO UNDERSTOOD WOMEN

and other stories

ROSEMARY FRIEDMAN

ARCADIA BOOKS

Arcadia Books Ltd
139 Highlever Road
London W10 6PH

www.arcadiabooks.co.uk

First published in the United Kingdom by Arcadia Books 2013

A catalogue record for this book is available from the British Library.

ISBN 978-1-909807-25-9

Typeset in Garamond by MacGuru Ltd
Printed and bound by CPI Group (UK) Ltd., Croydon CR0 4YY

Arcadia Books supports English PEN *www.englishpen.org* and
The Book Trade Charity *http://booktradecharity.wordpress.com*

Arcadia Books distributors are as follows:

in the UK and elsewhere in Europe:
Macmillan Distribution Ltd
Brunel Road
Houndmills
Basingstoke
Hants RG21 6XS

in the USA and Canada:
Dufour Editions
PO Box 7
Chester Springs
PA 19425

in Australia/New Zealand:
NewSouth Books
University of New South Wales
Sydney NSW 2052

in South Africa:
Jacana Media (Pty) Ltd
PO Box 291784
Melville 2109
Johannesburg

For Dennis Friedman,
whose idea it was.

'This is an important book, the critic assumes, because it deals with war. This is an insignificant book, because it deals with the feelings of women in a drawing-room.'

Virginia Woolf

Contents

Acknowledgements

These stories have appeared in:

ADAM International Review, Cosmopolitan, Daily Express, Everywoman, Good Housekeeping, Homes and Gardens, Ladies Home Journal (USA), *Saturday Evening Post* (USA), *Sunday Express Magazine, Woman & Beauty, Woman, Woman's Day, Woman's Own, Woman's Realm, Woman's Journal* and many other publications at home and abroad.

Thanks are due to Shirley Conran, Guy Shapir, Ilsa Yardley, Christie Hickman and Barnaby Spiro.

Foreword

Rosemary Friedman has a wicked ear for dialogue and her stories illustrate fifty years of change in women's circumstances. In them we look back nostalgically at England as it was and at what it has become.

The short stories in this collection give a composite portrait of women and their feelings, as they gradually loosened their corsets and nervously rebelled against centuries of tradition. Little girls are now prepared to fulfil their own dreams and can no longer rely on the arrival of Prince Charming. 'What happened to Cinderella *after* she married her prince?' is more often the question as it becomes clear that marriage is not a woman's only socially acceptable destiny.

Through the imagination of this sensitive author we experience love, joy and happiness, we know what it is to feel sadness and loneliness and see the results of ambition, pride and hubris.

The warmth, kindness, humanity and compassion that shines through Rosemary Friedman's work reveals an author that most of us would like to meet in person, after meeting her in these pages and enjoying her charming views of what I think of as women's Great Escape.

Shirley Conran

Introduction

The master of the short-story, Anton Chekhov, wrote about ordinary people and their survival strategies; he held a mirror up to nature, and – without striving for a climax or a neat resolution – showed that life's most significant moments are often the least dramatic ones, for small things may be small only on the surface: the butter knife in the kitchen – 'a deep cave paved with linoleum' – can be as effective as a pickaxe.

Underplanted like forget-me-nots, among my novels, film scripts, TV episodes and plays, are my self-contained, short stories, which showcase the changes in the lives of Western women over the last half-century. *HouseWife, Good Housekeeping* and *Woman's Realm* are some of the women's magazines in which my stories appeared from 1956 onwards, and those titles are a direct reflection of their readers' place in society.

In the post-war period, working-class women still slaved to make ends meet and put up with multiple pregnancies, while the upper classes hunted and socialised. Middle-class women were kept busy, playing second fiddle to their husbands – if they were lucky enough to have them – and managing their nuclear families; their sons were educated to follow in father's footsteps and their daughters groomed for marriage.

By 1956 women had been enfranchised for over twenty-five years, yet often they voted as directed by their husbands and were far from emancipated. The clientele of Miss Phipps, the librarian protagonist of 'The Magic' (1956) consisted mainly of middle-aged matrons who shopped daily in local high streets and then returned to a suburban home with a neat garden. A woman's life was at the bottom of the excitement scale, so women relied upon novels – often recommended by the librarian – to open the gate to a dream life in which their fantasies were fulfilled.

Yet within thirty years, their daughters would be running hospitals, banks and international businesses. Like Ibsen's Nora, they had struggled successfully to escape from the Doll's House.

In the sixties, a new phenomenon – teenagers – were no longer unpaid apprentices but earned proper wages, and with that came financial independence. British fashion icon, Mary Quant, showed them how to present themselves. Women's magazines now carried advertisements of girls in miniskirts and hot-pants, with sooty eyes and short, sharp haircuts. Role models were pop singers and actors, athletes, hairdressers, photographers and models.

As these teenagers grew up, electronic machinery made housework easier. Women began to enter the workplace, which unleashed a relentless torrent of criticism, and discussion about the exact location of a woman's place.

'A decade later, women wore trouser suits with exaggerated shoulder pads that said, 'Don't you dare', as they became lawyers and politicians, and Margaret Thatcher, who became prime minister in 1979, made the eighties her own.

By the nineties, women MPs were the norm and it had become clear, even to the long-married Maisie ('The Moules Factory', 1998) that her 'days of domestic servitude passed in a bungalow in Burlington, Massachusetts, had hardly amounted to a full life'.

By 2000, independent women did not necessarily believe that marriage was for life. In 'A la Carte' (2010), a divorced primary school teacher, fifty-three-year-old Helen, road tests Dominic, whom she meets through the Internet. She feels empowered by her considered decision – *not* to embark on a new relationship.

While most of the stories portray women, as they began to overturn centuries of tradition, prepared to live fuller lives and to follow their dreams, I could not resist including 'Mea Culpa', (1960) – an *amuse-gueule* or grace note – in which women do not feature at all.

Rosemary Friedman

2013

The Magic

1956

Miss Phipps knew what they said about her in the library. With her eyes cast down and seemingly intent on a list or catalogue she would listen to their conversation.

'Ask her if this is any good,' young Mrs Withers would say to her husband, flicking over the pages of a green-backed novel marked with an 'R' for Romance.

Mr Withers would glance up at Miss Phipps and then move a little closer to his wife. 'Make up your own mind, dear. If the old girl reads at all, I doubt if she reads romance.' They would smile together and then bring the book over to the desk for her to mark neatly with her little rubber stamp.

From behind her desk, where she had to stand on a box because she was so small, Miss Phipps watched her customers. In more ways than one they were her bread and butter and they were a constant source of interest. There was the Colonel, six foot two, with his purple face and his grey, waxed moustache. He came in regularly for the stories of famous battles and famous generals and life in the colonies – you'd think he had had enough – which she put aside for him. While she was removing the ' reserved' label from its metal clip, the Colonel would clear his throat with a rumbling roar and out would come some gallant remark.

Sometimes he'd look down at her, standing there so demurely in her flowered smock, and say, 'Y're such a bit of a thing, m'dear; could pick you up and put you in m'pocket, what!' Or at other times when she knew that his arthritis was bad because it took him so long to remove his gloves, he would look at her sadly and pat her hand. 'Don't work too hard, m'dear, there aren't so many good people in the world.' Then he'd pick up his book and his gold-topped stick, straighten his shoulders and, with the ghost of a once smart salute, make his way back to his service flat and his lonely gas fire.

There was Miss Loveday with her knitted stockings, her head held to one side and her passion for poetry; Dr Thomas who liked to relax with a 'whodunit'; a pair of newly-weds who came in, all moonbound with love, and asked for a good story to read aloud to each other curled together on their sofa.

Once a couple of sixth-formers, from the school round the corner, marched boisterously in, their long striped scarves trailing down their backs, but when they saw Miss Phipps with her neat grey hair pulled tight into its neat grey bun they looked uncertainly at each other and one of them muttered: 'Come on, Thompson, she's probably never even heard of Gerard Manley Hopkins,' and the glass panel quivered in its frame as the door slammed shut behind them.

Tonight the air was light and warm. Looking across the shop, past the skilfully displayed books and out through the window, Miss Phipps noticed that the pavement was dark with people strolling towards the park. Summer would not be long arriving and the busy, winter demand for cosy novels would soon be over. It was just on closing time and only Mrs Graves was still there. As soon as she had chosen her book Miss Phipps would lock up; there was work to be done in her little flat above the shop.

Empty-handed, Mrs Graves came over to the desk. 'Good evening, Miss Phipps,' she said. 'I was looking for another book by Vanessa Chase but I think I've read all you have.'

'There'll be her new one out soon,' Miss Phipps said, and picked up her fat pencil, blue one end and red the other. '*Amber for Love*, it's called, I'll keep it for you, Mrs Graves.'

'If you would, Miss Phipps. She's quite my favourite.'

Miss Phipps shut up the order book with a little thwack. Her eyes twinkled behind her glasses. 'To be perfectly honest,' she said, 'she's mine, too.'

Locking the door behind Mrs Graves and pulling down the blind with 'Closed' printed on the front, Miss Phipps smiled to herself. This was the time of day she liked best. Working quickly and with the agility born of use, she unfolded the dust sheets and unfurled them in the air, watching them sink down sighingly on to the tables of new books that stood in the centre of the shop. When all was tidy and the fat pencil lay neatly on the desk, carefully sharpened for the morning, she switched out the light and climbed the narrow staircase at the back of the shop to her little flat.

There was no one to welcome her in the living room, yet Miss Phipps, as soon as she had opened the door, said, as she always did: 'Hello, my darling, I've had such an interesting day.' As she spoke she looked towards the mantelpiece at a faded sepia photograph in a black frame. The picture was of a young, very handsome man. He was wearing the uniform of an army officer in the First World War and underneath his likeness was the inscription: 'They shall grow not old, as we that are left grow old.'

Miss Phipps put a match to the fire, ready laid in the grate, and kneeling on the rug, watched the growing flames licking up towards the neat spindles of wood. As she watched she thought, as she always allowed herself to think, in this lost moment between her two lives, of The Magic. The magic that began and ended with Captain Albert George Alexander Chase who looked down at her from the mantelpiece.

Miss Phipps, owing to the premature and tragic death of both parents – and this was many, many years ago – had been brought up by an aunt. The aunt, a Christian woman who knew her duty, took the orphan in and cared for her, as the years went by, with large helpings of the Bible and the stodgiest cabinet pudding in the world. Small wonder that when the handsome Captain Chase appeared on the scene in her eighteenth year, her ward lost her head as well as her heart and ran away to Brighton.

It was only a weekend. Two ecstatic days in a topsy-turvy world, then he had, heartbreakingly, gone off to meet his maker in the mud of France and she had returned to grim, silent lips and cabinet pudding.

Two days, among all the days it takes to make fifty-seven years, yet because they were magic days they had been enough. Miss Phipps listened to the wood in the grate crackling and snapping as the flames, now roused, curled angrily round it; but the sound she heard was the low call of seagulls swooping over the pebbled beach at Brighton.

It had been hot, she remembered, very hot. The French windows that looked out over the sea were flung wide open, and they had sunbathed, naked, in the big armchair in the bedroom. She could see the bedroom now with its giant bed between two rows of polished brass knobs; the fern, its edges brown and curling, in the fireplace; the green plush cloth on the table; the rose-patterned china wash-bowl and jug with the third piece to the hideous set in the pedestal cupboard beside the bed.

Two days, and in them he had tried to help her forget the twelve years she had spent in the tall old house – with the Bible but without the love that it taught. He had loved her, cherished her and brushed her long, jet-black hair. In return she had given him all the devotion no one had wanted from her ever since she could remember.

A fussy cascade of notes, sounding the half-hour, reminded Miss Phipps that she had dreamed for long enough. She looked up gratefully at the marble clock on the mantelpiece, which never failed to remind her of the too-swift passage of time. The clock had been presented to her on her fiftieth birthday by the governors of the orphanage to which, for many years, she had devoted all her spare time and money, and to whose small inmates she was known as Aunt Phipps.

The wood was now well alight, and, leaning one hand on the coal box, Miss Phipps got up off her knees. Slivers of pain shot up into her thighs as she straightened her legs. It was only when things like that happened that she remembered she was rising sixty. The magic had kept her mind young but it couldn't do much about wrinkles or rheumatism. Unbuttoning the flowered overall she wore, because she thought it looked the part in the library, she thought about other people's magic. Miss Loveday had her poetry; the Colonel had his memories of an adventurous and colourful career; the schoolboys had the magic of an uncharted future and the newly-weds had each other.

Reflected in the glass front of the bookcase the orange-tipped flames twirled higher up the chimney. Miss Phipps looked at the row of books on the top shelf; they were all by Vanessa Chase. What she had said was true when she told Mrs Graves that she was her favourite author. As she took the cover off her typewriter, which stood on the centre table, Miss Phipps smiled contentedly and thought of the millions of words which, taking her strength from the magic, she had written. She had given them all personality with the combination of the names of the only two people she had ever loved: Vanessa, her mother, and her darling Albert Chase.

The Square

1958

On the hottest of a stifling spell of summer days, Christopher Aldington lost something and found something. What he lost was gone for good but what he found was only a beginning.

Of course, he had known for weeks that Grandfather was dying. Grandfather himself had told him, when the nurse was out of the room, but Christopher had sat silent, embarrassed for the first time by the old man, his friend, and unwilling to believe.

Last night, unable to find a position in which he was cool enough to sleep, he had read his book until his eyes ached, then slipped silently out to the bathroom for a glass of water. He knew that it must be late, very late. Yet downstairs on the lower landing outside his grandfather's room he saw his mother, Aunt Evelyn, Dr Matthews and a strange nurse he hadn't seen before, in whispered consultation. He had gone quickly back to bed, unwilling to know what was going on, and fallen asleep immediately. This morning he had been reluctant to wake up, keeping his eyes tightly shut against the sunlight that spilled over his bed. He heard his mother open the door and by the tone of voice in which she said: 'Christopher, wake up, dear!' he knew that it was all over and that life would never be the same again.

In the stuffy, darkened, blind-drawn dining room he forced himself to eat a piece of toast. Aunt Evelyn was crying and his mother put her arms round her sister and said that it was a ' blessed release'. Christopher looked at her scornfully, but she was too busy comforting Aunt Evelyn to notice. He took the large iron key from the mantelpiece. 'I'm going into the Square,' he said, but his mother didn't even say

'Don't be late for lunch, Christopher'; she was busy with a tiny lace handkerchief.

Coming out of the gloomy hall, he had to stop for a moment on the top step to accustom his eyes to the brilliance. Being Sunday morning the Square was quiet, and the plane trees sheltering the gardens stood, black-green, majestically against a breathless blue sky.

The warm iron gate creaked as he opened it. The seats were occupied by the usual assortment of navy-blue or grey-hatted nannies, rocking their shiny prams or knitting. He walked on until he found one on which there was only a girl in a pink summer dress and white socks. She was sitting at the very end of the seat. Christopher walked to the other end and sat down.

He knew that he had come to say goodbye, that he would never again in the holidays sit in the garden. Everywhere he looked he saw Grandfather and the pain was too great for him to want to come again. Grandfather with his stick in the autumn crunching round the little paths, the red and yellow tight-rolled leaves like cornflakes crackling underfoot; Grandfather with his muffler and galoshes, stepping carefully in the snow, holding tightly to Christopher's arm, fearful of slipping, the trees stark against a winter sky; Grandfather, a lighter step for spring, unearthing the first primrose with his stick, glad that the weather was warm enough to sit for a while. Grandfather, a few weeks ago, a red rose in his buttonhole, ashen-faced, sitting slumped upon the seat while Christopher ran frantically for help.

The girl in the summer dress was swinging her legs; Christopher could see the flash of white socks from the corner of his eye.

Now he was the only man in a household of women. His father had died in an air crash when he was nine, and in the holidays Christopher came home to the tall old house in the Square where he lived with his three small sisters, his mother, Aunt Evelyn and, until today, Grandfather who every holiday greeted him with the same words: 'Thank goodness you've come, Christopher. I'm fed up with all these women.'

Every morning after breakfast he would go into the old man's room and discuss the ailments of the world, or his own particular problems, until Grandfather wanted to get up. When it was time for him to go, Grandfather would let him get as far as the door, then say: 'Christopher, would you like a piece of chocolate?' And Christopher would say: 'Yes please, Grandfather,' and have to go back all the way across the room to get it. Two squares of the same make of chocolate every day that he had been at home since he was five, and now he was fifteen. It was always two squares only and never offered until he had his hand on the doorknob. Today, against his mother's wishes, he had gone into the bedroom to say a last goodbye to his grandfather. The nurse, bustling starchily about, looked at him disapprovingly. Grandfather, it was true, was paler than usual, but looked only as if he were sleeping. There seemed nothing, as he had told his grandson, to be afraid of. At the door, Christopher had found himself hesitating and, meeting the nurse's curious stare, realised that he was waiting, as he had always done, to be called back. 'Christopher, would you like a piece of chocolate?' But it was only in his own head. His grandfather lay peacefully silent, and the nurse said: 'I think you'd better go now.'

He felt something warm and damp on his knees and, looking down, saw to his horror that great teardrops were soaking through his trousers and making dark patches on the grey flannel. He reached for his handkerchief but found nothing except a Victorian half-crown, his talisman, and a piece of string. The feet in the white socks shuffled nearer and soon a fold of pink cotton lay across his knee.

Nothing was said but he had to look up. There was no choice but to accept the proffered handkerchief. Accustomed to the continual baiting of his sisters, he waited for the caustic comment. After all, tears in a fifteen-year-old boy could provide the material for a whole afternoon's entertainment. There was no comment. Christopher dabbed at his eyes and his trousers and then handed back the little white square. The eyes above the pink cotton were large and black. He felt a strange, drowning sensation and it was a few minutes before he was able to look away.

'I've seen you here lots of times,' she said.

'I've never seen you.'

'I know, you were always talking to your grandfather.'

'I shan't be any more.'

'Is that why you were crying?'

Christopher nodded.

'It's very sad,' the girl said, 'but beautiful. I know because of my granny. He was a nice old man, wasn't he ?'

'He was my friend,' Christopher said. 'I told him everything.'

'What was that pink newspaper you were always reading?'

'The *Financial Times*. Grandfather taught me all about shares and used to ask my advice. Sometimes he even took it.'

'What else did he teach you?'

Christopher considered. It was a difficult question. They had discussed together everything from Horace's Odes, Grandfather disagreeing with his pronunciation, to modern youth, which Grandfather, contrary to most of his generation, considered no worse than his own, only different. Sometimes they didn't talk at all. The old man would bury his nose in *The Times* leaders, and Christopher would think about whatever happened to be on his mind. At times they both just sat, silent. But it was always a restful, amicable silence, a silence of perfect understanding.

On wet days they stayed at home and played Scrabble.

Christopher had been ten points in the lead in their fierce contest, which carried on from one holiday to the next, when Grandfather had played his last game. He'd never again find such a keen opponent. He let his mind slip back over the years but could think of not one thing his grandfather had actually taught him.

He only knew that because of Grandfather he would always be tolerant and true to himself. 'He taught me to be a man,' Christopher said, and waited for the girl to ask him what he meant. They always did. It was irritating.

She said: 'You're going to miss him.'

Christopher sighed. He felt a hand, cool and firm, close over his.

'It's always worse at first,' she said, 'like when you fall over.'

He thought her awfully sensible for a girl and liked the feel of her hand on his.

They talked. About television, books, their families and finally, at first shyly, themselves. Each laid out for the other to see, what they thought lay before them, sure that in the sunlight of the garden their dreams would not be trodden upon. Several times Christopher glanced quickly at the dainty profile, the gently tilted nose, the inky lashes, the pale soft lips. He liked it best when she turned right round to face him and he was caught in the level stare of her enormous eyes. He was unaware that the morning had passed. When he looked round the garden there was not a nannie or a pram to be seen. The sun was high in the sky. Guiltily, he thought that, for the past little while, Grandfather had been out of his thoughts.

'I'd better go back for lunch,' he said.

'Me too.' She stood up and shook out the folds of the pink dress. Side by side they walked along the path. At the gate he held it open so that she could go first. She lived at the other side of the Square. 'I go back to school next week,' she said.

'So do I.'

'I shall probably be in the garden in the mornings until then.'

Christopher remembered his promise to himself never to sit in the Square again. He looked at the girl, almost as tall as himself, graceful, with one foot on the first step, her long hair shading her face, a watercolour, black and pink, except for the face, pale.

'I shall probably be there myself,' he said and, turning, walked back across the shimmering, silent Square to the waiting house where the blinds were drawn, but not against the sun.

No Christmas Roses

1958

It started, like a bad play, with the ringing of the telephone.

In the spacious, centrally heated flat, high above the traffic and with a clear view over the park, everything was ready for Christmas. The Georgian furniture, each piece exactly right, stood elegantly polished; greetings cards and messages from all over the world were piled neatly on a silver salver; the piano had been tuned and the Aubusson rugs shampooed; in the kitchen, quietly, confidently, Maxine and Odile from Jamaica were making the early preparations for the two dinner parties and the one cocktail party that had been arranged.

Fleur herself, satisfied that nothing had been forgotten and that all was going exactly as she had planned it should, was resting with her shoes off and her legs up on the pale gold damask sofa, reading beauty hints for the over-forties in a shiny magazine. Her hair had been done, her nails manicured, and she had already arranged the flowers for the table decorations. Nothing had been left until the last minute, for today was Christmas Eve.

The telephone was by her side and its ringing shattered the excited silence of waiting for Christmas.

It was a Continental call, and Fleur sat up, the magazine sliding to the floor, as she waited to be connected with Paris.

'Mummy?' The voice was faint, the line crackling.

'Noelle! How are you, darling?'

'I'm fine. Mummy, I'm coming home for Christmas.'

'Oh, Noelle, that makes everything perfect. I shall keep it as a surprise for Daddy. What time do you arrive? I'll come to meet you.'

'There's no need. I'm at the airport now, waiting for the plane. And Mummy ...'

'Yes, pet?'

'Mummy, I'm bringing someone ...'

'That's fine, darling; the spare bed's made up. What a wonderful Christmas we'll all have together. Who is it?'

'Mummy, it's Graham.'

'Graham?'

'It's Graham I'm bringing home. Graham Gardner. We want to get married.'

Fleur held the telephone receiver away from her a little and stared at it. Then she said, 'Noelle, darling, what on earth are you talking about?'

'Graham's here in Paris. He's been here ages. He has a wonderful job in Kenya, starting after Christmas. I love him and we want to get married.'

Fleur blinked at the Christmas roses in the silver vase on the mantelpiece and said nothing.

'Mummy, are you there?'

'Noelle. Noelle, dear, you must come home at once. We'll have a talk. I should never have let you go. We can discuss everything with Daddy. Of course you can't get married, not for ages. Don't worry, dear. Just come straight home. We'll sort everything out. It's so difficult with this crackly phone ...'

'And it's all right to bring Graham?'

Fleur thought. 'Yes,' she said. 'I think Graham had better come with you.'

When Noelle had rung off, Fleur replaced the receiver and put on her shoes. There was a knock at the door.

'Come in.'

A head appeared. 'The pineapple au kirsch in the silver or the crystal, madame?'

'Not now, Odile.' Fleur waved her hand. 'The silver ... no, the crystal. Anything you like; don't worry me.'

She dialled the number of the gallery where Simon had an exhibition of his paintings, and waited for what seemed far too long while they tried to find him. When he finally came to the phone, he listened carefully to what she had to say. Then he said, 'I've always rather liked Graham. He's a good chap.'

'Simon, do be sensible; she's talking about marrying him and going to Kenya or some such place. We shall have to be absolutely firm, Simon, without being too unkind. What time will you be home?'

'Not before eight. I have to see that everything's properly covered.'

'Try to be earlier. Noelle always listens to you. And do remember, Simon, she's only a child.'

'Of course,' Simon said, 'it's out of the question. Don't worry, my darling. See you later.'

From across the park, drowning the noise of the traffic, Christmas bells began to ring. Fleur shut the window to keep out the noise so that she could think. Sitting tensely now on the very edge of the sofa, she lit a cigarette and remembered that it had been the week before Christmas that Noelle was born. But then there had been no Aubusson, no gold damask and no Christmas roses.

Noelle had been born in Paris, in a room at the very top of a tall old house on the Left Bank. It was snowing. Large flakes drifted down from an uncompromising sky, covered the Ile de la Cité and settled on the rich apartments of the Avenue Foch and the blank-eyed dwellings of Montparnasse with silent impartiality until everything was white and frozen. There was no escape from the cold. They had an oil stove that did little or nothing to heat the vast, draughty room, which was bedroom, living room, dining room, nursery and studio, and whose rent they could barely afford to pay.

It was the coldest Christmas Fleur had ever known, and her first away from the comfortable home where she had been born. Looking back, she was unable to feel the draught that swept day and night through the shut windows and under the door, or the icy chill of the floorboards beneath her bare feet, as she slipped reluctantly out of a warm bed at the first thin, pathetic wail of her week-old baby. On Christmas Eve, Noelle, born a week early, lay sleeping in her crib. Fleur, in layers of jumpers, with her dressing gown topping the lot, watched from the window, searching the early twilight for Simon. It was Christmas, but there was only ragôut for dinner, and there would be no presents. In Paris, city of dreams, artists were two a penny. Fleur's parents, unwilling to see their daughter living in one room, had been helpless in the face of Simon's pride.

When he came, his stiff, cold fingers fumbling with the doorknob, he was smiling and there were parcels in his arms.

'I sold a picture, Fleur. They want more!'

She kissed him, brushed the snow from his hair and opened the wine he had bought and the babas au rhum which would turn the dinner into Christmas. Little Noelle slept, and they sat huddled together round the stove, stiff with cold but oblivious with happiness.

One parcel was yet unopened and Fleur could still remember the thrill of her first Christmas present from Simon, the cheap red slippers with the silky pompoms to keep her feet warm when she got out to see to the baby in the night. That Christmas Eve had been the first rung of the ladder and they had never looked back. Today everyone had heard of Simon Bellamy, and he often joked that he couldn't afford to buy his own pictures. After Noelle, there had been no more babies, but Fleur saw to it that she grew up unspoiled. When she'd left school, Fleur had sent her to Paris for a year to learn the language, and next year she planned a big coming-out dance for her before she went up to Cambridge. As for Graham, the son of good friends of theirs, the Gardners, she had nothing against the boy, but the idea of Noelle marrying him, before she had really had a chance to meet anybody else, was quite fantastic. She tried to recollect what he had taken up. Photography or something, she thought, but couldn't quite remember. Fleur was a great planner and the plans she had made for Noelle were the biggest and best of them all. They did not include marriage for many years to come.

The peace of waiting for Christmas had melted in the heavy, centrally heated atmosphere. Fleur inspected the already tidy flat, told Odile that there would be two extra for dinner, put soap in the guest bathroom. She looked again at her present for Simon – a slim gold pencil with his initials on it – and wondered whether he had remembered about the sapphire pendant from Cartier. She was sure he had.

They always adhered to the same routine. Simon was the most generous husband in the world but, like all men, he hated shopping. A few weeks before Christmas or her birthday was due Fleur would say casually, 'I saw the most wonderful clips at Asprey's. They match my ruby set and they're keeping them for me ...' or 'My crocodile handbag is absolutely finished and I saw exactly the one I wanted at ...' and she knew that when the time came Simon would solemnly present her with the gift she had chosen herself. There seemed too many hours until Noelle was due to arrive, and she wished Simon were home so that they could agree on what they were to say to her without upsetting her too much.

Fleur was in the bathroom putting on her mascara when Noelle arrived. She looked even younger than she was, her face flushed with excitement above the fur collar of her coat and her dark hair shining.

When she had hugged her, inhaling the cold air clinging to Noelle, Fleur said, 'Now tell me all about it, darling.'

Noelle needed no encouragement. Graham was a journalist. He had been offered a wonderful job as a foreign correspondent in Kenya. They were in love. They wanted to get married. It was as simple as that.

'How long has this been going on?' Fleur said.

'About three months. Ever since Graham's been in Paris.'

'You never mentioned him in your letters to us.'

'We thought there was time. We didn't know this job was going to crop up.'

Noelle sat on the edge of the bath. 'Mummy,' she said, and her face was serious. 'I know what you're going to say about being too young. But I'm not too young, and although one part of me doesn't want to leave you and Daddy and go so far away, Graham and I love each other, and that's all there is to it. I'm sorry to spring it on you like this, but it just couldn't be helped.'

'How much does he earn? How will you live?'

'We'll manage.'

'Manage!' Fleur thought of the life Noelle had led. Her bedroom with everything a girl could want, her wardrobe, expensive schools, riding lessons, violin lessons, dancing lessons, skating lessons.

'Have you thought,' Fleur said, carefully outlining her brows with a pencil, 'that things might not be just as you've been used to? The life abroad; the heat ...? It may all sound very romantic and adventurous, but I'm older than you, darling, and ...'

Noelle stood up and she was no longer smiling. 'I don't think you quite understand, Mummy. I love Graham and I don't care where he goes – I'm going with him. I want you to understand.'

Fleur looked at her daughter's determined face in the mirror.

Her own was equally determined. 'I'm sorry, Noelle,' she said, 'it's quite out of the question.'

Noelle turned and left the room.

It was after eight o'clock and still Simon didn't come. The atmosphere was getting unbearable. Fleur had exchanged all the pleasantries she could think of with Graham and he sat, his long legs jutting awkwardly, on the spindly chair by the window, holding his drink.

Fleur could understand Noelle's falling for him. He was tall, good-looking and had deep brown eyes, which almost every moment sought her daughter's blue ones. 'Noelle,' she wanted to say, looking at her daughter, beautiful in midnight-blue velvet, 'you have it all before you. Please, please, don't throw everything away.'

She thought she could stand it no longer when at last she heard Simon's key in the door. He looked tired in his distinguished way. He kissed her, hugged Noelle and shook hands with Graham.

'It's started to snow,' he said. 'Sorry to keep you all from dinner. I must just have a drink, then I'll be ready.'

Fleur gave him a drink. 'You look tired, darling.'

'I shall have a rest over Christmas. Noelle, you'll find some presents on the hall table.'

Noelle brought in three parcels. Fleur looked for the long slim box she expected from Cartier. It was a family tradition to open their presents on Christmas Eve.

Noelle hesitated. 'Which is Mummy's?'

'The large oblong one.'

Fleur looked at Simon, but he was busy with his drink.

Puzzled, she undid the string, then the paper, then slowly took the lid off the shiny, oblong, white box. From what seemed miles away she heard Noelle exclaiming excitedly over a bracelet, and Graham thanking Simon politely for his tie.

She took her box over to the window where the curtains were not yet drawn, and watched the snowflakes drifting softly through the darkness. She saw them fall not on to the park but, as though it were yesterday, on the corner patisserie, the naked chestnut trees, the muddy waters of the Seine.

'Mummy, what have you got?' Noelle's voice was insistent.

Slowly Fleur drew from the box the shoddy scarlet slippers, their pompoms already damp with tears.

Not understanding, Noelle looked from her mother to her father, trying to interpret the look that passed between them.

Fleur bundled the slippers back into the tissue paper.

'Thank you, Simon darling,' she said. 'They're just what I needed. Now do let's have dinner. If you two are going to get married, we shall have a great deal to discuss.'

A View to Marriage

1958

Abbie MacFarlane was a spinster for the simple reason that no man had asked her to marry him. She was quite pretty, although inclined to be a little stand-offish; had a lively mind and beautiful manners. The most important thing about her, in her own opinion and that of her friends, was that she was twenty-seven.

Beryl, married to an engineer and with three children, said that she was too reserved and frightened the men away. Mavis, wife of a brilliant archaeologist, advised her to appear more helpless and less intelligent.

Abbie herself gave the matter a good deal of thought. She was happy in her job, happy at home, where she lived with her parents, but realised that time was getting on, and that she had no desire to progress, with the years, from a young spinster to an old one. Abbie was basically a loving girl and, although she had never tried it, believed marriage to be a good idea.

She had never been short of boyfriends. At eighteen she

had met them at parties and dances, gone out with them a few times then lost them in the crowd; at twenty she had met them at home and abroad, and stood by while they married her girlfriends.

After twenty-one she found them in the interesting places to which her work took her, and left them abruptly when they began to tell her their wives didn't understand them. Recently she had found them thrust upon her in an embarrassing though well-meaning way, and this was a situation she was determined to end. Her resolve was strengthened when the telephone rang late one night as she was about to get into bed. It was Marguerite, bubbling over with happiness because she was going to have a baby.

'Darling,' she said, 'we're having our last fling while I can still see my feet. Saturday at eight, only about twenty, cheese and wine. You will come, won't you?'

'What's he like?' Abbie said.

'Who?'

'The man you want me to meet.'

'Don't be ridiculous,' Marguerite said. 'It's just some friends of Hugo's and mine. I expect you'll know nearly everyone. You'll come?'

'Yes,' Abbie said, 'I'll come.'

Marguerite's denial had not for one moment deceived her. She recognised the tone of voice too well. The man she was invited to meet was usually somebody's cousin from Australia or long-lost schoolfriend or sister-in-law's brother-in-law.

He was the survivor of an unhappy marriage and was now

looking for the right girl – what about Abbie? Or he had been too busy previously working on a thesis to meet any girls – Abbie's intelligent; what about Abbie? Or else there just didn't seem to be any girls good enough in Bonga-Bonga or Bangor or wherever he happened to come from – don't you think that he'd be ideal for Abbie?

He was usually planted with dreadful cunning in the thick of somebody's cocktail party, tennis afternoon or evening of serious music; once, even, he had been hidden among the daddies at a children's party. No matter how neatly he was wrapped up, however, Abbie could spot him immediately. Always he knew, and knew that she knew, why they had been introduced.

Occasionally, she admitted, she had had fun for a few weeks after one of these meetings; more often than not, though, she found that she had nothing at all in common with the man she had been brought along to meet, and might just as well have spent the evening making polite remarks to the mantelpiece.

When she agreed to go to Marguerite's cheese and wine evening there was the light of battle shining in her eyes.

The party was well under way when she arrived, a little later than she had intended, but with the aid of her private radar she spotted him immediately. Not that it was very difficult, for apart from the tall young man and a pretty girl in leopard trousers dancing together with expert abandon, she had met everyone else before.

As was the usual procedure, Marguerite introduced Abbie to the young man last.

She was then able to say: 'You must excuse me, darlings, I have to go and do things in the kitchen. Abbie's in advertising, Charles; I'm sure you'll find heaps to talk about.'

Abbie waited for him to say: 'Can I get you something to drink?'

'Can I get you a drink?' he said.

She sipped her wine cocktail and waited for the inevitable discussion on her name.

'Did Marguerite say your name was Abbie?' he said.

'Yes. Short for Abigail.'

They agreed it was old-fashioned, rarely encountered now-adays. They discussed his job, her job, holidays abroad, the new films.

Then he said: 'How do you come to be here? Are you a friend of Marguerite or Hugo or both?'

She replied: 'You know perfectly well why I'm here, don't you? Marguerite introduced us with a view to our getting married.'

His face remained serious. He was good-looking in a slightly rugged way; middle thirties, Abbie guessed. He had an imperious air, which was rather attractive. Abbie could imagine him directing some big project deep in the wilds of Africa.

'Interesting,' he said, and although his expression remained serious she detected a glimmer of humour in his eyes and felt that her direct and unusual approach had perhaps cleared the air.

'Frankly, I find it most embarrassing,' she said. 'I know that people mean well when they ask me along to meet the only unattached man they know but they don't take the slightest trouble to find out whether we would have anything in common at all. Take tonight for instance,' Abbie went on, 'I suppose Marguerite said to herself: "Charles is a nice, sensible chap, about the right age, tall, intelligent; we'll introduce him to Abbie. Mustn't make it too obvious, of course; we'll have a party; there are a few people we have to ask back, anyway." So here we are, thrust together simply because we both happen to be unmarried.'

'So?' Charles said.

'So I'm tired of it!' Abbie said. 'I'm tired of being thrown at everybody's unattached male relations. Where do you come from, by the way? Bonga-Bonga?'

'Holland Park,' Charles said, 'on the Central Line.' And this time the twinkle in his eyes was unmistakable.

Abbie suddenly felt relaxed and happy. 'Well, that makes a change,' she said. 'You won't want to tell me how the natives wear rings in their noses or how many sundowners you had on the other side of the world.'

'No, we don't go in for that sort of thing in Holland Park,' he said.

'I expect you have exactly the same trouble as I do,' Abbie said. 'Wherever you go, your married friends probably dangle bachelor girls under your nose. I'm sure they simply don't care whether you like them tall, short, fair or dark; they'll put them all on the hook and hope that one day you'll bite.'

Charles looked enigmatic. 'Let me get you another drink,' he said.

Abbie held out her glass. Marguerite swept in through the door with reinforcements of wine.

'Come on, everyone,' she said, 'don't be shy.'

Abbie finished her second drink and Charles excused himself to help Hugo bring in some chairs. Abbie found herself swept up in a group of old friends. After supper Charles stayed at the other end of the room. Feeling suddenly unaccountably flat, Abbie went to fetch her coat.

Marguerite was in the kitchen and turned to kiss her. 'I'm sorry, darling, if you haven't enjoyed it. I really asked you to meet Hugo's cousin from New Zealand but he had to go away on business.'

'I thought you asked me for Charles,' Abbie said.

'Charles?' Marguerite said. 'Darling, Charles has just got engaged. Didn't he tell you?'

Abbie slowly buttoned her coat. 'I don't think I gave him a chance,' she said. 'Who's his fiancée?'

'The pretty girl,' Marguerite said. 'The one in the leopard-skin pants.'

Abbie's cheeks were still burning when she got home. Never in her life had she felt so small, so stupid.

During the next months Abbie kept away from Marguerite and Hugo. In fact she kept away from almost everyone. She was convinced that if ever she met Charles again – perhaps now married to the girl in the leopard-skin pants – she would pass out on the spot. The mere mention of Holland Park was sufficient to upset her for days.

When Marguerite's baby was born and Abbie was asked

to be godmother, she was unwilling to offend her friend by refusing. She bought a silver mug and presented herself at the christening.

When she caught sight of Charles in the church, she wondered whether she would be able to get through the afternoon. Of the leopard-skin pants there was no sign.

At the tea afterwards Abbie admired the baby, a dear little girl with Marguerite's eyes and Hugo's chin, chatted to everyone she knew and kept well away from Charles. She escaped as early as possible and, running down the garden path, whipped off her hat.

At the gate a car waited, the door open. An arm reached out and pulled her in.

'What on earth are you doing?' she said, shutting the door hurriedly, as Charles, his face impassive, drove off down the road. 'And where's your fiancée?'

'I'm a nice, sensible chap, tall, intelligent,' he said, taking a corner too fast, 'and I have no fiancée.'

Abbie held on to the door handle. 'What happened to the girl in the leopard-skin pants?'

'She decided she'd like her freedom for a few years more. And don't hang on to the door handle.'

Abbie let go the handle. 'And where are you taking me?'

'Holland Park,' he said firmly. 'With a view to marriage.'

Thank You for Everything

1958

Hubert Wilson, impeccably dressed, sixty-five but looking younger, held out a penny and a halfpenny to the conductor. About to turn the little handle smartly on his ticket machine, the conductor stopped and stared at him.

''Ow long since you bin on a bus, mate?' he said.

Hubert thought. Eight, nine, possibly ten years. He opened his mouth.

'Where yer going?' the conductor said.

'To the park.'

'Frippence to the park. Frippence is the cheapest 'nless yer under fourteen.' He zipped the handle round, tore off the length of flimsy paper and handed it to Hubert.

The two women on the opposite seat, clutching shopping bags to their bosoms, exchanged glances. Hubert was upset. He opened his newspaper.

It was all upsetting. For the first time in fifty years he had nothing in the world to do. Yesterday he had been Hubert

Wilson, head of 'Wilson & Sons', sitting in his pine-panelled office, Dictaphone at his elbow, directing a worldwide organisation. Today he was nobody: Hubert Wilson, man in the street, butt for bus conductors. He had been retired for less than twenty-four hours and already it was making him feel quite ill.

That it was not unjust, Hubert, who was a just man, understood. His three sons, fine men all of them, were perfectly capable of running the business between them. He knew also that they had meant it well and, backed up by his wife, had succeeded in doing him what they considered a good turn. Yesterday, on his sixty-fifth birthday, they had made him retire. They presented a number of irrefutable arguments: he had worked hard for fifty years and was entitled to some relaxation; he had sufficient money not to have to lower his living standards one jot; the business would continue to flourish equally well without him; he would at long last be able to spend more time with his wife. They were faultless reasons, all of them. All the time, though, while his retirement was under family discussion, Hubert had felt unhappy, vaguely uncomfortable. It wasn't until this morning that he had understood why. They had taken everything away and given him nothing back. They had relieved him of twelve crowded hours and left him with as many interminably long, empty ones. It was unfair and it had upset him.

He would be able to spend more time with his wife! That had come unstuck at the first touch.

'Muriel,' he had said at breakfast, which, from habit, he

could not help eating hurriedly, 'would you like me to take you out somewhere today? '

Muriel, drinking coffee in her quilted, peach-satin house-coat, had looked surprised. 'Hubert dear, it's the Bazaar. I promised to be on Fancy Goods until lunch; then I'm meeting Annabel at Fortnum's to help her with a rug for the nursery. I've got my hair at three and then I promised Michel faithfully I'd go for a fitting today, so you see ...'

'It doesn't matter.'

'I suppose you could come to the Bazaar,' she said doubtfully. 'But it will be mostly women.'

'Don't worry. I'll find something to do.'

'It's a lovely day,' Muriel said, handing it to him like a consolation prize.

He looked out of the window at the tops of the trees washed with sunlight.

'Yes. It's a lovely day.'

Like a small boy on whom she had taken pity, Muriel had given him an errand to do. He was to go to the hand-knitted woollies shop that she patronised and enquire whether the pram-sets she had ordered for their twin grandsons had arrived. It had been a horrible experience. The girl in the shop had called him 'dear' before he explained who he was and she had gone to fetch 'Madam'; with Madam he had had to enter into an embarrassing discussion about the babies' latest developments; the pram-sets were not ready. Fed up, he had taken the bus for the park, only to be made a laughing stock by the conductor.

Hubert realised that he was out of touch. But it was hardly his fault. If he wanted any shopping done, his secretary had always done it, as she wrote his letters, arranged his travels, booked his theatre seats. If he wanted to go anywhere, he sent for his car and chauffeur. How was he supposed to know it now cost threepence to the park?

In the park he scrutinised the ducks, nodded approvingly at the neat rows of dahlias and looked at his watch. It was still only half-past ten. He felt he had been up for hours and was as weary as if he had done a day's work. What did other retired men do? He looked about him. Nannies with prams, a few small children feeding the ducks, a tramp with a long, dirty-looking beard, muttering as he walked. The only able-bodied man appeared to be the park-keeper locking up his hut.

He sat down on a bench. It wasn't kind and, what was more, he wouldn't be able to stand it. The inactivity would kill him. He had heard of it happening. It was not even as if his health was bad, or his faculties were failing, or his business acumen. He was sixty-five, it was true, but he had never felt better. Suddenly he came to a decision. He was going to the office and would tell the boys that he had changed his mind. He was going back to his desk and would review the situation in ten years' time when he might begin to be feeling his age; five if they liked, anything at all! But he must get back to work. Pleased to have come to a decision, he stood up.

'Oh, please don't move! Please.'

Hubert looked round. The voice had come from a girl, a

modern girl, wearing long black trousers and her hair tied back in a ponytail. Her hands were black from the charcoal with which she had been sketching him.

'I'm awfully sorry,' she said, 'but I had practically finished. Couldn't you sit down again just for five minutes? It's a lovely day,' she pleaded. Hubert sat down.

'Would you like to see it?' the girl asked, after a while. She handed her sketchblock to Hubert.

With a few black lines she had drawn a man staring into space; a man with lifeless eyes; an aimless, empty man who looked older than his years; an unhappy man.

He handed it back.

'It's good. Very good. I wish I could draw.' There was nothing he knew how to do except to run his business.

'Anyone can draw,' she said, 'but first they have to learn to see.'

'How do you mean?' he said.

'Well,' she was packing her papers into an old canvas satchel and fastening her tin of broken charcoal sticks with an elastic band, 'you've got to look with more than your eyes. You have to put your heart into it.'

He waited for her to go on. She was very young but self-assured.

'When I was drawing you,' she said, 'I saw more than a man with grey hair, an expensive overcoat, a pearl tiepin, and hand-made, recently polished shoes. I saw a man with a look in his eyes as if he was lost – didn't know where to go. I saw money in the bank, an elegant wife in an elegant home. I saw a pure silk dressing gown with a monogram, a dressing room, Mediterranean cruises ...'

'Stop,' Hubert said. 'It's uncanny.'

'It's not,' she said. 'It's merely a matter of training oneself. I tried to put all that I saw into my picture.'

'And was that all you saw? ' Hubert said. ' The shoes, the dressing gown ...?'

'I looked for happiness,' she said carefully. 'But it wasn't there.'

'You should have come a week ago,' Hubert said, and sighed, then pulled himself together. 'So you really think,' he asked, interested, 'that if I learned to see, really see, I too could learn to draw, to paint perhaps?' It crossed his mind that here might be something he could do if they really wouldn't let him go back to the business.

'Why not?'

'How do I start?'

'Turn round,' she said, 'and look at me.'

Hubert turned sideways on the bench and looked at the girl. He had a granddaughter of her age. She came closer and, raising her chin, looked into his face.

'Tell me what you see.'

Hubert was embarrassed. She was pretty. One of the prettiest girls he had seen. He waved his arms vaguely.

'Hair,' he said. 'Hair. And eyes. Long eyelashes.'

'All right,' she said. 'We'll start with that. Describe in your own words my hair, my eyes, my lashes. Tell me what they look like to you.'

Hubert looked at her amber hair, soft and gleaming, drawn back from her face.

'Moonlight,' he said.

'That's good. And the eyes?'

It wasn't difficult. He remembered them growing in the garden beneath the trees when he had been a boy.

'Violets,' he said firmly.

They smiled at him. She closed her eyes and the unbelievably long black lashes lay straight against her smooth cream cheeks.

'Park railings!' he said.

She opened her eyes and laughed. 'You're wonderful.' Hubert laughed too. He was enjoying himself.

'If you keep on at this rate,' she said, 'you'll very soon be able to take one long look at me and say to yourself: 'Eighteen, art school, bedsitter in Bayswater, engaged to be married.' She waved the tiny stone on her left hand. 'Lively disposition, flat broke.' She looked at him, not smiling now. There was something very sweet about her face.

'Why are you unhappy?' she asked.

'Because I retired from business yesterday and I've nothing to do. I'm not used to it.'

'Are you rich?'

He nodded.

'Not a care in the world,' she said incredulously, 'and plenty of money. Good-looking, too.'

He smiled at her youth. 'What would you do? In my position.'

She took a deep breath and stared with her violet eyes towards the lake where a white swan glided silently by.

'I'd go to Rome,' she said, almost reverently, 'and I'd look at the achievements of men who lived and died for their art. I'd stand in the Borghese Gallery before Pauline and her golden apple and stroke her gown to see if it was really marble; and I'd look upwards at the ceiling to which Michelangelo gave years of his life, working under the most trying conditions, regardless of himself, to leave something of his greatness to posterity. I'd look at all the wonder and the splendour and the majesty of art, which knew nothing of pleasing society but was an expression of the very soul of man. And I would probably cry.'

Hubert watched the violet eyes – gazing at the lake but, seeing the Sistine Chapel, fill with tears – and reached for his handkerchief. It wasn't necessary because just then she smiled, and he almost looked for the rainbow.

'And when I wasn't doing that,' she said, 'I'd ride on the buses with the natives, breathing in the garlic, pushing back when I was pushed. I'd eat tagliatelle in the trattorias, where the menu would be written in ink on a piece of cardboard, and see moonlight silhouette the Colosseum; I'd put on my best dress and watch the smart women meet their lovers in the Via Veneto and at night dream by the fountain in the Barberini.'

Hubert thought of the countless holidays he and Muriel had taken: the luxury cruises with the deluxe cabins on A deck; the best hotels in Monte Carlo, Paris, New York, where the maîtres d'hôtel knew how Muriel liked her steak (two-thirds cooked) and that he always had two boiled eggs for breakfast. Pushing on the buses, the girl had said, the menu written in ink; it might be interesting but ...

' I don't think my wife ...' he began doubtfully.

' Of course, you don't have to rough it,' she said. 'It isn't necessary, and you're too old ...'

Hubert winced.

'... But I bet you've never even looked when you've travelled around. Not really looked. Have you? Take Paris,' she said. 'I've been there once.'

Hubert thought of Paris. All he could call to mind was the inside of Maxim's and the suite they always had at their hotel.

'Have you ever wanted to paint the children on a Sunday morning in the Parc Monceau? Listened to the roadsweeper's brush against the cobbles as he swept the water from the early morning gutters? Felt the sadness of the Rive Gauche or watched the sunlight in the Champs Elysées sprinkle the tops of the cars with diamonds?'

He couldn't in all honesty say he had, but he was suddenly excited. The girl made him feel that he hadn't perhaps done everything, seen everything. She made him feel, in fact, as if he, Hubert Wilson, widely travelled, rich in worldly goods, was a small child standing naked before an undiscovered world.

The church clock struck one sombre note. He waited for the others. 'Good Lord,' he said. 'It can't be one o'clock!'

The girl laughed. 'It is.'

'Come and have lunch,' Hubert said, wondering for a moment what Muriel would think, then not caring. 'I'll take you to the Ritz.'

She laughed. Her teeth were white, he thought, then checked himself. Not white. Like ... well, like pearls; small, even pearls.

She showed him her hand, black from the charcoal and shook her ponytail. 'You're awfully sweet, but I'm sure they wouldn't welcome me at the Ritz.'

He was determined not to let her go.

They had lunch at a coffee bar where it was he, in his too well-cut overcoat and his pearl tiepin, and not the girl with her trousers and her suede jacket, who looked out of place. She taught him to see that the bearded man in the corner was waiting for his girlfriend because every time the door opened his eyes grew wide, expectant, then disappointed, sad again, and that the waitress snapped at them because in all probability her feet hurt. Hubert had never, ever, considered such matters.

In the afternoon they wandered round London. She laughed because he wasn't used to strolling in the streets and got cross when people bumped into him. She showed him a woodcut in a shop window, a patch of sunlight on a street corner, a Titian in the National Gallery. He bought her an ice-cream cornet and, because she insisted, ate one furtively himself.

Before he realised it, it was five o'clock. She had to meet her fiancé and he had to go home. She gave him her address, which he asked for and, lifting her face to his, thanked him for her lunch and tea.

He dropped a kiss on the smooth forehead, then watched her disappear in her flat-heeled shoes, straight-backed, into the tube station.

Hubert went home.

The next day he got out of bed with the same sense of urgency as he had had before his retirement. Feeling like a naughty schoolboy, and as young, he kissed Muriel goodbye. He stopped at a stationer's where he bought pencils and a drawing block, then took a bus for the park.

'Lovely mornin'!' the conductor said, taking his threepenny piece.

'Lovely,' Hubert said confidently, and smiled. He even hummed a little tune.

In the park he drew a small child with eyes like black diamonds, a nannie with a hatchet face, and a boat. When he turned to the dahlias and noticed for the first time that they were royal scarlet or tender blushing apricot, he wished he had paints.

At lunchtime he thought about the Ritz, his club, the office. He had lunch in a coffee bar.

On the way back to the park he stopped at a flower shop.

'Yes, sir?' the lady in the floral overall asked. She had a nervous tic. He wondered what was worrying her.

'Some flowers for a young lady.' He looked round the shop, the tall roses, carnations, orchids. None of them seemed right. Then he saw them in a corner, just as he had remembered them as a boy. They were the exact colour of her eyes beneath the hair that was moonlight.

'I'll have those,' he said, pointing, 'and I want them sent right away.'

'Violets, sir?' the woman said.

He understood that they would hardly cover the cost of

transport to the bedsitter in Bayswater. He ordered two dozen of the best roses to be sent to Muriel. Red, to contrast with their French-grey walls. He wrote out two cards, paid the bill and went back to the park.

By the time the light began to fail, the nannies had taken their babies home to bed and the scarlet dahlias were turned almost to black, his sketchbook was full. The drawings were atrocious, barely recognisable, in fact, but Hubert was happy. He had seen a child's ribbon fly as she bowled a hoop, two lovers kiss, a young tree bent by the wind. He hoped that tomorrow it wouldn't rain.

In the drawing room at home the drinks were ready on the silver tray. He had just poured one for himself when Muriel came in. He looked at her, puzzled, then thought that perhaps it was because of his newly opened eyes. He saw for the first time that her hair was like silver smoke, her skin delicate as the petals of a pale rose, and her eyes the same blue, he could almost swear, as the summer sky.

But perhaps she was different. She was looking at him strangely.

She came towards him.

'Hubert,' she said, and her voice was softer, gentler, 'you sent me violets!'

He followed her eyes towards the mantelpiece. There, in a tiny vase, against the French-grey walls, were the violets he had sent the girl. Taking his drink with him he went over. She had propped the card behind them. He picked it up. 'For your kindness, sweetness and patience,' he read.

'You don't know how happy you've made me,' Muriel said. 'All the years that you've been sending me flowers, or rather your secretary has. The roses, the orchids, whatever was out of season, regardless of cost ... or thought. These are the first flowers for more years than I can remember that are really for me, from you. Thank you.'

He looked down at his sherry.

'Muriel,' he said, 'I was thinking of going to Rome ...'

Muriel said: 'Oh! We've missed the spring collections and we're too early for the autumn!'

'For what we're going to see it's certainly not too early and I hope it's not too late,' he said.

Muriel bent her head and smelled the violets. 'I'll do anything you like,' she said. 'You know, Hubert, you've made me feel like a young girl.'

Mea Culpa

1960

I should have been at a board meeting, but I was standing in the graveyard, the wind like a pain round the neck and ankles, staring at the fresh mound. There was only one other mourner. Two quick and row after row of dead. Another day there might have been children, but it was too cold. The swing park was empty.

Heatherington was already there when I arrived. We hadn't spoken. I didn't think he'd recognise me. The twenty years had turned what I could see of his hair beneath the black Homburg grey, and made him appear shorter and wider – unless it was his heavy coat – than I had remembered. They had changed me from a boy into a man.

He was still looking at the brown, unrevealing earth.

He said, 'Hello, Dawson,' and I, surprised back into the disciplines of youth, replied, 'Hello, sir.'

'Just the two of us,' he said. 'It doesn't seem much. Not after a lifetime. What brought you here?'

'I read the announcement in *The Times*.'

'I mean why?'

'He saved my life.'

'Old Partridge! What was it, drowning? Partridge couldn't swim. Death on the road? He could hardly see an inch in front of him.'

'Not from death,' I said. 'Deformity. I was thirteen at the time.'

The brief business at the grave being over, we fell into step and walked away from the brown hump beneath which lay old Partridge, and circled the cemetery, the leaves snatching angrily at our shoes. As we walked I told Heatherington my story, about old Partridge and the ink.

'It was soon after you became Head,' I said. 'About a year, I suppose, because that was the time it took to get the new floor in the library. We all subscribed, if you remember, boys, old boys, parents, masters, everyone. We'd all loved Mr Potter and when he retired we were glad to do something practical so that the school would remember him.

'The new floor for the library was decided upon. By the time it was ready we'd got used to you, as Headmaster, and almost forgotten Mr Potter, so perhaps it was just as well about the floor. Every one of us was proud of it and small boys are not very house-proud. Each time we went into the library we'd walk gently, trying to make ourselves lighter, as it were, our black lace-ups seeming clumsy on that pale gold surface. It was parquet, a great smooth expanse of it replacing the uneven stained boards we had always tramped upon unheedingly. We talked about it, gloated over it. For a few weeks it gave us something to write home about. Then there were other things to think of: maths and history and, terribly important, cricket. It was the summer we were to play Lakeside. Our heads were crammed with these and other small-boy thoughts and gradually we forgot about the new floor in the library. We grew accustomed to walking on it. Perhaps it did still give us a tiny surge of pleasure just to see it as we opened the glass swing-door, but after that it was as though it had always been there. Except for the Rule. That reminded us. You had made it up, signed it, and attached it to the door. "No ink may be taken into the library under any circumstances." I can still see the signature: "VS Heatherington". It took up the width of the page and the sight of it struck terror into us all.

'On the evening that it happened I hadn't been thinking. I really hadn't. We were rehearsing a play to be presented on Speech Day. I had two lines to say at the end of the last act. They wouldn't be wanting me yet, they said, so I thought I might as well get on with my prep. There was no one about in the school wing. Only those who had stayed behind for the play. The others had gone over for tea. It was terribly quiet.

'I took my books into the library and spread everything out on one of the round tables – physics, I think it was – and settled down to work. I remember a last ray of sun low down in the long window picking out a white rhomboid on the floor. It was as I went back to the physics from noticing the sun that

I spotted the bottle of ink. I had set it neatly on the table with my books and my ruler and things. You see I hadn't intended coming into the library. It was because of the rehearsal and they didn't want me yet. It was silly to hang around doing nothing. I did weigh it up for a moment in my mind. I knew it wasn't allowed but there was no one else in the library and I had no intention of opening the bottle. My pen was full. What harm could it do?

'I suppose I had been at the physics for about half an hour, because the sun had disappeared and the floor gone back to unlit amber, when I thought I'd better hurry, they must be getting near the last act, and started to clear my possessions.

I don't know what I tripped over. Perhaps the leg of the table. Possibly the chair. I didn't fall, but everything went flying out of my arms. My books, pencils, ruler, compasses, protractor, everything that had been in my satchel. I couldn't say exactly what was there. All I was aware of was the sea of deep, permanent blue spreading over the floor. Our floor.

'It was as though I were dying. I had the sensation that my heart had stopped beating from pure fright. I would never have dreamed there could be so much ink in one small bottle. I had some blotting paper but it was soon blue and saturated. I used my handkerchief, some pages from my rough-book. My hands screamed out murderer. On the way to the cloakroom to wash them I met nobody. I managed to take a towel from the roller, squeeze it under the tap, run with it to the library and clean up, what still remained on the surface of the ink. I hid the towel, the handkerchief and the pages from my rough-book in the boiler room. Through the open doors of the Hall I heard Johnson Minor announce that they were about to start Act Three. I went back to the scene of the crime.

'The ink had seeped in, stained and roughened the shiny surface. On our golden carpet was a hideous and unsightly patch. I, out of nine hundred possible small boys, had been the one to do it. I blamed God for allowing it to be me.

'They would have to do without their Third Courtier. I told them I had a headache and they sent me to Matron. It was the spring, she said, and gave me an aspirin. All night I lay with my foul deed.

'Next morning, solemnly, at Assembly, you told the whole school what had happened. There was a stirring of horror. They loved their floor. Not only was it a crime, you said, but one to which no one had had the decency to confess. Would the boy who had committed the heinous offence report to your study before noon. It was a dastardly occurrence. There must be shame, you knew, in the breast of some coward who stood before you, damning his fellows by his reticence.

'It wasn't cowardice. It was the foolish hope that by keeping it to myself some magic wand might be waved and it would turn out to be no more than a figment of my imagination, a bad dream, a boyish fantasy from which I might shortly be released. No punishment could bring more suffering than that which was within me.

'"Before noon," you said. At break I wandered off to where the willows leaned towards the brook and daffodils and grape hyacinths interrupted the greenness of the bank. I wanted to think. I didn't hear old Partridge, he must have followed me, until he said, "How did it happen, Dawson?"

'"How did you know it was me, sir?" I said. It was my conscience speaking, gently.

'"I," he corrected me automatically. "There were ink stains on your Unseen."

'He stood there in that ancient suit of his, his hands knobbly with arthritis, waiting for me to answer.

'"It just happened," I said inadequately, and again he waited.

'It was like that in the Latin lessons. He had all the patience in the world, old Partridge. He knew that you could make no impression upon small boys' brains with a steamroller. If he was teaching us a verb that we had difficulty in memorising, he would demonstrate it in such a way that it would stay with us for ever. Until my death I shall remember *nubere,* to marry, and the sight of poor old Partridge pacing before us with the blackboard duster on his head to represent a wedding veil. At the time we laughed, of course. With old Partridge there were so many causes for amusement. His misshapen fingers, how painful they must have been; the pebbly glasses through which we liked to imagine he could not see us in our mischief; the bushy eyebrows, each one like a small moustache.

'He stood there by the brook, his cracked shoes shabby on the tender grass, waiting for me to explain.

'When I didn't, he said, "It isn't the end of the world, you know, Dawson."

'"Our worlds are not the same," I said, for I was on the threshold and he an old man.

'He put a thin, almost weightless arm round my shoulders and said, "There is only one reality. If the whole of mankind were to perish tomorrow, it would remain."

'"The floor was so beautiful," I said. "Why did it have to be me?"

'"Life is beautiful, Dawson," Partridge said. "Nobody's sheet remains clean."

'"What can we do?"

'"Only our best. Inflicting the least pain."

'"The others will hate me."

'"Never do anything worse, Dawson, and you will be a man."

'As he went up the bank he stumbled over a root of the willow. I didn't laugh. I think the growing process had already begun.'

We had by now made three turns of the graveyard. Or perhaps it was four. I had been talking all the time.

Now Heatherington spoke: 'And at noon you came to my study and confessed.'

'Yes,' I said. 'Could you distinguish my knock from the beating of my heart?'

'You were pale, but I expected it. Old Partridge was a wise man.' Heatherington, his chin huddled into his scarf, looked sideways at me. 'You don't know how wise.'

I raised my eyebrows in query and clapped my leather gloves together against the cold.

'We knew it was you who had the accident with the ink.'

'You did, sir?'

'Partridge saw it happen. He was passing the library and saw it through the door. He told me immediately. I was furious. I wanted to come down straight away. Catch you red-handed as it were. Try to do something about the stain before it was too late. Partridge wouldn't let me. He said, "If you go down now, the blot will never come out." He wasn't referring to the floor.'

We had come round to the grave again and this time we stopped. I knew that both of us were for the last time seeing the shiny suit, the kind face that radiated love of a humanity that was not easy to love. The rare genius of a man who could put first things first in a topsy-turvy world.

'What about a headstone?' I glanced at those about us in varying stages of neglect and decay.

Heatherington fixed me with the flint-blue, uncompromising glance born and bred in all headmasters. 'Partridge has a hundred living monuments.'

I took out my wallet. 'Nevertheless, I'd like to do something.'

'It's very kind of you.'

'I can afford it.'

He took the money I held out and folded it neatly. 'Any particular wording?'

'Just "A wise man", I said. 'In Latin, of course. I'm afraid I don't remember the exact words.'

'Chisellings on stone,' Heatherington said. 'Partridge would forgive you.'

He turned up the collar of his coat and looked at his watch.

We shook hands, stamping our feet, cold in thin shoes, and said goodbye. It was unlikely that our paths would cross for a third time.

Heatherington, head down against the wind, set off across the park. I looked after him. I had meant to ask if, after twenty years, the blot had faded.

Tomorrow Will Be Welcome

1961

Sara Parker awoke to an autumn morning scarcely able to believe that a year had already passed. Was it possible that she was able to face the sight of the trees, their leaves already turning from green to gold, in a world that no longer held her beloved Roly?

It was possible and even more. Turning her face into the pillow until the pale sunlight was blotted out, she admitted to the darkness that she was contemplating marriage to another man. Not that he had actually asked her to marry him.

In the six months that she had known him, the subject had not once been mentioned. But today he was going back three thousand miles across the Atlantic and she knew, as women always know, that he would not leave without asking her. Of that she was certain. She, who had been so sure that there could never be a life without Roly, was now contemplating an entirely new one with someone else.

Would anyone believe that she would not be replacing Roly

with Judd? She would simply be living the only life she felt that it was possible to live. In the warm blackness of the pillow she was back for the millionth time in that other autumn morning, the rain beating against the bedroom window.

Roly was in the bathroom. He called to her, 'If you don't get out of that bed, lazybones, we're going to be late and Simon will take a very dim view of that!'

Sara smiled a fulfilled smile into the bedclothes, happy at the love in her husband's voice and because they were going to see their son Simon at school, whom, by half-term, she always missed terribly.

When they set out, they found the tarmac glistening and the traffic heaving. Once on the open road, Roly put his foot down.

'The roads are awfully skiddy, Roly.'

'Don't worry, darling. Simon will be upset if we don't arrive on time.'

She remembered the bend in the road and the dripping hedges. She would remember for ever the sickening, frightening slide as they negotiated it, which left them spinning like a top on the wrong side of the road. She remembered how huge, almost like the prow of a ship, the approaching hulk of the furniture removal van had looked. After that she would not allow herself to remember.

At the hospital they had avoided telling her the news for as long as possible. But because she knew, she did not press them. 'In a day or two,' they said, 'when you're stronger.' She made no effort to get stronger to greet the husband she knew would never come. When the doctor in the long white coat came finally to sit on the bed and take her hand she was able to spare him his embarrassing task. The only thing she hadn't known was that Roly had died instantaneously. She was supposed to derive some comfort from the information.

The weeks immediately afterwards had not somehow been so bad. The sickening, engulfing grief, the grief that was impossible to live with, somehow slid past in an anaesthetising wave. It was a bad dream, and she had wakened one morning to find that reality was far, far worse.

For the children's sake she had tried, but she found that without Roly she did not know how to live. There was no one even to quarrel with. Noisy, shouting quarrels whose course was satisfying and whose end was always certain.

She felt alone, as if she were standing on a high rock. Beneath her, kind arms waved to welcome her, but the arms she searched for were not there, so she remained alone on her rock and soon the arms stopped waving. The children made it possible – essential in fact – to carry on, but sooner or later children had to go to bed and she was left, wandering around the house, which brought back too many memories. She did not go out. She could not bring herself to make the effort.

There were problems. She found that Roly had left her enough money to live on and support the children, but she would have to cut down their standard of living. Should she stay on in the roomy old house, sell up and move into a small flat, or take the children and move in with her mother? There were problems she had to face.

On the evening when Judd had first called she was kneeling on the floor of the sitting room cutting out a dress for her daughter, Harriet, from a paper pattern. It was a task in which she was inexperienced and the concentrated effort had wearied her. Simon and Harriet, in pyjamas and barefooted, sat cross-legged before the fire eating their supper. Everywhere there were pins, material, books, games and vital pieces of her pattern.

The bell surprised them all. Nowadays no one ever visited them in the evenings. Sara got up and went to answer the bell, shutting the door behind her so that whoever had arrived would not see the mess.

A stranger stood on the doorstep, large, loose-limbed and blond. 'I hope I'm not intruding,' he said, certain of his welcome. 'I'm Judd Morphy from Washington. I met your husband when he was in the States. He told me to be sure and call when I was over here. I just got in.'

'He told me about you,' Sara said, facing him through the twelve inches she had opened the door.

'Is your husband home, Mrs Parker?'

She looked at him. 'Roly's dead,' she said, and it was the first time she had spoken the words aloud. She watched the large, bland, all-embracing American smile fade from his face. She was glad he didn't say he was sorry.

'May I come in?' Sara had heard Americans had no sense of occasion. She shrugged and opened the door wider. In the sitting room he tried not to put his large feet on the paper pattern. She made no attempt to clear up or apologise. She never bothered to make up for her evenings with the children and knew her hair needed washing. She didn't care, she hadn't asked him to come in.

He said, 'This has come as a shock. All the way over on the plane I've been thinking of Roly and the good times we had.'

'How long are you here for?' she asked politely.

'Six months. What happened to Roly?'

'It was a car accident,' she said, 'last October.'

'Daddy's died and gone to Heaven,' Harriet said calmly.

'Oh, shut up, Harry!' Simon said fiercely, kicking her with his bare foot.

Judd stayed only half an hour. When he got up to go she realised that she had offered him nothing, not even a cup of coffee. She was far too weary and she hadn't even washed her supper dishes.

At the door he said, 'I'm sorry for pushing in, but I know what it's like. I lost my wife to cancer soon after our marriage. Of course, it's a very long while ago now, but I remember how it feels. It doesn't do to be too much alone. I'll call you some time, Mrs Parker.'

'Sara,' she said. He had been a good friend to Roly. He didn't telephone her, probably anticipating what she would say. He just came back frequently and rang the bell and stood patiently on the doorstep waiting for her to let him in. She made no effort to entertain him. He had supper with her in the kitchen, listened, relaxed, to the radio, helped her get the children into bed. She scarcely noticed whether he was there or not until after two months, during which time he had visited them at least three or four times every week, he quite suddenly stopped coming.

The sitting room, cluttered as it was with furniture and toys, seemed empty. The children missed him. For the first time in a long while Sara looked into her long mirror and was horrified at what she saw. She hadn't bothered about her hair, her skin, her face, her clothes, the things she had cared for so proudly for Roly. She looked like an old woman and not a very tidy one. She wasn't even standing up straight. She braced her shoulders. The effort was painful but it took a few years off her age.

They heard nothing from Judd for three weeks. When he did come he said he had been in Europe on business. He made no excuse for not letting them know. Why should he? If he noticed that Sara had a new dress and had had her hair done, he did not say anything.

One day he noticed the golf clubs that were kept in the cupboard under the stairs.

'They're Roly's,' Sara said. 'I don't play.'

'Well, I do,' Judd said. 'How about walking round with me?' He didn't say it would do her good to get out into the fresh air, but she knew that that was what he meant. He was quite right. She had hardly been outside the house for months.

And on the golf course she would not have to face people.

It was not long before she bought a waterproofed jacket, trousers and shoes, and borrowed a bag of lightweight clubs from a girlfriend. In the weeks preceding Christmas she trudged miles over sodden grass, pulling a trolley uphill and down dale behind her. She learned to relax her knees, keep her head down and take the club head back slowly and follow through, and there were hours at a time when she did not think about Roly. When it snowed and they could not play she was upset and practised in the hall.

Slowly, week by week, with Judd she learned to laugh again. He made a Christmas tree for the children. He took them skating on a frozen lake. She found herself looking forward to his double ring, punctual as a grandfather clock.

By the time her drives were landing, time after time, on the fairway and her iron shots stopping neatly on the green, she began to be sure that Judd wanted to marry her. She knew that there would never, ever, be a love like hers and Roly's, it was something past. One could not live in the past and Judd had broad, comfortable-looking shoulders.

As the weather grew warmer and their golf games more frequent, she began to expect his proposal. She wondered when it would be. That he was fond of her was obvious. A woman did not have to be told.

One after the other, their days together slid quickly by and the proposal of which she was so sure was never mentioned. Before she realised where the weeks had gone, it was time for Judd to return to Washington. Still nothing had been said. That there was no one else, she knew. He told her all there was to know about his life at home and she was certain he had no woman waiting to welcome him.

Today he was going home and, dreaming on her pillow Sara guessed that before his plane left he would ask her. She was ready with her answer. She dressed carefully and was annoyed with herself for being in a dither of excitement.

They had lunch at the airport. She thought to herself how familiar his large, kind face with its straight mouth and receding hair had become, how much she had grown to depend upon him.

After the coffee he held her hand for the first time, filling her with a sense of security.

'Sara,' he said gently, 'I've known you long enough to ask you something.'

She watched him stub out his cigarette; then he was holding her hand in both his own.

'Would you think of getting married again?' he asked.

She thought of Roly and, knowing that his memory would always remain untouched, said yes, she might, and waited for what would come next.

He leaned forward. 'You mustn't mind what I'm going to say, Sara,' he said, 'because I say it for your sake. If you should think of getting married again, I ask you to wait. Wait until your heartache's gone and there's no need to seek the comfort of the first pair of arms that comes along. When you've had a shock, such as you have had, your judgement goes haywire and your imagination may give to any man qualities he does not really possess.

'And there's another thing, Sara. Marriage is for two. It needs giving as well as taking. You cannot expect to give yourself over to the task of building a new marriage and making it work while you are still recovering from Roly. Whoever you marry you will have to meet halfway.

'You don't mind my saying this?' he asked. 'Look at me, please, Sara.'

She managed to raise her head but knew her eyes were full of tears of disappointment.

'I'll go and get my baggage cleared,' he said, standing up. 'Wait for me downstairs.'

Before he got into the plane he held her very close and very tight, and she tried not to cry when he kissed her. He left her holding a large square box, his parting gift. As she waved goodbye to the plane the tears slid unrestricted down her face.

When she got home the children were waiting for her, busy with the presents Judd had given them. They wanted to know what was in her parcel so she sat on the settee, red-eyed, to open it. There were three-dozen brand-new golf balls in the box and she started to laugh hysterically through her tears. When she was calm she realised that it was not such a stupid present after all, and that with each one she would learn to live a little more, concentrating on something she was anxious to do really well.

'Is Uncle Judd coming back?' Harriet asked from the floor where she was busy with her new doll.

Sara shook her head. 'I don't think so, Harriet.'

Simon said, 'I think he is, Mummy. He's left his golf clubs in the hall.'

Sara ran across the polished floor. The large, heavy leather bag leaned solidly against her own light one as it had done for months. She knew that he had not left them by mistake.

Rosita

1961

I had been married for ten years when I heard from Rosita. It was not so strange, really, when you considered that she inhabited one planet and I another. At first I couldn't make out who the letter was from. It was on very thick white paper written in very black ink and began 'Helen darling'. Since I had only one lover and he sat not two feet away spreading marmalade on his toast, and none of my women friends ever addressed me as 'darling', it had me puzzled for a moment or two, and I picked up the envelope to see if perhaps it wasn't for another Helen at a different address.

Having made sure that I was, in fact, the 'darling' concerned, I turned over the page and looked at the signature. It occupied the entire width of the page and was in itself a conceit. How did she know my life was not peppered with Rositas? What made her imagine that after twelve years the mere sight of her name would crowd out the teeming events of a decade and take me back to my schooldays?

Yet had she added an explanatory 'Your old chum, remember?' or more explicitly, 'Barclay, that was', it would not have been Rosita.

'Who is it from?' Mitchell asked, not raising his eyes from the share prices.

'Rosita.'

'Rosita?'

'Rosita Barclay.' My brain did a quick flip down the years and back into school. Rosita Barclay with the face of an angel; wide blue eyes and long blond hair; at sixteen a perfect figure; legs destined for things other than tearing down the right wing; darling of them all. Particularly the men.

Yes. The men. Fat Monsieur Bonnard devoid of breath after toiling up the three flights of narrow stairs, mopping his brow as he stood at his desk on the rostrum, chest heaving as the minutes ticked. A voice at last: '*Et bien mes enfants.* But why must I have *toutes mes petites fleurs* in the back row? It is not a pleasing arrangement.'

All the little flowers, but he'd be looking at Rosita, tenderly, speculatively. Some would pick up their books and shuffle forward good-naturedly, not Rosita. She didn't need to. Where she sat, eyelids lowered, indolent, was the centre of the class. Did she still remember the French for a 'double-edged sword'? I wondered.

And it wasn't only fat Monsieur Bonnard, the essence of Gallic goodness, who really believed that to understand everything was to forgive and tried to teach us to understand.

Nor was it only Mr Jarvis, the human hairpin who taught

us to fence in the dingy gym; taught us, a white spider, dancing, lunging, never still, his eyes on Rosita. She was, of course, the best – accurate, quick on her feet – but did he always have to pick her to demonstrate a point, illustrate a common fault?

As they stood, backs straight, foils raised in salute, before commencing the thrust and parry, every one of us was uncomfortably aware that there was more to it than the points that Mr Jarvis allowed Rosita to score on the white front of his target; more to the terse instructions he called to Rosita as they danced back and forth between the lines of we who were watching.

When Rosita took off her mask and shook loose her hair the spell was broken. Mr Jarvis would choose another partner but it was not the same, the power had gone out of the battery; Mr Jarvis's feet, though they twinkled just as fast, seemed no longer inspired.

Nor was it only the men. For that we could have forgiven her, not fully understanding, yet not unaware of the power of sex appeal. The women too responded to her magnetism with a predictability that sickened us the more because we knew that we too, in spite of ourselves, were not immune to the eyes that brainwashed as they looked.

To be late for a class was a heinous sin. But not for Rosita. We could all be deep in Addison, Swift or Livy, when the slowly opened door would reveal the shining head, and with a silvery laugh she would proclaim: 'Sorry. I'm late again!'

'Settle down quickly, Rosita, you're holding up the class.'

But there was no venom in the remark, which was no more than a half-hearted rebuke. Anyone else would have found herself in disgrace, the subject of a lecture on punctuality. Sometimes we thought it was because Rosita's father was a film director, and you could read about him and his various wives and not-wives in the newspapers. We knew that from time to time he sent tickets to the headmistress and the staff for film premières. But I don't think it was only that, because people who didn't know about her father were not immune.

We travelled home on the bus, she to her father's penthouse overlooking the park, I to the aunt with whom I stayed in term time. I gave up making bets with myself that the conductor, no matter how busy, would stop for a chat with Rosita, It was inevitable and you knew that selling Rosita a ticket would cheer him up however morose he had been before, and that afterwards he'd probably be singing.

'Do I know her?' asked Mitchell.

'I've shown you her picture in the newspapers. You met her once, remember?'

'Oh, that Rosita!'

He looked eager, investments forgotten. One meeting and the odd photo on the Society Page. That was the effect she had.

'What does she want? She's never written to you before.'

Neither had she. Curious that she should do so now. I held up the letter. Rosita and I had never been close friends. Because she was always head and shoulders above everyone else in looks, in knowledge (knowledge of the world, that is, not academic) and in worldly wealth, Rosita never formed one of those passionate, vulnerable, adolescent alliances common among girls. But, looking back, I suppose I did know her a fraction better than any of the others.

She chose me because she had to talk to someone and, out of the whole class, I was the one who wanted nothing from her. She was too remote. Our main point of contact began and ended with our common need of the number 12 bus to carry us to and from school. Those who were nearly beautiful envied her her perfect features; those who were wealthy, her disdainful use of money; and those who aspired to fame, her father whose name was a household word.

I think, perhaps, I alone had no snag. I wasn't pretty, my education was paid for by my aunt, and I knew with the utmost certainty that whatever my future held it would have nothing to do with fame or fortune, both of which waited like toys to be played with in Rosita's lap.

Of course we talked a good deal on the bus but it was mostly Rosita telling me about the men her father entertained and who were old enough to be her father. She hinted at things, wicked things. I pretended to understand, but I often puzzled about those hinted things, together with my geometry or my algebra, when I got home.

On one memorable occasion she asked me to the penthouse to tea. I thought in my naiveté that tiger-skin rugs, silk-panelled walls and blinds that slid up to reveal giant television sets existed only in novels and films. That Rosita actually lived with such refinements widened the gap between us. We didn't even have tea. We helped ourselves to milk and little bits of toast with caviar left from the night before, from the fridge that was large enough to put your bed in.

Later, Rosita said: 'Let's have a drink, I'm gasping,' and a whole section of what I had thought were books disappeared to reveal what must have been a hundred bottles. I've never really trusted people's books since and usually go around taking surreptitious prods at them.

I invited her back, diffidently, out of politeness. I warned my aunt that she came of film people and was a little unconventional. I underestimated Rosita. When she'd gone my aunt was positively bubbling over and demanding to know why I hadn't introduced her to my charming friend before.

The bus journeys and those two visits, and of course the brief times we chatted to each other at school, was the extent of our friendship. Since we had left school, I for my physiotherapist training through which I ultimately met Mitchell, and Rosita for the great wide world that was lying at her feet, I had seen her only once. I had been dining with Mitchell in a basement restaurant, which was enjoying a wave of popularity at the time. It was our wedding anniversary, fourth I think, and we were dancing, happy with each other, on a minute, crowded floor. Suddenly a voice screamed: 'Darling!'

Drowsy with champagne, I looked up idly to see who it was that was being hailed. On the edge of the floor, attached by two fingers to a man whose antics on the racecourse and elsewhere frequently filled several columns of several newspapers, was Rosita. And she was looking at me.

We pushed our way over to her and when I introduced Mitchell, Rosita kissed both of us, Mitchell not objecting in the slightest.

'Helen, darling, how exciting!' Rosita exclaimed, her eyes bright. But I couldn't quite see what it was that she found so exciting.

We stood talking for just a moment and then her boyfriend – she never did marry that one, whose type we were not at all – pulled her away and Rosita blew kisses at us as they weaved towards their table. Afterwards the bandleader, shaking his maracas, looked at us with different eyes and I swear we had better attention from our waiter. Our claim to fame was manifest. We knew Rosita.

The incident, though leaving me quite unmoved, had obviously seared itself into Mitchell's memory. He leaned forward, waiting eagerly to hear what was in the letter from Rosita.

There was no address or date.

'Helen, darling,' I read aloud. 'White sand and blue sky as far as the eye can see, you'd think that nothing else existed ...'

'Wait a second,' Mitchell said, 'there were no foreign stamps.'

I looked at the envelope again. It had been posted in Streatham. I continued to read.

'... and that everyone in the whole world was lying in the sun. I came today from Tangier and it's not so. Helen I must see you. At Bellotti's on the thirty-first at one? Have you changed? I visualise you in your green coat going back and forth on the number 12 to eternity. I'll try not to be late. Yours as ever, Rosita.'

'The thirty-first,' Mitchell said, 'that's tomorrow.'

'She might have meant last month. She could hardly have been lying on the white sands in Streatham.'

'Last month had only thirty days. Shall you go?'

I read a certain urgency into the phrase: 'Helen, I must see you.' 'I'll take a chance,' I said.

Quite apart from the fact that the letter had obviously been written in one place and posted in another, there were several things that puzzled me. How did Rosita know my married name and where I lived? As far as I knew, we had no mutual acquaintance and she could not possibly have followed my career as I had hers in the newspapers. How did she know whether or not I could keep the appointment when there was no indication of where I could contact her?

And, most odd of all, what did she mean by her reference to Tangier? Rosita had never had a social conscience.

The rest of the day I spent in speculation. What could she want? Had she perhaps fallen on hard times and needed help from an old schoolfriend? Bellotti's hardly suggested financial difficulties. Might she have come to realise the folly of her roaming and unstable life and want from me the recipe for a settled existence in suburbia? Was she in some sort of personal trouble, ill maybe, and needing someone upon whom she could rely or confide in?

The possibilities were endless.

The next morning I stood before my wardrobe knowing that no matter what I wore it would not be up to the standard of Bellotti's. Mine was not that sort of life.

I dressed in the best I had and, knowing that I looked nice but not outstanding, set off, feeling doubtful that Rosita would be there at all, almost certain that it would turn out to be a wild-goose chase.

The lobby of Bellotti's was full of people waiting for other people and for tables, nibbling olives and sipping at glasses of sherry. There was a girl, a paper cut-out from a fashion paper in a fabulous pink suit, and another in mink with banana-coloured hair, but no Rosita.

'Madame has a reservation?' the head waiter murmured.

'No, yes, that is I'm waiting ...' and then to my horror I realised that I did not even know Rosita's name. She had been married to an Alsopp and after that to a South American millionaire called Diaz but according to my newspaper all that was in the past. Messrs Alsopp and Diaz had long ago moved on to pastures new.

I took a chance. 'I don't know if Rosita has booked a table,' I said, and had an unsolicited view of half a dozen gold teeth as the head waiter embraced me with his smile.

'Aha! Rosita,' he made the name a caress. 'Lady Harrington. Yes, we are waiting for her to arrive.'

At least I had not come all the way for nothing. I squeezed in on the banquette between a young man with a red carnation in his buttonhole and an American matron with a whimsy veil, and watched the revolving doors. I finished the sweet sherry I had ordered to while away the time and had almost worked my way through a dish of peanuts when the doors were suddenly hurled into motion and there, deeply tanned and gorgeous as ever, was Rosita. I had a moment to examine her before she saw me, and noticed first that her handbag was such that its price alone would have dressed me from head to foot. It was as if an alarm had been rung. Everyone, the head-waiter, the barman, my neighbour with the red carnation, the American matron, was looking at her.

Helen!' she exclaimed as dramatically as if I were her long-lost sister, and held out both her hands. I stood up and she kissed me. Her skin was cool and had the exotic tang of expensive perfume used lavishly. She took my arm, clinging as if she'd never let me go, and we followed the headwaiter to a table by the window.

When he'd left us I watched her go through the small set-tling motions of seeking comfort; I knew that Rosita had not fallen upon hard times. She hadn't changed, except that the long blond hair was now shorter in keeping with the current fashion and perhaps owed a little, but I could not really be sure, to artifice. She seemed unaware that everyone at the tables around us was watching her, admiring the chiselled perfection of her features, as she leant forward and said: 'It's so wonderful to see you.'

'How did you know my address?'

'I saw the birth announcement, a daughter, wasn't it? I meant to write to you.'

'The birth announcement?' My youngest child was four.

'I came across the piece of paper in my wallet. I often wondered what I'd done with it.'

'That was four years ago.'

'As long as that? I stick things away.' She opened her hand-bag. 'I bought a present. I should have looked at the date.' She handed me a jeweller's box.

Inside was an exquisite coral bracelet which would have fitted a baby no older than six months.

'It's very lovely,' I murmured. 'Thank you, Rosita.'

Rosita dismissed it with a wave of her hand. 'You can put it away for the next.'

The waiter asked me what I'd like to eat and it wasn't until he'd gone that I realised Rosita hadn't ordered anything at all.

'So you live in Sutton,' Rosita said.

'Yes,' I said, on the defensive although she hadn't attacked. 'Where do you?'

'All over,' she shrugged. 'London, Paris, Florida. Hooper's in oil.'

I only now remembered reading about her recent marriage to the Harrington heir. According to the papers they were blissfully happy. That put paid to my theory that Rosita was in some sort of emotional trouble, which she thought I might be able to sort out. She certainly looked happy enough and the personification of radiant health. All my speculations as to why she might want to see me became groundless in her actual presence and I waited, curious throughout the meal, for some logical explanation of why I was lunching with Rosita at Bellotti's on an ordinary Wednesday when normally I would have been at home boiling myself an egg.

The waiter brought the lunch I had ordered and the headwaiter himself brought Rosita a small portion of salad although I hadn't heard her ask for anything.

'You are a darling, Emilio,' she smiled at him and then at me. 'I never take anything more complicated at midday.'

I was a darling, too: 'Helen, darling.'

I asked her about the letter. She had written it in Miami, she said, and forgotten to post it. She had given it to Hooper to post when she'd returned. I didn't ask what Hooper had been doing in Streatham.

'What upset you in Tangier?' I asked. I pictured the beggars with their running sores, the waifs of children, ragged, barefooted, Rosita distributing largesse.

She wrinkled the peach-brown forehead. 'Tangier?' she said. 'Oh, yes, it was the rainy season ...'

She asked me and I told her about my life in Sutton, and about my marriage and about my two children. She was listening with only half her mind and I didn't blame her; it didn't sound much compared with Tangier, with Paris, with Florida.

'Have you kept in touch with anyone else from school?' I asked.

'No, no one.'

'Were you happy there?'

Rosita looked surprised. Happiness and its elusive quality was a subject I often pondered on and had long discussions about with Mitchell.

'I suppose so,' Rosita said.

I should have known that for Rosita life was for living and not for questioning.

'How long are you staying in London?' I asked, thinking

perhaps that her visit was only to be brief and there was something she wanted me to do for her.

'Oh, until one of us gets the urge to move, I suppose.'

I imagined her waking up in the morning and standing on the balcony in her negligée and deciding with no ado at all to transport herself to the other side of the world. Thus it was to be Rosita.

She was still terribly amusing. While we ate she told me stories about her life, her homes, her husbands. The people at the next table listened too. The fabric she wove was of bright colours, each stitch close to the next. There was no delicate shading of hope or of dream or of aspiration.

Was this scudding across life's surface perhaps happiness? Rosita certainly seemed to be content.

With the coffee, which Rosita had in a specially large cup brought again unasked-for by Emilio, I could not resist asking why it was that after so many years Rosita had wanted to see me.

Rosita looked puzzled. Then she said: 'Oh yes, I told you I came across the birth announcement in my wallet.'

I waited for her to go on. But she only said: 'I don't know about you but I'd like some more coffee,' and looked round vaguely for Emilio.

Of course I should have realised before. I prided myself on my knowledge of human nature yet I had in my imagination vested Rosita with a depth she did not possess. My presence in Bellotti's was, of course, the result of a whim. 'Helen, darling, I must see you.' How else would you put it if you were Rosita?

She signed the bill and allowed Emilio to kiss her hand. I had a sudden sharp vision of Monsieur Bonnard, long since dead, and Mr Jarvis unable to keep the devotion from their eyes. I wondered how it felt to have all men in love with you and to revolve steadily through life surrounded by a galaxy of desire.

Outside, a long, low car and a grey-uniformed chauffeur were waiting. 'I'll drop you off,' Rosita said. 'Where?'

I mentioned the nearest tube station from which I could get a train back home and found myself sharing a rug with Rosita, which the chauffeur tucked solicitously round our knees.

There was a lot of traffic round the entrance to the tube station, and because I was afraid there'd be a hold-up caused by the big car, which should not really have stopped just there, I tried to get out quickly and gabble my thanks to Rosita for the lunch. But she, seeming quite oblivious to traffic problems, followed me out of the car and stood on the pavement holding both my hands.

A man in the car stuck behind Rosita's hooted impatiently. Rosita turned her head and smiled at him indicating that she'd be no more than a moment and he grinned back and stopped hooting.

Rosita kissed me for the second time. 'It was lovely, we must do it again some time,' she said. 'Only we won't leave it so long.' I was about to suggest a future date and that Rosita be my guest for a return lunch when a look into the depthless eyes told me she was no longer interested, anxious to be gone.

I waved my glove at the car until it was swallowed up

between two buses and I found myself standing there bidding farewell to nothing.

There it was. I had been picked up and put down in whatever sense you liked. I walked into the draughty maw of the station.

When he came home at six Mitchell's first words were: 'Well, what did she want?'

And it was then that I realised how stupid my ideas had been about why Rosita had wanted to see me. The Rositas never needed anything from anybody; their lives were not dependent upon love or sympathy, compassion or understanding. And the material things fell from overladen trees.

I told Mitchell about our meeting, describing Rosita, and when I'd finished he was smiling, one could almost say glowing, and offered to put the children to bed. Usually he was tired after a long day and ready to collapse into his chair with his feet up, but now he seemed revitalised. And even I, after quite a hectic day, doing my usual chores and dashing up to town to meet Rosita, was aware of an extraordinary glow of elation.

Looking at Mitchell I marvelled that the effect of Rosita could be vicarious, too, and I thought of Monsieur Bonnard and Mr Jarvis and my aunt, and all the conductors on the number 12s, and Emilio and the people at the next table in Bellotti's and the man who had hooted in Oxford Street, and all the people she had made happy, if only briefly, myself included. And I did not at all mind being a whim.

The Crowded Room

1962

My name is Susan Slade and I hate cocktail parties. Not just the weary excrescences on toast and the faceless waitresses with their inevitable offerings of mouthfuls that disintegrate at the touch or are too hot, but the very format of the things.

The desire to turn and flee for home that comes between the ringing of the bell and the opening of the door. The self-confidence of which one is divested with one's coat. The bitter taste of smoke and the back-to-front tape of a hundred unintelligible voices. With assimilation, a drink, exchange of pleasantries with a familiar face, things usually improve, only to turn sour when on the doorstep, whipped back to reality by comparatively unpolluted air, you realise that you are partly full, partly drunk, partly satiated with partly heard conversation.

Drusilla's party was on Sunday, which made it worse. It meant stepping out of the comfortable morass of unmade beds and Sunday papers and *The Critics*, and dressing, as one did every other day.

Informal, Drusilla said, don't bother to dress, but of course just as much effort was needed for the 'thrown together' look as for the biggest gala appearance. It was just a figure of speech.

I don't think Drusilla would have cared for my Pyrenean wool housecoat against her Chinese Chippendale, nor Simon's glad rags, which bore abundant testimony to the Sunday he creosoted the side gate, and pruned the roses a little too enthusiastically, and the dog who had a fit in the scullery, and the sailing dinghy –begun a hundred Sundays ago and now languishing in the garage.

Knowing Drusilla's crowd and unable to compete, I chose an understated tweed suit, the most expensive garment I had in my wardrobe, and Simon, begging for one more moment in his slippers, settled for the natty fisherman's pullover I had bought him for his birthday in which he would never have dreamed of going fishing.

Reluctantly we kicked the newspapers into a semblance of tidiness – my skirt was too tight to allow me to pick them up and Simon was too lazy – admonished the children to behave, turned the oven down upon the lunch and set off.

Drusilla was the sort of woman who collected people as others did jade or old sugar tongs or first editions. She strung them on the bracelet of her basic loneliness and insecurity, and the moment she felt the slightest sign that life was passing her by she took them out and looked at them. Mostly they were glad enough to dance for a while to Drusilla's tune.

Many of them were poets, writers, musicians, painters, rarely averse to the hospitality or adulation that Drusilla dispensed unstintingly.

To be fair to Drusilla herself, she was beautiful and indefatigably cheerful, and there were few who did not benefit from an hour in her company. Lavished by her kisses and caresses, by her endless sincere insincerities, there was not a woman who did not feel more feminine, a man more manly, in the rosy aura of her charm. If we had to waste a Sunday morning, there was no one more capable than Drusilla of sugaring the pill.

Naturally there was nowhere to park. Drusilla did not believe in doing things by halves and the cars filled the not inconsiderable carriage drive and spilled along the kerb a good half-mile down the road.

'Simon! Simon!' The door was flung wide and immediately one was in Drusilla's arms pleasantly anaesthetised by 'Moment Supreme' and struggling to remind oneself she didn't mean the praises she showered on one.

'Simon, you're handsomer than ever! He doesn't age a day. Susan, darling, what a dream of a suit!'

Thoroughly kissed, we had a chance to look at Drusilla. It was always a surprise. Today she had on a baby-pink dress and pink phosphorescent shoes. Her hair was pink, too; Drusilla could do things like that and get away with it.

I was about to compliment her on her appearance but the door had opened behind us and someone else was drowning in her welcome, so we allowed ourselves to be carried on the tide into the depths of the party.

There was the usual nucleus of familiar faces. Drusilla always made use of the hard core of her acquaintances, of which Simon and I were a part, and embroidered it with her latest acquisitions. We waggled our fingers at those similarly extricated from their Sunday limbo and did what was expected of us by chatting amiably to the newcomers.

I lost Simon in what was now a reasonable facsimile of the platform of Tottenham Court Road station in the rush hour and was attempting manfully to keep a guard on my third champagne cocktail, an oozing asparagus roll and my tongue, when Drusilla in her pinkness appeared beside me and said: 'Susan, darling, I want you to come and meet someone special.'

There was always a 'someone special'. A particularly succulent morsel gleaned from studio or stage, frequently in transit between exciting places and dished up as the *pièce de résistance* at Drusilla's parties.

Her slim arm round my waist, she steered me across the room, clearing a pathway with friendly hugs and squeezes to her guests as we went. The noise had become intense and reminded me of the parrot house at the zoo.

By a group near the concert grand, which took up only a corner of the great room, Drusilla stopped. A ring of upturned, attentive faces, some with cigarettes stuck in them, were listening to a tall man in a black, cable-stitch jersey. Obviously the lion, I thought. Drusilla stroked the back of his neck with slim, pink-tipped fingers. He turned round and with a zoomp of the time-machine I was face to face with my past.

The group that had been hanging on his words knitted together and left the three of us a separate entity.

'This is Stefan,' Drusilla said. She put the accent on the last syllable, conjuring up an image of some colourful eastern European village.

'Hello, Steve,' I said.

'Susan!' He was as shattered as I.

In the hubbub Drusilla hadn't even noticed. She hugged us both to her and said: 'Stefan paints. You simply must see his exhibition at the Cotterell. For fabulous sums he'll paint your portrait, won't you, darling?'

Fabulous sums! He must have covered over a hundred canvases with my face and I hadn't paid him a penny.

With a delighted smile to each of us Drusilla was gone and we were left on an island of silence to roll back the years. He looked first at my hair, no longer the savage jungle it had been when I was eighteen, to be posed over my shoulder or across my mouth, but a neat tribute to fashion and my hairdresser, then at my understatement of a suit which in his eyes I could see was the grossest of overstatements.

'So you're really a cake-eater ...'

'And you,' I said quickly in self-defence, looking pointedly at his champagne glass. But I knew it wasn't true. Nearing forty he was still as thin as a lathe, hollow almost in the middle, and I could tell he had never returned to the petit bourgeoisie of Blackheath where he was raised.

It was a game we used to play in the nasty cynicism of our tender years. Looking out of the gritty window of his studio through a peephole we had rubbed with our fingers in the dirt, we'd watch the shoppers in Fulham Road disappear with predatory faces into packed shops and then reappear laden with weekend joints and teeth-rotting, fruit-filled pies. 'Cake-eaters', we named them disparagingly for their philistinism.

At night we watched the 'fat' cake-eaters, an even more despicable class, shrugging off fur coats at restaurant tables, through lighted windows in the King's Road. Ourselves, we lived on beans and tea and love. In summer, dust griming our sandalled feet, we roamed like an 'entwined dryad' in the parks; in winter we huddled in front of the electric fire in Steven's studio.

As if I had spoken my thoughts aloud Steven, his black hair still at sixes and sevens, though greying elegantly now above the ears, reached for my hand. He turned it over gently in his own and looked at the white scar that puckered the palm. I could feel the pain of it now.

We used to do our cooking by turning the little stove on to its back and standing the saucepan or the kettle on its bars.

It was snowing, I remember; snow that drifted unhurriedly in fat flakes past the window. Steven had been painting all day and I sitting. We were both exhausted. I had grabbed hold of the stove too quickly, not thinking what I was doing, and the next moment was screaming hysterically in Steven's arms.

Our idyll had lasted until the term before we were due to finish our course at the art school. To hear us talk you would have thought it infinite.

I had been home for the mid-term break and there, neat and tidy, living the other half of my chameleon existence, I met Simon. With the part of myself that recognised the need for stability and family and roots, and a thousand other things we had derided in the cake-eaters, I fell in love. For the other half, for my dream self, there was no one but Steven.

For the rest of the term I managed to keep my two lives separate. I dined with Simon in fashionable restaurants, dressing myself suitably, and discussed the future.

With Steven there was no future, only the intensity of existence from day to day. Because I was afraid of him I put off the moment when I must tell him. When I finally did I made the terrible mistake of throwing a sop to his disappointment.

I had always refused to sit for him in the nude. Not for any reasons of modesty, three years at the art school had put an end to any pretensions I might have had of that, but on the odd grounds that if Steven ever became famous and his pictures hung, I might be exposed *toute nue* to the horrified gaze of my relations.

A week before the end of the term in which I had met Simon, Steven had asked me to sit for a study of Ariadne, a painting he was doing in a series of scenes from Greek mythology. Without saying anything I took off my clothes and arranged myself on the couch he had prepared. He gave me a long look, but with no more comment, squeezed Chinese white on to his palette and started to paint.

He painted all that week and I don't think that we even stopped for our customary diet of beans. At the end of it we could hardly stagger, but on the canvas was the finest painting Steven had ever done. Wrapped in his dressing gown I looked at it with tears in my eyes; it was an inspiration of Steven and myself and paint and canvas: it lived.

'What made you change your mind?' Steven said, as he cleaned his brushes, and I knew the moment had come.

He looked at me, happily saturated with achievement. 'Don't bother to answer,' he said. 'It doesn't really matter. We're on to great things, Sue. This is only a beginning. Next term we shall conquer the world.'

'There'll not be a next term for me,' I said. 'I'm going to be married.'

He stopped with his brush in mid-air and cocked his head as though he hadn't quite heard.

'I'm not coming back.'

The next five minutes were the worst I had lived through to date and even now I cannot think of any experience since that made me feel so bad.

With the brush he had been cleaning, Steven attacked his palette savagely, and white-faced, desecrated Ariadne from top to toe until there was nothing to be seen on the canvas but a hideous, glutinous, string-coloured mess weeping great tears of viridian.

That was my first love and that was how it ended. After almost twenty years I could relive the vicarious suffering I was unable to assuage.

I didn't see him again but I learned from a student at the art school that my place had been taken by a girl called Nadia who had Russian parents and hair she could sit on.

'So now you charge fabulous sums to the cake-eaters?'

He had the grace to blush. 'I don't paint just anyone. I have to want to.'

'Of course,' I said, helping him, and we smiled the smile of friendship into each other's eyes to hide the love that was almost, but not quite dead.

'Stefan!' a voice from the present said, and a girl with pure black hair to the waist, a blue canvas tube of a dress and no make-up, came from nowhere and leaned her really beautiful face upon his shoulder.

'This is Katya,' Steven said.

We shook hands politely, although she did not really look at me, but hung on to Steven as if she would never let him go.

'The lunch will be burning,' Simon's voice said from my side; and my eyes met Steven's, laughing, the old lines of communication still open.

'This is Stefan,' I said, introducing Simon. 'He has an exhibition at the Cotterell Gallery.'

'My wife was at art school when we met. You've always been keen on painting, haven't you, Sue?' Simon said.

'I was never any good, though, at painting.'

'Stefan, Katya, you mustn't monopolise my friends!' Drusilla said. 'Susan, darling, I want you to talk to the Walshes. They come from New York and are in biscuits in a fabulous way and are on their way to Madrid.'

'We have to go, Drusilla.'

'The lunch is burning,' Steven said.

I looked him in the eye. 'Indeed it is.'

He took my hand, running his thumb along the scar. 'Goodbye,' he said, and I knew that this and not the volcanic separation of twenty years ago, was really the parting.

In the crowded room at Drusilla's I realised the futility of an ageing Ariadne and knew that only Steven's work had identity and that whatever happened, there would always be a Nadia or a Katya with hair to her waist; there had to be.

We said our goodbyes slowly, gradually making our way to the hall in the now dispersing crowd.

In the car my mind went to the lunch in the oven and the children and the now thinning dream of Steven. I pulled the fine kid gloves on to my carefully manicured hands, obscuring the cicatrice and the odd illusion that my fingers were covered with paint.

When I was settled in my seat I smiled up at Simon who was waiting, as he always did, with infinite patience. He smiled back at me, turning the day once more into an ordinary Sunday, and unequivocally shut the door.

Mrs Pettigrew's Cheque

1962

Mrs Pettigrew pulled on her gloves with no enthusiasm and waited for the car. From her window she could see that the lawns had never looked so flawless, or the roses so perfect, but the sight failed to move her. She made a mental note to tell Ackroyd that the far bed was getting perhaps a shade overcrowded, and turned, with no joy at all, to check her appearance in the mirror.

The reason for this despondency, which frequently overwhelmed Mrs Pettigrew but today was particularly bad, stared back uncompromisingly at her from the large expanse of peach-tinted glass. Mrs Pettigrew was fat. She was not only fat, she was extraordinarily ugly.

The gods, who for their sport create us, were certainly having a field day when they went to work on Mabel Pettigrew. Her upper arms, emerging from the neat navy-blue print, were of phenomenal circumference, the flesh wobbled as she moved. It was no consolation to Mrs Pettigrew that the skin that covered them and indeed the rest of her body was of a texture and translucence enviable on less ungainly contours.

As her arms were large and fleshy so too was her body, losing its battle with the best in corsetry, and her legs, tree trunks only less graceful, overflowing at their termini her fine-quality shoes.

This mountain, then, this over-liberal dollop of humanity in its faintly ridiculous, unambiguously costly petalled hat, was the image of herself with which Mrs Pettigrew's mirror faithfully presented her. It was also the likeness reflected, frequently with derision, in the eyes of those who beheld her.

That it was not the private vision of herself perceived by Mrs Pettigrew's inner eye was beside the point. She was not a stupid woman and she was well aware that if within she felt like ten ballerinas, each more ethereal than the next, and had the beauty of Garbo and Dietrich and Bergman rolled breathtakingly into one, it was of no avail. It was the outward appearance that counted and about that she could do nothing.

Not that she hadn't tried. They never told her, of course, with their hands outstretched and their obsequious leers in the slimming clinics and the beauty parlours, at the hairdressers and at the spas, that hers was a hopeless case. They were not so foolish, but then neither was Mrs Pettigrew.

On some days it was not so bad. There were times when Mrs Pettigrew was able to console herself with her fabulous house, its priceless treasures and impeccable staff. Times when she listened to the coos of admiration and adulation emitted by the so-called friends with whom she was surrounded and pretended to herself quite successfully that they meant it. There were days when she found herself quite tolerable to live with. This was not one of them.

A discreet tap on the door of the bedroom was followed by the announcement that the car was ready.

Mrs Pettigrew took a last despairing look in the mirror and with a final adjustment of her mink tie she made her way downstairs noticing with some irritation as she did so, a wilted dahlia and a strand of cotton on the Aubusson about which she would have to speak.

Mills, inclined from the waist, head slightly to one side, held open the door of the car neatly inscribed with the Pettigrew crest, and remarked upon the splendour of the day as if she personally were responsible.

Mrs Pettigrew agreed that it was warm again and, puffing slightly, sank her own upholstery into that of the car and directed him to the Park Hotel.

Under the competent leather-gloved hands of Mills, the car, whose engine was the quietest in the world, scrunched ever so lightly over the gravel drive and floated like a shiny black swan out into the main road.

Mrs Pettigrew was unimpressed. She looked at the summer-green plane trees lining the avenue of houses, each vaster than the next, and thought exactly how it was going to be.

She would arrive on time. She always did. And would be greeted with tremendous effusion by the Functions Committee members whose sighs of relief at her appearance would be almost audible. How nice of her to come, they'd say, how well she looked. One of the more inspired would in all probability admire her hat. What else about her was there to admire other, of course, than her chequebook, which they would all be praying she had remembered to bring.

After a glass of indifferent sherry, which always seemed to go directly to her feet increasing their swell, she would, from her seat of honour at the top table, be lunched, wined, cosseted, mollycoddled and fawned upon until they were finally forced to leave her in peace in order to listen to the speeches. After the speeches, impassioned, indifferent or downright incompetent, would come the appeal. After the appeal they would turn expectantly, hands outstretched to catch the fruits of their eloquence, to Mrs Pettigrew.

Had they known that Mrs Pettigrew was quite unmoved by their oratory they would have been deeply shocked. Had they in their innocence been present in the Pettigrew dining room at breakfast time they would have been even more horrified. It was not the scene that would have surprised them, the Pettigrews were sitting very nicely before their silver-topped jar of Dundee marmalade and their Queen Anne coffee pot, it was the conversation.

On this particular morning Isaiah Pettigrew had been in an exceptionally 'bonhomous' mood. Not that he was ever downhearted, not for long at any rate. The fact that Pettigrew's plate glass covered the windows of two-thirds of the houses in the country was more than enough to keep him happy. Unlike his wife, the fact that he was fat and not particularly prepossessing did not bother him in the slightest. But then, of course, he was a man.

'What is it today, dear?' Isaiah asked from behind the pages of the pink newspaper in whose columns he noted daily and with satisfaction the outward evidence of his many commercial successes.

'The Bancroft Home,' Mabel said, hoping he would not emerge from his paper and notice the quantity of butter she was spreading on her toast.

'That was poor old Harry's effort, wasn't it?' Isaiah said. 'What are they: deaf, blind or incurable?'

'I don't remember,' Mabel said. 'Pass the marmalade.'

'Fifty?' Isaiah asked, pushing the jar across the highly polished tabletop. 'Fifty guineas should be more than enough.'

'As you wish,' Mabel said removing the lid. 'Did you remember to ask Ackroyd about the compost?'

In this way the contribution that the Bancroft Home was that day to receive from the purse of Mrs Pettigrew was arbitrarily decided. Lest it be thought that the attitude of either Mabel or her husband to those less fortunate than themselves was one of callousness, it must be remembered that on practically every weekday Mrs Pettigrew was 'guest of honour' at some luncheon or another and she coped uncomplainingly, in addition, with a formidable programme of coffee mornings, bring-and-buy sales and bazaars, all of which made deep inroads upon her purse.

Mr Pettigrew himself dealt with an equally full diary of similar but more masculine activities and in this way between them they disposed philanthropically each year of a large slice of the Pettigrew income. That they were unable to identify themselves personally with each and every cause was hardly surprising. That the extent of their generosity was determined before their attendance at the various functions was only reasonable, too. The Pettigrew Charitable Trust had to be stretched in an infinite number of directions.

Had the Chairman of the Functions Committee of the Friends of the Bancroft Home known all this she would very likely not have been in such a tizzy. As it was she stood in the foyer of the Park Hotel glancing at her watch every few minutes, waiting for a glimpse of Mrs Pettigrew's Rolls.

If only she played her cards right, she thought, Mrs Pettigrew would be moved to donate an outstanding sum and others at the luncheon, holding tight to their purse strings, would be shamed or inspired into following suit. If only she got on the right side of Mrs Pettigrew her period of office as Chairman of the Functions Committee would go down in history. No one would forget Drusilla Fenwick; her name would be on their lips for years. Had Drusilla Fenwick known Mrs Pettigrew a little more intimately, she could have saved herself much worry and doubt concerning her arrival. If Mrs Pettigrew promised to be at the Park Hotel on a certain day at a certain time, there, in the absence of Riots, Strikes, Civil Commotions, War, Invasion, Acts of Enemy Hostility or any similar upheavals beloved by insurance companies, she would be.

At exactly twelve-fifteen, therefore, on the agreed day, Mrs

Pettigrew was handed into the swing doors of the Park Hotel by Mills and extracted from the scarcely large enough compartment, when they had completed their semi-circuit, by Mrs Fenwick.

Mrs Fenwick whose blood pressure dropped slowly but several degrees with relief, led Mrs Pettigrew firmly into the room where the reception was being held and now the charade with which Mrs Pettigrew was so familiar began.

Like bees round a honeypot, in their carefully selected headgear, they surrounded her.

How well she looked, the Vice-Chairman said. 'What a delightful hat,' the Hon. Sec. enthused. 'Something to drink,' the Treasurer insisted, and 'How is Mr Pettigrew keeping?' one of the more enterprising Committee members wanted to know.

Mrs Pettigrew smiled, she knew they had their jobs to do, accepted the drink, answered their questions and let it all flow over her head. It was a trick she had acquired early on in her public life and one that was very useful.

Almost before she was aware of it she found herself sitting at the top table in the private room where they were to lunch, between the Chairman and the Vice-Chairman, having been applauded as she entered.

Out of a sea of three hundred faces Mrs Pettigrew was able to distinguish several that she knew. She smiled amicably at those who sought her eye, her mind on other things. Wedged between Mrs Fenwick and her faithful helper, the wedging due rather to Mrs Pettigrew's proportions than those of the other two ladies, Mrs Pettigrew was plied with lunch. And she was also plied with endless bright chatter, but since she dealt with this with only a small portion of her mind it did not weary her.

After years of practice she was now adept at simulating attention to things that did not interest her. She was even able to interpolate yes and no in exactly the right places in a conversation she scarcely heard.

When Mrs Fenwick turned briefly to the representative from the Bancroft Home, who sat on her other side and excused her inattention with the sotto voce confidence that they were working on a whacking cheque from Mrs Pettigrew, Mrs Pettigrew, as if every word had not been audible, applied herself diligently to her dessert. She had no illusions about herself or any of them in their smart hats. There was nothing that she hadn't heard before.

The coffee dispensed – a tiny cup, Mrs Pettigrew could have drunk three – the Chairman rapped importantly upon the table with her gavel and informed the assembled ladies that the time for idle chatter was at an end and the serious part of the luncheon was about to begin.

One thing that Mrs Pettigrew never objected to on this and similar occasions was the speeches. It meant that her immediate neighbours would stop talking for a while and leave her in peace. That she was free to doze, provided, of course, that she did so attentively and with her eyes open. To slip off her shoes and to digest her meal.

At every reference to 'our dear Mrs Pettigrew' or our

'Honoured Guest', Mrs Pettigrew smiled and inclined her head in acknowledgement. Her torpor was never deep enough to cause her to miss a cue. She was too old a hand.

By the bursts of enthusiastic applause, in which of course she participated, Mrs Pettigrew was able to pinpoint the beginning and end of every speech and to assess the progress of the luncheon. The function, like most things, had a shape, and with no reference to the diamond-studded watch embedded in her wrist Mrs Pettigrew was able to assess its every contour.

When, out of the mists, she heard the words '... and now, ladies, I am sure that not a single one among you can fail to be moved by the splendid work the Bancroft Home is doing ...' Mrs Pettigrew knew that it was time to wake up and feel surreptitiously beneath the table for her shoes.

In a very few minutes she would be invited to start the ball rolling with her contribution to the Bancroft Home, would whisper 'fifty guineas' in the ear of the Chairman, the amount agreed by herself and Isaiah at breakfast, would be loudly applauded, thanked publically and finally released.

Mrs Pettigrew winced as her oedematous feet forced their way into the shoes that only an hour ago had not really been too uncomfortable.

Mrs Fenwick, standing before the microphone, smiled encouragingly at Mrs Pettigrew, and Mrs Pettigrew smiled back indicating that she was prepared to do that which was expected of her.

Mrs Fenwick turned once more to her audience from whom wafted drifts of idle smoke. 'Before we call upon our

Guest of Honour,' Mrs Fenwick said, 'to start the ball rolling with the gift she has so graciously consented to make to the Bancroft Home, we have a little surprise for you. One of the girls who has been brought up in the Home is here today to offer a token of appreciation and, incidentally, a sample of the fine work done in the Home, to Mrs Pettigrew.

Mrs Fenwick looked towards the door. The incomplete silence granted to Mrs Fenwick became complete as they too twisted their heads to look towards the door. Mrs Pettigrew, from her seat of vantage, patted her moist upper lip with her table napkin and, watching expectantly too, waited.

The door immediately opposite Mrs Pettigrew opened, and into the room, up the gangway, slowly, came the most beautiful girl she had ever seen. She was no more than sixteen, tall, slim as a reed, walked like a princess and had honey-coloured hair cascading right down her back. She held a bouquet of apricot roses as fine as any that Ackroyd had ever produced, and she was the embodiment of everything that all her life Mrs Pettigrew had ever wanted to look like but never for one single moment had.

Her progress towards Mrs Pettigrew was painfully, laboriously slow. It wasn't, however, until she extended a milk-white arm and an artist's dream of a slim hand to feel for the edge of the table that Mrs Pettigrew realised that the girl was blind. With almost more of a shock she realised, too, that the apricot roses were artificial. The girl, chin lifted, extended them to her, dropping a straight-backed curtsey as she did so.

Mrs Pettigrew, with the kind of tenderness with which she

could have held a newborn baby, took the flowers. Her eyes on the girl's grey, unseeing ones, she was quite unable to speak.

Amid a thunder of applause the girl turned, and as slowly as she had come, one foot carefully in front of the other, made her way to the door. Until she had gone from the room Mrs Pettigrew kept her eyes riveted on the slim waist.

Mrs Fenwick was holding up her hand for silence. 'And now,' she said when she had obtained it, except for the occasional small snuffle into the odd handkerchief, 'I will at this point call upon our dear Mrs Pettigrew to make the first donation to our new drive for the maintenance and improvement of the Bancroft Home.'

She looked nervously, expectantly, at Mrs Pettigrew who was gazing fatly down at the apricot roses and fingering them delicately with her short plump fingers.

'One hundred guineas,' said Mrs Pettigrew.

Taormina

1962

'Taormina?' Iris said, threading her needle with blue wool. 'Surely, darling, that's a place, not a person.'

'This is a person,' Jonathan said.

'It's like calling somebody Bexhill or – or Clacton.'

Jonathan perched on the stone coping of the terrace and looked down at his mother who was squinting at her tapestry.

'I'd like to explain about Taormina.'

Iris decided on the right-hand corner as being as good a place as any to begin and inserted the needle.

'I shouldn't bother, darling. We survived the others, no doubt we shall survive Taormina.'

'Taormina's different.'

'I'm sure she is, darling. So were Bo-Peep and Mary Grey and Samantha what's 'ername, and Joanna, and the one with freckles, and who was that extraordinary creature with the orange hair your father couldn't stand?'

'Diana.'

'That's right. Diana.'

Jonathan dismissed them all impatiently with a wave of his hand.

'Mother, this is serious ...'

Iris was holding the tapestry at arm's length and looking at it over the top of her glasses.

'I do believe they've sent me the wrong blue,' she said slowly. ' They have, you know. Look at this!'

Jonathan sighed and jumped down on to the black-and-white tiles.

'That blue is not the same as this, is it?'

'More or less. No one will notice.'

'That's beside the point. Aren't they the absolute end. You can't rely on anyone.'

'About the weekend,' Jonathan said, leaning now against the balustrade and looking out on to the garden.

'I've asked the Watsons for Saturday. Serena Watson's been driving me mad for weeks trying to find out when you'd be down. One mustn't be harsh. I suppose if I had three daughters, each plainer than the next, although I must say the youngest one's improved tremendously lately ... Jonathan!'

Iris took off her glasses and watched him in his dirty white plimsolls walk down the steps and on to the lawn.

How much taller was he going to get? Surely he must now have stopped growing. How old was he? Twenty-four, nearly twenty-five. He dragged his feet along the grass, leaving marks in the dew, for it was still early, and slumped on to the wooden seat facing the pond. Adonis, Iris thought, looking at his profile, the personification of careless youth: slim, no fat, cleanly outlined features, the flop of the fair hair. The age had an insouciance about it, a sort of unconscious splendour employed arrogantly, extravagantly, by those who were unaware of its ephemeral nature. No wonder the girls were mad about him. He hadn't even to speak, just to lean, he was always leaning, against the lintel in a crowded room ... and they'd be round him like butterflies, gazing up at him, eager ...

Iris put on her glasses again and turned her attention to her tapestry. She had every reason to be content.

Taormina arrived on the six-ten. She wore blue jeans and sandals attached to her feet by a single thong between her toes whose nails were scarlet. From the window Iris watched Jonathan help her down from the shooting brake and kiss her. She came no higher than his shoulder. The embrace was a long one, and when they'd parted they stood with linked hands, gazing at each other. Such capacity to love, Iris thought, such vulnerability. No one can help them. They have to grow their own shells.

'This is Taormina,' Jonathan said at the dinner table. 'My parents.'

She had changed into a silk cheongsam and very high-heeled white shoes. Her small, oval face was animated, only the grey eyes were wary, watching Iris and Miles.

'There's one thing about Jonathan,' Miles said, taking her hand in his, 'he has exquisite taste.'

Iris watched her turn to caress Jonathan for a moment with her eyes and Jonathan, equally volubly, return the love, and thought next month it will be Dawn or Sandra or Pollyanna – how they delude themselves.

Over dinner Taormina, vivacious, laughing as easily as she talked, kept them amused. She flirted mildly with Miles who, through Jonathan's girlfriends, tried to recapture his youth, if only for the odd moment. Jonathan himself, an anxious impresario, watched her every move.

It must be difficult for her, Iris thought, helping Taormina to strawberry cake. Soon the others will come.

But Taormina seemed to be happy. After dinner, when the Miller boys came and the four Sutherlands and the Farrows' house party complete, they drifted noisily towards the sitting room, leaving Iris and Miles on the terrace with their cigarettes.

'Thank heavens it's not every night,' Miles said as the music, blasting out of the open windows, became more and more deafening and the laughter and the clapping drowned out the evening serenade of the crickets.

They looked in through the open window on their way to bed. The oldest Miller boy, sleeves rolled up, red-faced, feet thumping on the floor, was at the piano; Jonathan sat tailor-wise on the floor with his electric guitar; and on the marble table in the centre of the room, barefoot, arms above her head, hair flying, Taormina was dancing.

'I hope they remember to lock up,' Miles said.

Iris yawned. 'From the look of them, I doubt if they'll be gone by breakfast-time.'

'At least Jonathan is over the Finals,' Miles said. 'He can dissipate with a clear conscience.'

'He always has done. I keep forgetting he's a doctor now.'

'It's difficult for us to remember that youth is anything other than young.'

In the morning, by the time Miles appeared, Taormina and Jonathan were on the terrace sunbathing, Taormina in a pink bikini.

'The energy of it,' Miles said, 'Taormina, where did you get your lovely name?'

'Born or conceived on the Island, I should imagine,' Iris said coming out through the French windows. 'Sicily is so intensely beautiful, I think it was extremely clever of your parents.'

'They had never been further than Brighton,' Taormina said.

Jonathan jumped up. 'Taormina, come for a swim!'

Ballet dancers, they leaped down the steps and over the lawn.

'Odd,' Miles said; 'we don't care to discuss our antecedents.'

'She's an odd child,' Iris said. 'Jonathan always picks slightly "off-beat" ones.'

'Amusing, though,' Miles said. 'I shall be quite sorry when he starts bringing home plain Janes with glasses.'

'He'll have to settle down some time, especially if he's going into general practice.'

A shriek of laughter floated over the hedge from the swimming pool.

'I think I'll go for a dip myself,' Miles said.

Iris smiled. 'Give my love to Taormina.'

For lunch Taormina changed into skin-tight pink trousers

and piled her hair into a knot on top of her head. Her nose had started to peel from the sun. She looked enchanting.

Next to the Watson girls, earnest in white, ready for tennis, Taormina looked not quite real. She didn't play but picked up the balls for them, clowning all the while.

After tea, languid on the terrace, Jonathan played snake-charming music on his harmonica; Taormina, lithe, apparently boneless, was the snake.

Miles, watching her, said: 'She's extraordinarily graceful.'

Iris, from behind her sunglasses, was watching the movement, and the sunlight through the balustrade, and the faces of youth, and listening to the music and the laughter.

'I wish it was always like this,' she sighed.

'We shall be glad of the peace on Monday.'

'I have a horrid feeling that it can't last, a sort of premonition.'

'It's always like this when Jonathan's down.'

'I get the impression that this is the last time; that it will never be quite the same again.'

'It's obvious,' Miles said, getting up, 'that you could do with a Pimm's. You're getting broody.'

Iris was watching Jonathan watching Taormina 'There's something going on,' she said. 'I feel it in my bones.'

After dinner there were twenty of them, most of the girls in floating dresses. Jonathan got out the floodlights and the record player and they danced on the lawn, Taormina, in gold lamé trousers, took off her shoes and leaped to the music like a firebird. Wherever she was, always laughing, was the centre of the crowd.

When Iris was woken by the birds at six next morning she heard them calling 'Goodnight.'

Miles went to church alone, Taormina had letters to write, Iris had a headache, and Jonathan was waiting for a telephone call.

At mid-morning Iris, topping and tailing gooseberries in the shade of the big elm, watched Jonathan, in his open-necked white shirt and grey trousers with grass stains at the knees, pace up and down kicking at nothing on the lawn.

'Want any help?'

This was unlike him. Iris showed no surprise. 'That would be nice.'

He squatted beside her and picked up a gooseberry.

'Mother?'

'Mm?'

'About Taormina.'

A sudden crystallisation of her earlier premonitions swept over Iris. She put a gooseberry in the colander topped but not tailed.

'There's something I have to tell you,' Jonathan said. Iris looked at him.

'You want to marry her,' Iris said slowly.

'No, it isn't that.'

Iris let out a breath of relief.

'We're already married,' Jonathan said.

The gooseberries, topped-and-tailed and not-topped-and-tailed, scattered over the lawn.

'I'm sorry to spring it on you like this ... I tried on Friday ...'

'Just say it again, will you, dear? Slowly,' Iris said. 'I have a bit of a headache and I'm not sure that ı heard you correctly.'

'Taormina is my wife,' Jonathan said. 'We were married last month in Cambridge.'

'Jonathan,' Iris said, 'you'd better explain quickly because I feel very shocked and I simply don't understand. There was no reason why you shouldn't get married, we expected it. You've passed your Finals and you're going into partnership with Dr Slocombe, but why the secrecy?'

'I'm afraid that's something else I have to tell you,' Jonathan said, throwing the gooseberry he had been holding into the pond. 'I'm not going into practice with old Slocombe.'

'You'd better start at the beginning,' Iris said, and noticed the bead of sweat on Jonathan's forehead although they were in the shade.

'Taormina's parents died when she was small,' Jonathan said, 'within a year of each other. I might as well explain about her name. They hadn't a lot of money, her parents, but a great deal of imagination. Each year before their annual holiday in Brighton they'd go to the travel agent and get all the leaflets and information about a glamorous holiday resort somewhere in the world. In their dreams they'd go there. In the year that Taormina was born it was Sicily.

'Anyway, after they died Taormina was looked after by an aunt. Because she seemed to have talent the aunt put her on the stage when she was fifteen, and she became a dancer. After a couple of years she decided that she would rather do something for mankind other than entertain it and she took up nursing. She was doing her final year for the SRN in Cambridge when we met.'

'Taormina a nurse?' Iris said. 'I can't believe it.'

'She is,' Jonathan said, 'and a good one.'

'But I still don't understand ...'

'The next bit is more difficult. Taormina and I got on together right from the start. Taormina will surprise you when you get to know her ...'

'She seems a sweet girl,' Iris said. 'Why didn't you bring her home and get engaged and married in the usual way? There's nothing sinister, is there?'

' Nothing at all. Taormina, I told you, has no parents. Her aunt isn't very well off ...'

Iris sat up. 'You were worried about the wedding. Darling, you know that Daddy and I ... You are our only son, we could have had a marquee in the garden and Follis to do the catering. They did the Beauchamps' superbly.'

'That's just the point,' Jonathan said.

'What is?'

'That you would have been willing to spend hundreds of pounds feeding strawberries and cream to half the county.'

'Why on earth not? Your father can afford it.'

'Because we want you to give us the money instead. The money you would have spent on our wedding if we hadn't got married in Cambridge.'

'The money, Jonathan? What on earth for?'

'To feed bread and potatoes to people who have never seen strawberries and cream.'

Iris waited.

'Taormina and I are young. All over the world there are people suffering, children dying. I'm a doctor and she is a nurse. We are going to help them.'

'Darling, it's terribly high-minded of you,' Iris said, 'but there are people needing your help in Dr Slocombe's practice. I really can't see why you have to go to the ends of the earth ...'

'For the most part, the crowd in Slocombe's waiting room won't die for lack of attention. Besides, there'll never be any difficulty in finding someone to take over there. It's a plum practice. Any young man would be glad of the opportunity in this county, particularly with the lure of the Watson girls.'

'Whose idea was all this?' Iris asked.

'Taormina's. We're starting off in Algeria. We leave at the end of the month.'

Iris looked around. 'There'll be no elms,' she said, 'no dancing on the lawn, no tennis ...'

'We'll be back from time to time.'

'I knew it couldn't last. I told your father.'

'What's that?'

'Nothing. I'm going in to lie down. You'll pick up the gooseberries?'

'Of course, and I'm sorry ...'

But Iris had gone.

When Miles came back from church he went up to change. Iris was lying on the bed.

Dangling his tie, Miles looked out of the window. Suddenly he chuckled.

'What is it?' Iris said.

'Taormina. She's wearing scarlet trousers and she's walking round the pond on her hands.' He turned to Iris, rolling up his tie neatly. 'Excellent company, I must say, but I doubt if she's a thought in her pretty little head.'

Iris got off the bed and stood where her husband had been watching the flash of red slowly circumvent the pond in the washed sunlight of the garden.

'You know, Miles, there are times,' she said, ' when one can be hideously, hideously wrong.'

Peeping Tom

1965

We met at the Ritz, the Lisbon one. I was dining when she came in, and all through the potato soup and the beef with mustard sauce I had been wondering who she was. I say came in. It was not so much a coming in as an ingression, an intrusion upon the suitably muted brouhaha of the Grill. She was cocooned in mink under which there was the suggestion of nothing, for she did not remove it, and flanked – or more precisely, followed, so fast was her progress from door to table – by two alpaca-suited, be-ringed youths too old for sons, too young for ... No, perhaps she liked them tender. One felt one should know her face. An examination of it brought hints of gossip column and glossy magazine. She looked at no one, occupied only with her paramours and the undivided attention of the maître d'. She was satisfied to be looked at. Every pair of eyes was turned in her direction, openly or secretly. One sensed she recognised this as her due. She had not so much beauty as presence, an élan vital, the current of which had charged the entire Grill, waiters and diners alike. Her hair (burnished copper was too dull, red misleading, more I would say autumn leaves of a particular variety brought to a high gloss) was done up in a kind of cone effect, its symmetry perfectly balancing her face. I have said it was not beautiful, the eyes rendered her remaining features superfluous. From where I sat I could not distinguish their colour, but the light that emanated from beneath their shadowed periphery dimmed the two small, shaded table lamps. They were truly enormous. The maître d', inclining from the waist, almost drowned, the attendant circus danced in their fulguration. The slim hands, illustrating her requirements, were good too, pale ambassadors of her desires. I had seen her before. The name was titillating my tongue. Actress? Screen star? I could almost, but maddeningly not quite, recall.

The beef had lost its savour. I was forking it into my mouth, although it might now have been hay, and looking in her direction when she glanced round. I am forty-two and personable. The touch of grey above my ears lends an air of board or consulting room. I am intimate with my looks and the effect they are likely to produce, I have lived by them and my wits for a great many years.

She did not look away. Not until a delicate frisson of rapport had woven its web between her table and mine. I wondered what was under the mink. Predictably, aware of my interest, she turned her attentions more animatedly, or so she intended it to appear, to her companions. Their hands made brief contact, they raised glasses, shared intimate, divinely humorous jokes. I wagered with myself that before I laid down my fork she would look at me again. She did. With immense subtlety, of course. I was merely in her line of vision as her eyes swept the room seeking some elusive face-saving figment of her imagination. The field, I sensed, was open. Madame, for all her entourage, was bored.

I was feeling in my pocket for five escudos with which to bribe my waiter for her name when the very good King Wenceslaus of a diminutive page hopped down the marble steps and into the restaurant. Less elevated establishments might call their guests over speakers. Not so the Ritz. Unwilling to shatter the dearly priced silence, they dispatched a page, for whose buttoned uniform the ragamuffin youth of the city would give its eyeteeth. He passed from table to table with a neatly lettered billboard held proudly at chest level. Madame Gonzalez was wanted on the telephone.

Gonzalez. Of course. The Madame was a courtesy. She was one of the famous Gonzalez sisters. Of course I knew her, everyone did. There were three: a pianist, a physicist and a social butterfly. The hands, nails almond-shaped, that gesticulated less than ten feet away were not on close terms with a keyboard, their owner, I was willing to bet, was ignorant of the simplest scientific formula, she blazed a trail, though, from Madrid to Monte Carlo, settled, for no longer than a moonbeam, in London or New York. Her pace was matched, but only just, by the newshounds. Lucia Gonzalez.

The page had reached her table. One companion touched her sleeve, the other held her chair. She looked at me for a brief moment, clutched her coat more tightly round her, elevated her head and was gone. Everything went with her.

Noses were back in the soup. I glanced up to see if the lights had really dimmed. She did not return.

I was due to drive next morning to the Algarve. At nine the car, a Mercedes, was at the door. I instructed the girl from the hire company to park it. I would leave later in the day. She shrugged. 'It is a six-hour drive, señor.' I told her not to worry and she got in the car with a final word of warning to take the Villafranca road if I delayed my start later than three o'clock.

All morning I haunted the foyer, having ascertained from the desk that Madame Gonzalez was still in residence. By three o'clock, when I should have been speeding south through the cork trees and the rice fields, I was hungry and nauseatingly familiar with every item of local art and craft in the gift shop. I lunched hurriedly – well, hurriedly for the Ritz against whose tradition it was to hasten – and emerged, coffeeless in my anxiety, in time to see the copper-red-autumn-leaf-burnished coiffure disappear, minion-flanked, in the back of a matching sedan.

For ten escudos I learned that she had left for Estoril where the weary croupiers raked the tables laid only sparsely with plaques after the summer season. I coaxed the Mercedes to action and took the Auto-estrada, rehearsing my speech of introduction en route. In the casino parking lot there was no sign among the Fiats and Studebakers of a bronze car of any description. The man at the door was helpful. The señora had looked in for a moment only and had gone on, he thought, eyeing the crumpled note in my hand, to Cascais.

The boats at Cascais siestaed still in the sun of what, to the local inhabitants, was winter, but would have done an English August proud. Two mottled, scrawny dogs chased each other and their tails outside the bay hotel. A waiter cleared away debris from the few outside tables. He had not seen a señora with red hair. Yes, certainly he would have noticed. Perhaps she had gone to Sintra.

The afternoon was heavy, the square at Sintra empty except for cab drivers waiting for fares. Yes, a señora with red hair had driven up, to the Palace.

The scent of camellias on the steeply winding road almost overpowered me. I drew the Mercedes perilously close to the edge to allow a coach to pass. A huddle of sightseers stared from the courtyard at the grotesque contours of the Palace. Slightly apart, a girl with red hair leaned against her companion in a stance that cried out honeymoon.

I drove back along the coastal road. By now I could have been in Faro. Women had always been the primroses in my path.

No, the hotel said, Madame Gonzalez had not returned. Next to me an American enquired about tickets for the bull-ring. I could no longer tolerate the sight of the gift shop. I decided to be bold.

A chambermaid who supported a family of six let me into the señora's suite. For the second time in one afternoon, I was almost anaesthetised by the fragrance of flowers. The paramours had done their work. The sitting room was a veritable bower. I telephoned for champagne and two glasses, and settled into an armchair behind one of the floral tributes from where I could see the door. This time she couldn't escape. It didn't occur to me that it would be I who would wish to.

The waiter came, fussed over the ice bucket and left. Apart from the flowers and one photograph, the room was impersonal. The photograph was of a schoolgirl desperately plain.

At five-thirty it grew dark. I lighted one lamp, not wanting to frighten her, and wished I had brought the English newspaper. I think I must have dozed, drugged by the flowers. I was awakened by the sound of the door opening. I hadn't heard the key. Madame Gonzalez extended a limp hand into the corridor for kissing. She wore a greyish jersey suit. It sculpted contours of which an eighteen-year-old would not be ashamed. I knew she must be almost twice that age.

She closed the door, turning the key in the lock, and leaned against it breathing a sigh of what sounded like relief. The beautiful eyes were closed. I waited a moment, not wishing to scare her, until she emerged from her reverie. I had my mouth open to say 'Madame Gonzalez' in as gentle a voice as I could when she did something that cleaved the words to my tongue. I thought she was running her fingers through her hair. She did in fact put her hands to her head. When she lowered them the burnished-copper what-have-you hairdo was between them. What remained was a short crop of dull, indeterminately coloured strands, springing from a crown lamentably flat. I shut my mouth unable even to think. She set the wig, like an empty busby, on the table near the champagne and walked to the mirror on the far wall. Facing it, she cupped one hand beneath her eye, extended the lid with the other and blinked; when she had repeated the process with the other eye she set two tiny objects into a small box which she took from her handbag. Before I had decided what to do she disappeared into the bedroom. I knew I must go. I was a crafty operator at best but did not care, unless the occasion provided no alternative, to wound the susceptibility of others.

I took two burglar-worthy strides to the door. She had not only locked it but removed the key. I was trapped, an unwilling peeping Tom. I resumed my seat behind the flowers and was wondering what I should do, wishing I had driven, as planned, to the Algarve, when she came out of the bedroom. I assumed at least that it was Madame Gonzalez, for it was she who had gone in. The woman who walked slowly into the sitting room reading a letter would scarcely have raised a flicker of desire in the least discriminating man. The straight crop was brushed behind her ears, which were none too small, she wore glasses with unflattering frames and heavy lenses, her silk wrap clung to her flat figure.

I was not ignorant of women and their wiles, which were as ancient as time. It was the complete metamorphosis that threw me. Somewhere I had seen this woman. I refused to admit even to myself that this was Madame Gonzalez.

'Madame Gonzalez!' The words came, ejected by my conscience, softly.

For a moment her eyes remained on the letter; from there they swivelled to me and from me to the red wig shining in the lamplight on the table. She might have been naked.

Her hand was on the telephone. 'I shall call the manager.'

'No, please; let me explain.'

'How long have you been there?' She was looking again at the wig.

'Long enough. I had no intention ...' I took the receiver from her hand. 'Let me give you some champagne.'

She sat down abruptly and I could see that she was trembling. The empty wig, like an evil eye, shrieked traitor, as I did battle with the cork. I looked from it to her in all her plainness, quite stupefied and trying not to let her see.

We both needed the drink. She didn't look at me. The scent of the flowers filled the silence. I cleared my throat. 'Madame Gonzalez, I would like to explain ...'

She held up her hand. 'It is all the same ...' She turned the photograph of the schoolgirl on the table towards me. Of course, the eyes. I should have known.

'My mother used to say, "You have beautiful eyes."' She spoke as if to herself. 'Eyes and hands. It was by way of consolation. I was neither talented like Maria or Rosanna, nor beautiful as she. I favoured my father. People remembered him by his nose. On him it was an asset. Maria had her piano, Rosanna her laboratory, Mother her looks, Father his nose. Wherever we went, the Gonzalez family made its mark. When I was with my sisters, one was begged to perform, the other to speak about her work. When I walked in the street with my mother, heads were turned at every step. When I walked alone I remained alone, attracting less interest than a paving stone. I did not want to be a paving stone. The nose was painful but soon over. That was the least. It takes me an hour, at the very least, to assemble Lucia Gonzalez for the street. You cannot know what it is like.'

'Is it worth the candle?'

'I am no longer a paving stone. Wherever I go heads are turned. There are three sisters.'

She picked up the photograph. 'There used to be two, Maria, Rosanna and that plain one, I cannot remember her name. I killed her long ago. Only when I am alone does she rise from the tomb – or when I think I am alone.'

Alone and lonely. I pitied her, desire long ago having fled. I tried to think of something to say. That she was more beautiful without her aids. She was not. A woman on a bus. A paving stone.

I changed the subject, my voice a decibel higher than was usual. 'Shall you stay long in Lisbon?'

'Who knows?'

She looked round at the room, the flowers, and said unasked: 'I have no home.'

'That makes two of us. I am building a house in the Algarve. I am forty-two. One needs a place for household gods.'

She looked up sharply, in control now. 'You'd better go.'

'I haven't explained. You don't even know my name.'

'It isn't necessary.'

'Will you have dinner with me?'

'I'm tired. I shall dine in my room.'

'Luncheon tomorrow?'

She looked at me, half-smiling, relaxed. 'One o'clock in the Grill.'

'I shall look forward to it, Madame.'

'Now go.'

'If you would kindly open the door.'

I could not sleep. At two I rang for whisky and a sandwich, pacing the marble floor. In the morning I rose late, jaded, and rang Faro saying I had been delayed. There were still two hours to kill. I wandered out of the hotel and into the dusty street towards the Liberdade. Lucia Gonzalez, the cobbles said. I saw a woman of remarkable plainness. Twelve o'clock, then one.

In the Grill I took my table but refused the menu. I was, I said, waiting.

At one-thirty I resolved to give her until two. At two I combed the foyer lest she had mistaken the venue. At two-thirty I demanded at the desk that they call her.

The clerk looked at me surprised.

'Madame Gonzalez checked out, señor.'

'Gone?'

'She took the morning plane to Madrid.'

My actions, of course, in surprising her with her hair down, as it were, had been those of a heel. She could not have done otherwise.

I lunched alone, liver, English style, washed down with *vinho verde*. I did not enjoy it. I felt I should set off for the Algarve but had lost my enthusiasm.

'A little cheese, señor?'

My rambling thoughts clicked suddenly, lucidly, into place.

I laid down my napkin.

'I'll take the cheese in Madrid.'

The Very Even Break

1966

It was seven-thirty when the phone rang. I had got into bed at four; it felt like five minutes ago.

'Ginger?'

I said nothing.

'Ginger?'

It was ten years since I had heard the voice, the nickname. Only the tone had changed, lost its note of patronage.

'Are you there?'

'I'm here.'

'This is Clint, remember?'

Remember; engraved like a scar on the tissue of my memory.

'Sorry to wake you, honey. Just touched down from the States. I have to see Rosensweig. He's casting this fourth-century epic, two thousand extras, greatest thing to hit motion pictures since ...'

'I heard about it.'

'You did? Who told you?'

'Rosensweig.'

'Did he mention Clint McGowan for the male lead?'

'No.'

'Listen, honey, I'm in a callbox and my car is waiting. I'm throwing a party. I want you to come.'

I made an unsteady grab for my diary.

'OK.' I had been waiting ten years for this.

'Tonight. Eight thirty on. The Starlight room.'

'Tonight!'

'I know you're a pretty busy woman ...'

Busy! June the first. Four fifteen: the Bardsley wedding at St Peter's Eaton Square; five thirty: cocktails with the Beckforth Smiths en route from New York to Paris; simultaneous drinks with the Cromer Waddells to celebrate their daughter's engagement; the Savoy at seven thirty to interview David Glover on his latest production; dinner and dance at eight thirty in aid of the Children's Winter Holiday Scheme. I had promised the viscountess ...

'I read your column every week. It's just great. You really go all those places, know all those people, or are you a syndicate?'

'Just little me.'

'I always knew you'd make it. Brother, I said, that ball of fire will go right to the top. You still ginger, Ginger?'

I took a pencil and queried the viscountess, hoping I could escape after the dinner. 'I may be a little late.'

'Bless you, and forgive me for waking you at this hour. What time's the deadline?'

I played dumb. 'Deadline?'

'Deadline for the Martha Munroe column.'

'Three thirty a.m.'

I thought I heard a sigh of relief. 'Don't worry, honey. I won't detain you.'

'I've never missed a deadline.'

It was too late to go back to sleep. Susan was coming to do my hair and I had ordered breakfast for eight. I lay back on the eau-de-nil pillow with its white lace over-slip, stretched like a cat, fine for the circulation, then relaxed, enjoying as always the space, the warmth, the outrageous luxury of my bedroom and allowed my thoughts to regress.

Clint McGowan. I had grown up immune to 'copper-knob', 'rusty', 'carrots', in my schooldays, but shaking like a leaf with humiliation on Clint McGowan's terrace ten years ago was the first and last time until just now I had answered to Ginger.

Since I was nine years old I had wanted to be a newspaper reporter. We lived in a flat in South London, two rooms and six kids over my father's greengrocer's shop. Shop, well, it was tiny really, most of the stuff outside on the pavement: grapes 'sweet as sugar', plums 'pick of the crop', tomatoes 'don't squeeze me till I'm yours'.

He got up at four to go to the market, Dad did, and it was always after six when the shutters went up. He never made a decent living. Too honest; not believing that the quickness of the hand deceived the eye and palming nobody off with rotten apples or overripe bananas.

My mother scrubbed the floors at the town hall, recognising

the dignitaries by their shoes as they muddied the steps she had just carefully washed, with never a word of apology.

I only ever saw two newspapers. The evening for the racing results, and the local rag, because my parents were both cinema fans and liked to know exactly what was on and where and who was playing in good time for Saturday night. I always waited with excitement for Wednesdays when the paper came but turned immediately to the 'weddings' page.

I would glance briefly at the photographs of the demure brides on the arms of their apprehensive grooms, then turn to the copy whose phrases read like poetry to my ears. 'The bride wore a dress of criss-cross taffeta, her bouquet was of tulips and freesias ... bridesmaids were her twin sister Janet and her cousin Linda Groves, charming in lemon tulle ... the bride was given away by her father and wore a wild silk dress, a train falling from her waist ... the Matron-of-Honour's lilac moiré full-skirted gown was sashed with green ... the bridesmaids wore Dutch bonnets ... dresses were made by the bride's mother ...'

At school I got Cs for my compositions. Miss Baxter, who took us for English and had, I was convinced, a heart of stone, said I allowed myself to be carried away by words, the meanings of which I had not the slightest idea, and neither, I am willing to swear now, had Miss Baxter.

I used phrases such as 'co-opted on to the local council', 'the growing threat to old people' and 'a warm welcome was extended to the Lady Mayoress' culled from the local paper and without exception in the wrong context.

I told her I wanted to be a newspaper woman, Miss Baxter

I mean. At first she thought I meant deliver them, but when the message finally got through she looked at me pityingly. I don't know whether because of my essays or because my poor little overworked dad dropped down dead one morning early, in the market, just as I was in my final term and about to leave school.

The only newspaper we saw now came with the chips for tea. The racing results were no longer of any interest and Mum had no heart for the cinema. I still brooded on the brides in guipure lace, however, carrying a simple hymn book.

I took a job in a shoe shop. The money was good but my mind was not on that but 'the honeymoon was in Jersey' or 'the happy couple left for St Mawes where the bridegroom's uncle is lending them a cottage'.

They suffered me for almost a year then fired me. I called at the local newspaper office. In a weak moment they said I could run errands, make tea, in exchange for a pittance. My mother created; scrubbing her fingers to the bone and all that while I … I loved her, but I loved ambition more.

I emptied waste-paper baskets, carried copy form desk to desk, inhaling the heady smell of newsprint and absorbing through every pore the jargon of the trade. There was no knowing how long I might have persisted in my monotonous ritual if something had not happened, resulting, for me, in an almost meteoric rise in my career.

I was waiting after work, in the bus queue, first on one foot then on the other, for both were aching, when a lorry which had been cruising steadily down the high street changed course quite suddenly and headed with determination for the very paving stones on which I stood.

Miraculously, like the waters of the Red Sea, the long line of waiting commuters parted, leaving alone, and directly in the path of the vehicle gone crazy, an oblivious and heavily pregnant woman with a child in a pushchair.

In the bedlam that followed it was impossible to see exactly what happened. A hand, I think, had pulled the pregnant lady free, she had lost her grip on the pushchair and, with the child in it, it was pinned against the wall.

I learned the hard way the meaning of pandemonium but this was the whisper of leaves against the primitive shrieks of the mother calling for her child.

The ambulance came, and the fire brigade with special tackle, and the police. When it was over, the ring of bells no more than an echo, and only the lorry lay drunkenly still on the pavement, I asked a remaining constable, my heart thumping, to which hospital they had taken the child. He told me and for the first time in my life I hailed a taxi.

Next morning I appeared at the office with red-rimmed eyes. Dana Luck who did the Woman's Page asked if I'd been crying. I said no, only hadn't been to bed.

The waste-paper baskets no longer of any interest, I made for the News Editor's office and knocked upon the glass with more confidence than I felt. Mike Munroe, unwed and everybody's heart-throb, had never looked anywhere but through me. I wasn't sure, in fact, if he knew I existed.

He said, 'Yes?' as if he too had had a rough night, and waited.

I laid thirteen sheets of blue-lined, handwritten paper from Mum's writing pad on his desk.

'What's this?'

'There was an accident. I was on the spot.' He waited.

'I wrote it up for the paper. You'll use it, won't you?'

He glanced at the top sheet and let me roast in hell on the uncarpeted floor until he threw back his head and started to laugh.

'What's wrong?' I could see nothing funny; its composition had after all occupied me the whole long night.

He stopped laughing and watched my tired eyes fill with hurt tears.

'There is something wrong?'

He nodded and looked at me, serious now.

'The first thing you must learn if you're going to be a reporter is never to use purple ink!'

Mike did use the paragraph, although by the time the thirteen sheets were cut to nine lines and the spelling improved upon, scarcely a word remained that was my own.

It appeared on the front page, though, and I was launched. My ascent, as ascents go, was swift. I liked to think it was because I was dedicated, but know it was because I married Mike. I had the talent, I suppose, and he taught me, with infinite patience, the technique.

Within two years I had achieved my ambition and my description of local weddings – she wore a red velvet dress and carried a basket posy – brought tears to the eyes. Within three I had thoroughly learned my craft. I was fed to the teeth,

in fact, with such items as 'Shoplifting pair fined', 'Vegetar-
ian movement spreads', 'Public ignores warning', 'Apathetic?
Not us, traders tell Chamber' and similar snippets of news.
Saying nothing to Mike I applied for, and to my amazement
was offered, for a trial period, a job on a national evening
newspaper.

I thought Mike would be angry, but he wasn't. There was
a new tea girl with a forty-inch bust and false eyelashes, so I
think he was quite pleased in a way.

On my first assignment for the new paper I thought I'd die.
Clarice Leighton, the second-richest woman in the world, was
at Claridge's, they said. Bring back a story, but quick.

I was still very much the local girl, unused to pile carpets,
commissionaires and lifts.

Clarice Leighton was a doll; a sad, rich doll.

'You're shaking like a jelly,' she said and made me drink a
vodka and tomato juice at mid-morning.

She rattled through the copy for me, walking barefoot in a
black negligée across the white carpet, until I had more than
enough to keep even the strictest editor quite happy.

When I'd put my pen away she took me over to her dressing table, pushed me on to the stool and put a cape round my
shoulders. 'Honey,' she said, 'with a face like yours you could
launch a million ships, but not the way you treat it.'

I got used to the carpets, the lush foyers, the hotel suites,
the celebrities. Not all of them were rich; some bored, some
drunk, some crazy. I interviewed them in penthouses and cel-
lars; in trains and ships; even on one occasion in the bath.

For the most part they saw at a glance that I was wet behind the ears and went out of their way to be kind. They refreshed me, fed me, saw to it that I never left without sufficient copy, even if they had to ask and answer their own questions.

I suppose their own days on the way up were not too far away and they were considerate.

With one exception. It was during my trial period on the paper and it almost cost me my job.

Clint McGowan was quite deliberately insulting and it was like a smack in the face.

He had just made a name for himself in films. One minute he was unknown and the next plastered on every billboard and in every magazine in the country. One week he had been 'resting' and on National Assistance, and the next he'd a mansion in Sussex with umpteen acres, a Bentley without and staff within. That was showbiz.

He had the good fortune to be around at a time when a 'Clint McGowan' was needed and his agent was quicker than quick off the mark.

It took me three hours to get to Sussex. The train was late; the local taxi had broken down. I thumbed a lift on a truck, laddering my stocking in so doing, hiked half a mile down a muddy road and arrived in a lather at Great Oaks, bad temper overlying my customary apprehension.

Dogs barked the minute I rang the bell and continued viciously until the door was opened by a manservant who looked at me as if he'd found a piece of old Camembert on the doorstep.

'Mr McGowan is expecting me,' I said.

He took from his pocket a gold watch as they did on the movies and raised his eyebrows at it then at me.

I checked my watch. Twelve noon. That was the time arranged for the interview.

He opened the door and left me cooling my heels in the hall while he disappeared into the bowels of the house.

When he returned the manservant motioned me to follow him and I did so through film-set decor – long low sofas, everything white and hi-fi everywhere – out on to the terrace.

He left me blinded momentarily by the midday sun and for the moment I could see nothing. I blinked, then looked around.

At the far end of the not inconsiderable terrace Clint McGowan lay spread-eagled, half naked on a sun lounger. A blonde, falling out of a bikini, was spread-eagled almost on top of him.

He wore dark glasses so I was unable to see whether or not he saw me although his head was turned in my direction.

I waited, not knowing quite what to do.

'Don't be frightened, Ginger,' he said finally. 'Come closer. I don't bite. She does.' He put a finger into the blonde's mouth.

I walked the length of the terrace on legs suddenly become fragile and took out my notebook and pencil. There was a trolley of drinks with ice in a flask.

'It's very kind of you to allow me to interview you for the *Echo*,' I said. 'I hope you don't mind if I ask you a few questions about your overnight success.'

'I dare say I can tolerate it.'

'How does it feel, Mr McGowan,' I asked, 'to jump so suddenly from rags to riches – to wake up and find yourself a star?'

He stroked the long hair of the blonde, no longer looking at me. 'Fabulous, doesn't it, darling?'

'Perhaps you could expand a little. I mean mentally, how has it affected your life, your view of the world, your philosophy?'

He smiled and raised the blonde's chin, kissing her long on the lips.

'I like it.'

'What about material things? I understand you have several cars, a yacht, a villa in Sardinia. Do these things mean anything to you, never having had them?'

He put a hand down the top of her bikini. 'I like it.'

'Have you found it difficult to adapt yourself to being a star, recognised in the street, followed by fans wherever you go?'

He gazed into the eyes of the blonde and I'd written it in shorthand before he could get the words out. 'I like it.'

I decided to change my tack. 'Could you tell me a little about your childhood, Mr McGowan, your background?'

He was stroking her nose. I thought perhaps he hadn't heard the question.

'I was born very young,' he said finally and I could feel my redhead's easy blush envelop me. I was almost in tears, this interview was important. I decided to throw myself upon his mercy.

'Mr McGowan,' I said, 'I haven't had this job very long; actually I'm still on probation. I want to make a success of this social column and you aren't being terribly cooperative.'

They were still gazing at each other. 'Would you say I wasn't cooperative?' he said to her. I waited patiently until they had disentangled themselves.

'Would you tell me something of your tastes in food, drink; have you any hobbies ...'

'Hobbies? Sure!' He patted her behind. 'Drink, never touch it.' There was whisky in a glass by his side. 'Food.' He looked at his watch. 'In precisely forty minutes we shall make our leisurely way through shrimp bisque, cold baked ham in champagne, Russian salad, raspberry mousse ...'

My mouth was watering.

'... so if you would be kind enough to excuse us, Ginger, we have to go and prepare ourselves for luncheon.'

They rolled themselves into an oblivious embrace and I stood wondering what my editor was going to say to a luncheon menu, in which I hadn't even been invited to join, as the sole outcome of my journey to Sussex and the interview with God's gift to women, Clint McGowan.

I cried with humiliation all the way back to London. At the office my editor went berserk and had to take tranquillisers, and it took Mike all night to console me.

Because of his intervention they gave me another chance on the paper, but the name Clint McGowan and the image of the splendid torso and the insolent voice were etched for all time in my memory.

Ten years later the memory hadn't faded, neither had the emotions it evoked.

In ten years much had happened to both of us. I was

Martha Munroe of the 'Martha Munroe column', the most sought-after and influential name-dropper in town, and Clint McGowan, after a brief moment of glory, was all but forgotten by most people.

His stay at the top was good while it lasted, but after a while his type ceased to appeal. He descended to B pictures, then television, then nothing. Not in this country at any rate. I'd heard he was drinking himself into premature middle age in the States, bumming around and living on the past.

In the powder room of the hotel where he was throwing the party I looked at my mirror image. 'Ginger!' My hair was still as red, I hadn't changed much, just matured, acquired confidence and was at the top of my profession; a very nice spot to be when it had been your life's ambition. I smoothed my white gown and put on my mental boxing gloves ready for Clint.

The noise in the Starlight Room hit me. I stood at the door for a moment to adjust. I thought of the first of these star-dusted parties I had attended for my paper and how I'd looked with envy on the older columnists who'd thrown their arms round the lion's neck cooing 'daaah-ling!' while I stood nervously hidden behind the canapés.

He saw me before I saw him. I had made my way to the centre of the room and had been greeted effusively by at least half-a-dozen celebrities, who would open their newspapers anxiously in the morning seeking for my column and their names, when Clint took my hand in both his.

'Darling!' he said. 'Long time no see. You simply haven't aged an inch.'

It was more than I could say for him. His chin was slack, the sandy hair had thinned and I guessed that the body beneath the frilled shirt would not now be quite so fine.

He turned to everybody. 'Ginger!' he said. He touched my hair. 'Have you ever seen such a fabulous colour, and it doesn't come out of a bottle either? Martha and I have known each other for years.'

'Ten,' I said, knowing my hair, which I wore in a chignon tonight, looked good.

He gave me a whiskied, double-sided kiss and halted a waiter with a tray of champagne cocktails. 'See that this lady has everything she wants. It should be your party, darling, not mine.'

He put a glass in my hand and drew me into a corner.

'This part,' he said, 'my agent fixed me a try-out. It's just a question of convincing Rosensweig. He's a simple guy, hasn't heard my name just lately. I've been busy, investments, real estate, you know, maybe he never saw my early movies. You knew me then; you know I went down big: I've got the know-how. Rosensweig don't like small people. If he likes you, all right. If he don't, ruthless.

'He's got so much money he don't give you a good morning. I don't like guys who don't like you when you're down on your luck. You know how much this part's worth? You'll never get to see that many dollars. I get that part, I'm made. I just need a little build-up, see, public image and all that, a handful of publicity, Martha ...' He was sweating. 'Name your price.'

'That's not how I work.' I sipped the champagne. 'Nobody buys space in my column. It just depends how I feel.'

He put an arm round my shoulders. 'Darling,' he said, 'drink that little drink, there's another where it came from and another after that. By the time you leave this room you'll feel like a million dollars. I'll see you home myself.'

There were plenty of people I knew and even more who wanted to know me. I circulated, making idle talk. Clint was never far away. Watching me like a lynx.

At eleven-thirty he put a hand beneath my elbow. 'I'll take you home,' he said into my ear. 'I know you have your column to write. Say goodnight to all these lovely people.'

The lovely people who had come to eat Clint's food and drink his drink – who was paying, I wondered? – said goodnight.

I collected my coat and he led me to a waiting Rolls, hired, I assumed, for the evening.

As we skimmed down Park Lane through the night-lit traffic he explained, desperately and at speed, sitting on the edge of the seat and talking right at me, how exactly right he was for the part he was after and all he needed was a little public acclaim.

He handed me a list of all the well-known names at the party, aware, as I was, that nothing appears to succeed like success.

As we drew near my beautiful house in its beautiful square he signalled the chauffeur who slid back the glass partition.

'Number seventeen for Mrs Munroe,' he said. The tone slipped back ten years to when tired, and hungry, I had stood nervously on the Sussex terrace.

'Not Mrs Munroe,' I said.

He raised his eyebrows.

'Mike and I were divorced four years ago. I just use the name for the column.'

The car purred to a halt.

'You're not married then?' I saw a calculating look in his eye.

'I married again.'

His face fell but only for a moment as he snapped, his fingers. 'Pipped at the post again!'

The chauffeur held open the car door. We stood on the pavement.

'You kept it all very quiet.'

'There was nothing to make a noise about.'

I smiled charmingly and thanked him for a lovely evening.

'I'll stay up till the paper comes out,' he said. He kissed me on the cheek. 'You'll give me a break, won't you?'

I looked him directly in the eyes. 'A very even one.'

'I knew I could rely on you, Ginger,' he said.

He kissed me once more and climbed back into the car. 'Take it easy,' he said, as the chauffeur was about to close the door. 'We don't want to waken the lady's husband, do we? Who's the lucky guy by the way?'

'You don't know?' Surprised, my key remained half-turned in the lock.

'Nobody told me.'

All at once I felt sorry for him, then I remembered Sussex, the blonde, my laddered stocking, the hot sun and the tray with the ice-cold drinks. I looked at him, handsome still I had to admit, across ten years and the wide London pavement.

He had grown small but had I grown big?

'Is it a name I should know?'

I turned the key fully and firmly in the lock.

'Rosensweig!' I said from the doorway. 'Goodnight.'

The Inner Resources of Mrs Prendergast

1967

The moment Mrs Prendergast opened her eyes she knew it had arrived. They had warned her about it, pestered her with it, cajoled and pleaded, all to no avail. The day with all its incipient and disturbing innuendoes was upon her. She had already glanced at the front page of the daily newspaper and noted that there had been no air disaster reported. That was one worry off her mind.

Warmed by the spring sun, she decided before rising to allow herself a little wallow in the events of yesterday. Not that there would not be days in which to wallow; days, weeks, months, years, in fact. She would probably spend her time in the past, and that was exactly what they did not want her to do.

She was not interested, however, in what they wanted her to do. Thirty years had been spent at their beck and call. Today belonged to Laura Prendergast.

They had predicted she would cry and she had indulged,

it was true, in a little weep. They had assured her that her feet would ache. In this too, they had been correct. Her feet felt like two balloons at the end of her legs.

'Wonder what it's like in Majorca?' Mr Prendergast called from the bathroom where he was shaving.

'I doubt if they've seen much of it yet.'

'Wassat?'

It was one of his more irritating habits. He would ask you something against the noisy buzzing of the electric shaver and expect to hear the answer.

Mrs Prendergast raised her voice. 'I said I doubt if they've seen much of it yet!'

She was just able to see him, slightly pot-bellied, through the open door of the bathroom. He was concentrating on the hard-to-reach part beneath his chin and was not listening. The sight of him carried her back to her own honeymoon, spent in Brighton, a not un-smart place at the time, where she had watched fascinated as he deftly wielded a cut-throat razor at the old-fashioned washstand.

She had returned to this scene – the carpet had roses on, she remembered – on each occasion. When Michael got married, very correctly, choral and floral, to Lydia, so perfect in every aspect that Laura felt secretly that if she fell down a drain she would emerge smelling of violets; when Richard had appeared one unexpected weekend from Cambridge with an ever-so-slightly pregnant sandal-footed Olivia and confessed shiftily to a register office 'quickie'; when Diana, all golden and dumb, had plighted her troth to Glint and flown away to California, which was a wonderful place, so they said, for the golden and dumb; when Nicky, creeping his way steadily up the medical ladder, had predictably married the theatre sister whose task it was to hand him scalpel and retractor while making love to him with her beautiful green eyes over the top of her mask; when Elizabeth (was it only yesterday?) had finally emptied the nest and given herself – for what Mrs Prendergast suspected was not the first time – to something that called itself Nigel and wore mauve button-down crepon shirts and yachting caps, whom she had privately christened Goldilocks (his hair was longer than Lizzie's) and who was said to be an up-and-coming Society photographer, a member of the new elite who, together with the up-and-coming, or already up-and-come, hairdressers, filled the discothèques by night and the Mayfair salons by day.

They were now, Mrs Prendergast assumed, safely in Majorca where later Lizzie, she guessed, would rub her spouse's delicate skin with suntan oil.

It was a long way from Brighton, in every respect. Geographically it was a fair distance; in terms of change it was a million miles. When she had sat on the beach with Jack, rugs cosily round their knees, holding hands demurely and now and again throwing pebbles into the Brighton waves, neither of them had heard of Hiroshima, Nagasaki, Korea or Vietnam.

Neither of them guessed that in years to come terms such as atom bomb, napalm, escalation, mescalin, psychedelic, astronaut, computer, inter-uterine coils, the Pill, Oxfam and Billy Graham would become everyday coinage. In those days, people were neither square nor switched on, gear nor camp, grotty nor fantastic, and neither one of them had been to an all-night rave-up. Times, Mrs Prendergast observed, had changed.

She was fully aware that in the palmy Brighton era those women who found themselves, after a varying number of years, with their families married and gone, settled happily into middle-aged atrophy or preoccupied themselves with their roles as grandmothers. At this last thought she allowed herself a smile. It was a role she neither wanted nor was prepared to play.

The nursery at Lowndes Square was rigidly and admirably administered at all times by Nannie Prendergast with whom the good Lord in his mercy had seen fit to endow Michael and Lydia in the early days of their marriage; in Cambridge – where Richard was now a don – Goneril, Regan and Cordelia born, Laura swore, with less than nine months between each, romped happily, grubbily and usually knickerless around a household whose vocabulary did not contain such philistine words as nursery and where Olivia, again merrily pregnant, knew nothing of nannies, nylon-trimmed cradles (the babies went straight into the bottom drawer of the chest in their bedroom), nor of the necessity, now and again at least, of wiping noses.

In California – according to the photographs usually taken round the pool – Joanna was growing as beautiful and as goldenly dumb as her mother, and Hank as broad, razor-cropped and all-American as his father.

From the deepest wilds of Chislehurst, from which he

commuted to his hospitals daily, Nicky had produced so far nothing but articles for various eminent medical journals, and his green-eyed goddess, who always for one reason or another made Laura feel terribly inferior, was still as far as she knew sterilely handing over scalpels and retractors to augment the family budget.

As a grandmother Laura was redundant; a fact in which, to the horror of her various offspring who declared she had no inner resources, she inwardly rejoiced.

'Enough is enough!' she said firmly, wriggling her aching toes.

'Wassat?' The shaver was still buzzing.

'I said "Enough is enough!"' Laura yelled.

Jack extracted the plug from the socket. 'I'm not deaf, yet. What are you talking about anyway?'

'Just thinking aloud.'

She watched him dress, as she had for thirty years, sure that he was the only man in the world who fastened his cufflinks then made his hand very small in order to get it through the aperture. He brushed what was left of his hair, selected a tie and tied it with care, chose a matching spotted handkerchief for the pocket of his city suit and smiled at his reflection in the mirror.

She hoped he would leave the bedroom with the affection-ate peck on the cheek that had become so familiar, the warm reliable hand resting for a moment on her shoulder. She knew he wouldn't. He didn't. He sat on the bed. He was as bad as the rest of them.

'They've all gone.' It was a statement rather than a question. 'Would you like me to stay at home?'

'The Bank Rate would fall at once!'

'What will you do?'

'Mind your own business,' Laura Prendergast said.

She saw the hurt in his eyes and that he was about to repeat the question.

'Mind your own business!' she said firmly.

'Would you like me to call Dr Littleton-Cooper?'

'Why, Jack? Aren't you feeling well?'

'It's you, you're overwrought. The excitement of the wedding has been too much for you!'

'I'm nothing of the sort,' Laura said. 'Now off you go and I'll see you tonight.'

He looked at his watch. 'Are you sure?'

She laid a reassuring hand on his. 'You'll be late.'

'You looked beautiful yesterday.'

'Thank you,' Laura said. 'My swan song.'

His hand was on the door. 'What did you mean, "Enough is enough"?'

'I was talking to myself,' Laura said, 'and it would take me all day to tell you.'

'In that case I'll be off. I'll ring you at lunchtime.'

'Don't bother,' said Laura, 'I shan't be in.'

'Lunching with Lydia?'

'With Laura Prendergast.'

'Dr Littleton-Cooper wouldn't mind, I'm sure ...'

She twiddled two fingers at him. 'Bye!'

The door closed gently and opened again a moment later to admit Jack's head.

'What did you think I'd be doing,' Laura said from her pillow. 'Dancing *The Firebird* in my birthday suit?'

Jack opened his mouth to speak.

'Yes, darling,' Laura said, 'I know all about Dr Littleton-Cooper. Have a good day.' He closed the door. 'And don't forget to take the things back to Moss Bros!' she shouted after him.

She waited, as she had every day, except of course for the unmentionable period of the war, for the front door to slam, then lay back to allow herself one more retrospective and enjoyable glimpse of her baby, Elizabeth, walking up the aisle in the wedding dress which did not, Laura was ashamed almost to think, cover her knees.

'Finished,' she said to herself firmly, and then wondered how many days there were in thirty years. She was not going to work it out but confident that there must be several millions if not more, Laura put one aching foot (she should have ordered the satin shoes a size larger) out of bed when the telephone rang, and after that seemed unable to stop.

First it was Anne to say at extraordinary lengths what a marvellous wedding it had been and that Laura was not to brood and must come to lunch; after Anne it was Clara to vow she had shed tears and that Laura must not let herself go to pieces; Muriel thought the mini-dress delightful (she had always told lies easily and transparently) and Laura must join them for bridge to take her mind off things; Poppy said what a charming couple (Laura noticed they all skated delicately round Nigel) and that Laura should go to evening classes, in the afternoons of course, and make pots or arrange flowers, just to keep herself occupied.

When Poppy had finished organising her life for her, she left the handset next to the telephone where it burped rudely and again put a foot out of bed. This time it was a knock on the door. Doris, who had worked for Mrs Prendergast for twenty-five of the thirty years she had been married and whose second name she could never remember, wept tears in recollection of her 'baby's' wedding down her nylon overall, and said that on Mr Prendergast's instructions Laura was on no account to be left alone. She picked up the breakfast tray and said she would be up immediately with another cup of coffee.

'No more coffee,' Mrs Prendergast said firmly, this time putting both feet out of bed and replacing the handset on the telephone.

'If anyone calls, I am not at home. I am going to take a bath and afterwards you can bring up a bottle of champagne if we have any over.'

The tray rattled in Doris's hands. Mrs Prendergast pretended not to notice and went into the bathroom. An hour later she was ready to go out.

In the morning room, into which she peeped from habit to see everything was tidy and the flowers fresh, she found Dr Littleton-Cooper. Her face tightened.

'Good morning, Mrs Prendergast.'

'Good morning, Dr Littleton-Cooper.' She wondered, as

she often did, where he had picked up that ridiculous name. He was no more than a youth and it added nothing to his stature. Dr Smith, whose practice he had inherited, was ten times the man of this one, for all his fancy waistcoat.

'I suppose my husband sent for you?'

'As a matter of fact, it was the maid.'

'Housekeeper. Maids went out with mob caps. Doris would be most insulted.'

'She was worried about you.'

'I can't help that.' Mrs Prendergast pressed the bell. 'You'll join me in a glass of champagne?'

This one needs treating carefully, his eyes said. 'No, thank you, really ...'

Doris came in with the tray and two glasses. Mrs Prendergast handed Dr Littleton-Cooper the bottle to open and sat in the easy chair. 'Since you have come, you may as well earn the ridiculous and exorbitant fee Jack is fool enough to pay when we have a perfectly adequate National Health Service.'

The cork hit the ceiling and the white bubbling foam of champagne trickled down Dr Littleton-Cooper's immaculate trousers.

'Perhaps I will ...'

'Of course you will.' Mrs Prendergast filled the two glasses.

'To Freedom!' Mrs Prendergast said, raising hers.

'As you wish.' Dr Littleton-Cooper stopped mopping at his trousers and raised his. 'I really shouldn't, when I'm working.'

'You'll need it by the time I have finished with you,' Mrs Prendergast said. 'Now just sit there and listen. How old are you? Twenty-eight? Thirty?' She answered her own question. 'Practically since you were born I, Laura Prendergast, have been occupied with my family. I have endured six pregnancies, two with unpleasant complications, three with extended and painful labours, and the last resulting in the easy birth of a blond angel who survived for an hour.

'While others have gone out into the world and achieved great things, I have been occupied for what seems eternity with nappies, bottles, prams, pushchairs, rented houses, buckets and spades and sandy swimsuits. I have staggered out of bed in the small hours more times than you have had birthdays, to soothe the pangs of mumps, chickenpox, whooping cough, measles, both the German and the plain varieties, tonsillitis, and croup.

'I have bathed a hundred grazed knees, applied simply countless sticking plasters, dried Niagaras of tears and nursed, at a quick reckoning, six broken limbs. And on Friday nights, when they were small, of course, I have cut a hundred nails, a hundred, Dr Littleton-Cooper, including toes, of course, and shampooed five separate heads. I have watched more haircuts, bought more shoes (indoor and out) and sewed on more nametapes than you could imagine in your wildest dreams.

'I have taken root, I swear, at the dentist's, the piano, the dancing, and the skating sessions I have been called upon to endure; I have sat through unending successions of conjurers, pantomimes, ice shows, circuses, Donald Ducks, Mickey Mouses and Punch and Judys. If I had to watch the "Dance of the Sugar Plum Fairy", no matter how exquisitely performed, just once more, I swear I would get the screaming abdabs.'

Dr Littleton-Cooper rose from his seat, mumbling something about sick patients to visit, but Laura Prendergast pushed him back and refilled his glass. This time he did not protest.

'I have not finished. In addition to the aforementioned trials of the early days, there are further delights of which you men of the world, of the mighty professions, know nothing ... nothing. There is at all times an endless river of garments to be taken in or out, let down or up, put away for the spring, retrieved for winter, to be ferried to the cleaners and be collected therefrom. Acres of cupboards to be tidied, hockey-sticks – you see we are older now – to be disentangled from ball gowns, football boots from clean tennis shorts.

'Often I have wanted to count the number of Speech Days, Parents' Days, End-of-Term Performances, Prize-givings, Sales of Work and Carol Concerts through which I have sat, but I have been too busy catering for seven ravenous mouths, and double and treble the number when Molly and Polly and Dolly, and Harry and Larry have come for a week and stayed for a fortnight.

'I have listened, Dr Littleton-Cooper, over the years to more fables than La Fontaine ever thought of, to more verbs, regular and irregular, than you would ever have guessed existed, and to my dying day I shall not forget the past participle of *se battre*.'

'They say that as you grow older life becomes easier. Dr

Littleton-Cooper, they lie! They grow hysterical with examinations, bewildered by choice of careers and entangled in the most bizarre relationships from which one is frequently required to disentangle them.

'When they finally decide upon their life partner, the fun, as they say, has only just begun. One becomes embroiled with living accommodations and wearing apparel, hysterical over whom to offend least over the wedding invitations, frustrated by landlords, builders, caterers, florists, plumbers, electricians and little men and women of every description. This, of course, is when they have finally made their choice.

'Dr Littleton-Cooper, if you had seen some of the sights that have walked during the past years through my front door you would not believe your eyes. Apart from the difficulties, to which I have become accustomed, of distinguishing the boys from the girls, I have said goodnight to creatures with unsavoury beards whom I have tripped over in the corridor next morning, emptied a Vesuvius of ashtrays and thrown out, I swear, about a million beer cans.

'I have seen romances broken and mended, listened in the small hours for keys turning in the door, waited in terror for imaginary policemen on the doorstep to tell me my son or daughter had wrapped the car round a lamp-post. I have lost one child to California (it always makes me think of figs), the others are despatched to Lowndes Square, Cambridge, Chislehurst and the Fulham Road.'

'Mrs Prendergast,' Dr Littleton-Cooper said, tilting his third glass, 'you are a wonderful woman ...'

'Oh, no,' Mrs Prendergast protested in horror. 'I am a mother.'

'You have had a hard life.'

'Please don't be ridiculous. I have enjoyed every moment of it and would do exactly the same were there a second time round. I am neither out of my mind, going to pieces, nor "on the turn". It is not mysterious, and I really think you've had sufficient champagne! You haven't, of course, understood a word I've been saying, despite your fancy waistcoat and your fancy name. Dr Smith would have caught on at once but has, of course, been kicking up the daisies now for a long time. I'll say goodbye and Doris will show you out.'

She left the room but a moment later was back.

'I'd be grateful if you didn't suggest to Jack that I now have "too much time on my hands", nor need "something to occupy my mind". The children have tried. Simply because I have no urge to work for the Council for Moral Welfare, the Family Planning Association, or the League for Penal Reform.

'I will not be a prison visitor, house a foreign student nor address envelopes for the International Friendship League. I shall not take up basketball, badminton nor book-keeping, mathematics, modern ballet, nor music, and haven't the slightest wish to learn Russian.'

'What are you going to do?' Dr Littleton-Cooper said.

'I am going to the park. The primroses and daffodils are in bloom now. I shall buy some sandwiches and throw the crumbs to the birds. I may come back before dark if it gets chilly, otherwise I shall not. I shall talk to no one and no one will talk to me. I shall not read a book and I am not taking my tapestry or my knitting.

'Should you want me you will find me on one of the benches every day until I'm an old, old woman. I shall think of my grandchildren occasionally, and when it is their birthdays I shall telephone my favourite stores. Are you sure you're all right?'

Dr Littleton-Cooper was distinctly glassy-eyed.

The telephone on the bureau rang.

'Don't take it,' Laura ordered, putting on her gloves.

'It may be for me,' Dr Littleton-Cooper said. 'I left your number with my secretary.'

Laura lifted the receiver. Dr Littleton-Cooper gazed out of the window on to the well-kept garden and wished his head would clear. When he looked round, Laura had put down the receiver and was taking off her gloves as though each finger was of the utmost importance.

'It was Richard from Cambridge,' she said. 'Olivia has toxaemia of pregnancy. She's going into hospital.'

Dr Littleton-Cooper pulled himself together and put a professional arm round her drooping shoulders. 'Don't worry, that's nothing these days. Bed, rest and perhaps a surgical induction when the time comes ...'

'That's not really the point,' Mrs Prendergast said. 'There is no one to look after the children.'

All my Love

It was the telegram in the Post Office that threw Iris off balance – not that it took very much to do that these days – the telegram that led her into the piped-music-washed womb of the coffee bar.

It was a very ordinary telegram clipped to the top of a pile of them on the clerk's side of the counter. It was upside down and she read it through the glass partition. The coding at the top and the time of despatch were of no interest. It was the message that sent her into the valley of despair, hurrying to the solace of coffee and cheesecake and the acquisition of goodness knew how many undesirable calories. '*All my love, Roy*'. Four words.

She turned from the counter without buying her stamps, walked agitatedly down the street, sat down at the nearest table in the nearest coffee bar.

'Yes, dear?'

The waitress, no more than nineteen, had black-ringed eyes with lashes so heavy it was a wonder to Iris she could see.

'Coffee, please.'

'Anythinktereat?'

Iris followed her gaze to the trolley laden with over-creamy cakes in papers, chocolate layer cake, humpbacked shiny éclairs, cartwheels of Danish pastry.

'I'll have some cheesecake.'

The girl scribbled on her pad, tore off the sheet, folded it and slipped it under the glass of paper serviettes. As she did so the man came in. They both saw him together, became linked, the nubile girl and the middle-aged woman, with a common bond of desire.

He walked like a panther, light and boneless, carrying his six feet like a feather, broad chest narrowing to slim hips, elegant suit following his every move. An actor, Iris thought, or could have been, more probably, an executive: authority radiated from him. He wore a red carnation in his buttonhole as if by right.

The waitress, rooted to the spot, sighed. 'They always sit at Jean's table. There's no justice.'

'Coffee and cheesecake,' Iris said. She was used to dealing with daydreaming juniors.

'Not one of our regulars. Wouldn't mind taking him home.'

'I am in rather a rush,' Iris said.

He had sat down and was studying the menu while the sharp-nosed Jean waited patiently by his side.

'I'll have a Welsh rarebit, and coffee.' He smiled dazzlingly at Jean, then, to her utter amazement, he smiled at Iris.

All my love, Roy. All her life, more often of late, she had longed to receive and, even more, to send so simple a message, so few words in which were implicit so infinite a meaning. All my love. She had so much to give, so very much. Sometimes it overflowed and engulfed her, reducing her to tears. She'd look in the mirror then, to dry her eyes and see what they all saw, a stout woman of middle age whom love had passed by.

It seemed incredible to Iris, incredible and indescribably painful, that no one realised that inside the fat and ugly body were thoughts, deeds, hopes and fears identical with those beneath the bosoms of the slim and beautiful. There was so much love within her unprepossessing exterior that sometimes Iris feared it would break its bonds and flow in a glorious river of beauty to swamp the nearest stranger. So much gentleness, so much compassion, she sometimes willed it to wither and die so that she might be left in peace.

The girl was right. There was no justice. She knew how to treat a man, had more love to give than the hard-faced bitches working through their second and third marriages, pitilessly reducing their mates to size; more than the pretty dollies who took and took; more than the moaners, the naggers, and the succulents who grew fat on the lifeblood of their men.

She knew they were weak and that she was strong, that they needed the comfort of her arms, the tranquillity of her bosom. She would be quiet, unshakable, always ready to give. She knew the secret, the strength, the ability to give and to give and to give ... He was still looking at her, more gravely now. She was undeceived by his air of authority. She knew he was tense, nervous, angry, demanding, thoughtless, selfish; that he was weak. ...

'Coffee and cheesecake,' the waitress announced.

'All my love,' Iris said.

'Pardon me?'

Iris looked at her. 'I didn't say anything.'

The blank, sooty eyes examined her.

'It was cappuccino you was wanting?'

Iris looked at the frothy, steaming cup. 'Yes, thank you.'

'The cheesecake's fresh.'

She smiled dismissal at the girl, and together they both had a final look at the man. He was waiting for his Welsh rarebit and still looking at Iris in what she could have sworn was an inviting way. She felt a slow blush creeping up her neck in the manner of a young girl, which she was not. Most decidedly was not. She started on the cheesecake. Perhaps after all there was going to be someone.

His order had arrived. She liked the way he ate, unhurriedly, calmly. He caught her looking and she turned her attention to the coffee, uninteresting and too weak. We would have a little house, she thought, perhaps by the river, not a so-called 'town house' made of matchboxes, something older, more mature, that's what she was, but that was what a man needed, someone to rely on, who would always be there.

She would give up work – he looked as if he could keep her – and economise by making things for herself, the house, growing vegetables if there was a tiny garden, she'd always had green fingers. They wouldn't need many friends, not when she had someone of her own, they'd be self-sufficient, stay at home most evenings, people's eyes would light up with envy – 'my husband, meet my husband'.

He was smiling openly now, she smiled back, her heart singing. The cheesecake was gone but she scarcely recalled eating it. He had finished, too, except for the last of his coffee. His smile was a bit lopsided really, rather attractive; lazy, dreamy eyes. He beckoned to Jean for the bill.

Iris called for hers, her hands shaking a little as she fumbled in her purse. Would he come over, or would they meet outside? She wished she'd worn her new suit, nearly had, but it still grew chilly in the evenings. *All my love, Iris*. On cards and telegrams. On birthdays and anniversaries, and sometimes on nothing at all.

He was standing up now and looking straight at her, or rather at her right ear. She glanced behind her, and a girl with green eyes, bathed in auburn hair, tall and reed slim, was getting up from her table. She wore a pale pink suit and her legs seemed to go on for ever. She insinuated herself past Iris's table and went over to the man. Together they walked out of the shop, he holding the door open for her. They stood for a moment on the pavement laughing into one another's faces, then disappeared down the street.

Iris waited for the pain, which started in her throat, to recede ...

It did so, slowly numbing as it went.

She was nothing; a fat fool. How could she have expected him to see inside her where lay all the love? Had there been a mirror opposite she would have been all right; would never have made such a stupid mistake, believing that she looked as she felt. In dissection she and the green-eyed girl would prove identical, except in Iris there would be more tenderness, more compassion, more love.

He probably hadn't even seen her at all, sitting there fat and flushed with her coffee and her cheesecake, and her kind but untidy face.

She saw the green-eyed girl in the house by the river. It would have to be the town house though, and no vegetables, quite definitely no vegetables; you couldn't grow courgettes and avocado pears. She'd lie there in a leisure gown waiting for him to come home; if he was late she'd scold and he'd soon grow tired. Tired of her green eyes and her auburn hair and her scolding, and their voices would rise, and they would live in toleration not in love, and most probably when his hair grew grey and she'd sucked him dry she would put on her town clothes and leave the river, and sit in a coffee bar where a man would smile at her ...

The Food of Love

1968

I have always loved Hermione. Always, that is, from the moment the lights changed to red in the Bayswater Road and I was halted, frozen-lashed in the traffic, not five yards from where she stood.

She wore long black boots and earmuffs, and changed her weight from one foot to the other, peering up the road for the bus. She was far too beautiful to have to work, yet I supposed she must: why else shiver in the queue for the 88 so early in the morning? It was almost the end of March and should have been less cold.

I wondered, had my motor scooter been pumpkinned into a saloon, would I offer her a lift? The lights turned amber, green, and the moment of speculation passed, or should have. All day it remained, although the colour of her hair evaded me; all night the lights-brief glimpse I had had of her kept me turning in my bed.

She was there next morning. It was snowing slowly and the

signals were green. I tried to idle past but a taxi hooted. Not much of a ration to nourish an entire day. By the end of the week there was little more: one morning she was obscured by the bus; another, her back was turned against the nasty wind that knifed over from the park. I spent Saturday and Sunday waiting for Monday.

There was a spare seat on the Vespa; girls had straddled it. Not plucked from bus stops, though, in snow, unsuitably clad. I could not remember their names.

On Monday the lights were red once more. A lorry driver who could have got across had the view of her; on Wednesday, too. By 8.15 my day was finished. On Friday I did not think I could endure the weekend. My mind works slowly, it must do, for a third week passed before the solution came. I would travel by bus; stand behind ... excuse me, I'm so sorry, a smile, may I introduce ... my name is ...

The willing Vespa, left behind, chid silently. The Bayswater Road extended itself. My heart chirruped; not the spring.

She wasn't there. Was not there. Not then. Not any day. Disappeared. Gone. I languished. Could not work. How could you lose a beautiful girl in the Bayswater Road? In the country perhaps, not in the Bayswater Road. To lose presumed having ...

I conceived a plan. An orderly plan, fruit of my orderly mind. I used my drawing board to etch a neat map embracing every street within a ten-minute walking radius of where she had stood. Must she not live somewhere within it?

The evenings lengthened, for me. I combed each and every

pavement, eliminating windows, passers-by. It pays, you see, to have an orderly mind. Within a week I found her. On steps in Chester Street with a bag of groceries, No. 4. Don Quixote, I patted my Vespa, sang home. Finding was one thing. I appealed to my orderly mind: nothing. To my mother's knee ... if you want a thing badly enough ...

Badly enough? I was lighter by half a stone, vague, irritable. The next night I bathed, changed, changed again, stood ten minutes limp-kneed on the step of No. 4, chic with window-box; rang the bell; Don Quixote. Ha!

Footsteps. I opened my mouth and she the door – wide.

'I ...'

'I'm so glad you've come. I thought no one was going to.'

I looked behind me. Only the Vespa, drunk again, at the kerb.

My luck, I thought, a party and no one's turned up. I followed her and, indeed, no one was there. It did not look as if she was expecting anyone. Books and busts in the tiny, elegant room, no bottles, ubiquitous party dainties. She took my coat. I did not protest. Unmanned. I could not. Without the boots she was ... I don't know. A scent, an essence turning your head, ingredients unidentifiable. She said, 'Sit down.' I sat. Would have stood on my head, in the fire ...

There was infinity in her eyes, unhappiness.

'I was so afraid no one would come ...'

I have come from the ends of the earth. The Bayswater Road.

'... where did you see the advertisement?'

Advertisement. What was it I was to be? Butler, valet, lodger, chef? I would be all or any. Lie down at her feet if necessary, die.

There was a ring on her wedding finger; not plain. I could not be sure. About the room no sign of a man: widowed, separated, divorced?

She sat down opposite me and leant forward until I saw my own reflection in her pupils.

'I did not know,' she said, 'which newspaper would bring the best results.'

A gardener perhaps, I could manage that ...

'So few people today,' she went on, 'seem to care for the violin.'

The violin!

If there is one sound calculated to arouse in me a combination of fury, anguish and hysteria, it is that of bow upon string.

That is not all. I am tone deaf.

'One has, of course, to have the physiological qualities in addition to the talent ...'

The chair and I became as one.

'... a left hand suited to the instrument, flexibility of both arms, and the ability to sol-fa with perfect precision. You have a violin?'

I was as likely to have in my possession a stuffed elephant.

I breathed a deep breath. 'No,' I said. 'I have no violin.'

'I have one you can use until we see how you progress. The outlay,' she was looking at my shoes, 'for any worthwhile instrument is quite considerable.'

Men have done many things for love: raced time, endured, slain dragons. I wished there had been a dragon.

For Hermione I kept the appointment for my first lesson.

She was more beautiful, a shade, perhaps, more sad. I sat, as one transfixed and watched her as she laid a violin case upon the table as tenderly as if it were a newborn babe. She opened the lid, removed a swathe of cloth in which it was encased and lifted the instrument from its velvet crib with love.

'The violin,' she said, 'is the smallest and highest pitched of one of the most important families of stringed musical instruments, to which it gives its name. Perhaps I go back too far?' She looked at me questioningly. 'You are familiar with the rudimentary principles?'

'I know nothing. Nothing.'

'It consists essentially of a resonant box of peculiar form, over which four strings of different thicknesses are stretched across a bridge, standing on the box in such a way that the tension of the strings can be adjusted by means of revolving pegs.'

There was a tranquillity about the room. Real chairs and rugs. No permutation – endless units on sterile walls. I could not picture her in such a setting.

'Many speculations have been advanced with regard to the superiority in tone of the old Italian instruments over those of modern construction.'

It was not the construction of the violin she held with such obvious pleasure at which I looked.

'The excellence of an instrument, according to the best authorities, is dependent upon its varnish and the method of application. In this respect there can be no doubt that the southern climate placed the makers whose work lies in higher latitudes at a disadvantage. In a letter to Galileo in 1638 concerning a violin which he had ordered from Cremona, a writer states that "it cannot be brought to perfection without the strong heat of the sun".

Not violins perhaps, but teachers?

'The violin, I must tell you, is not an easy instrument to master. The beginning is thankless.'

I prayed silently for its delay.

'One has to acquire precision and tone, and learn the necessity of going slowly at first ...'

I would be a very paragon of slowness.

'... in order eventually to acquire a sure technique. These are the parts of which the violin is composed. I do not expect you to remember them all at once.'

I stood by her. Her perfume convinced me that I should not remember even one.

'First the violin itself. The scroll, the pegs, the nut, the neck, the strings, the fingerboard, the belly ...'

I shut my eyes.

'... the button and the chin-rest. Now for the bow ...'

The bow.

'... the magic wand that does the trick.'

I needed no magic wand.

'It is nothing more than a modification of an archer's bow having, instead of a string, many dozens of fine white horsehairs that are coated with resin to give their surface some friction.'

The lessons took place twice a week. I would not have believed such exquisite torture existed. I, whom a thousand Menuhins could not educate in as many years to distinguish note from note, learnt with pain to up-bow, down-bow, to execute the minor sixth and the augmented fourth.

To the new pupil the teacher must demonstrate the model position of the violin. She controls his bow until he can play the first exercises while conserving perfect suppleness of arm and wrist. Needless to say, after several lessons, I had not mastered the requisite suppleness. She continued to control my bow; I, myself. I do not know which one of us it was who suffered more.

Our relationship made less progress than our lessons, which by any standards was little enough. Between the solfeggio and the manipulation of the left hand I told her about myself, my life and aspirations; she countered always with an exposition on the change of strings or the importance of the left elbow which must, she emphasised, fall under the centre of the violin.

It became urgent to clarify what was fast becoming an intolerable situation. I was willing to woo her, win her slowly, tolerate the perfect pain of Tuesdays and Fridays, but only if she was free, ultimately, to be mine.

Each direct question, however delicately put, was met with evasion or, infinitely worse, the sound of bow upon string.

I began to look for clues. There was never anyone in the hall or sitting room when I called, no sign of another person in the house; no photographs, no mention of a past.

Had she a husband, perhaps, who worked late on Tuesdays

and Fridays? I begged to change the nights of the lessons. She agreed. I came on Mondays; on Wednesdays and Saturdays; once, cunningly, on Sunday. She was always alone, impersonal. Sometimes I thought the hour passed without her seeing me at all. She looked often at the ceiling, unremarkable as far as I could judge, her mind seemingly on something else. The more remote she became, as the weeks went on, the more distracted I.

I could not go on for very long without declaring the reason for my visits, which had she not been so preoccupied she must have guessed, listening to my own cacophony.

Often I wondered why she persevered with so inept a pupil. It was almost summer and myself at breaking point, when I discovered.

One unsuspecting Tuesday I rang the bell, which must be worn with imprints of my finger. There were wallflowers in the window box.

She always opened the door immediately, but not today. When she did, I could see she had been crying. It had not made her ugly.

She wore a sleeveless dress. I followed her into the sitting room, where she told me to sit down, as I had on the first occasion. Usually I went straight to the music stand and examined with sinking heart what was to be the day's torment.

I did as she asked, preferring to take her in my arms and soothe with my lips her reddened eyes. I waited. What was to be? She could no longer dedicate herself to so incompetent a performer? The lessons were to end?

But no: she took the violin from the table, tightened the bow and tuned the strings, an accomplishment she had admitted I would never master. I was about to stand up to take the hated instrument from her when to my surprise she tucked it beneath her own chin. I say surprise because, although until this moment I had not realised it, I had never heard her play.

She looked at me just once, straight at me, forgetting this time the ceiling, shook the hair back from her eyes, inclined her head, then applied herself to the sounds she gradually released into the room. Even I, unable after countless lessons, diligently given, to distinguish note from note, knew this was music. I did not understand but was aware the cadence she produced was born of harmony, sincerity, inspiration.

She played for twenty minutes, although it seemed no more than five. As she played the tears slid down her lovely face to land, slow-rolling, on the violin.

If I had muscles they did not twitch, afraid with so much sadness all around that I too might weep.

When the music was done she stood, quite still, as if it still continued, in the soundlessness. If before I had not dared to move, now I was stone. She seemed to wait for the last echoing notes to return from the corners of the room into which she had released them, to the strings which spawned them.

Then it was over.

She put the violin, which must have been damp, away in its case, loosened the bow, packed all away and fastened the clasp with finality. There was obviously to be no lesson.

She dried her eyes, more red than previously, and sat beside me. What would we speak of? My pitiful scrapings? The reason for her tears?

'I have not been honest with you,' she said to me.

'Nor I with you.'

'It was obvious from the first that you would never master the violin. You have no ear.'

'It was not proficiency on the violin I was after.'

'I needed the money.'

I looked round the room, not having considered her desperate for funds.

'My husband was a lawyer.'

Was.

'Barristers don't earn much, when recently called, not even when they're working.' She glanced at the ceiling as I had watched her do so many times. 'It's a year since Basil worked. He's been ill. We knew there was nothing ... At first I went out to work ...'

It seemed a lifetime since the Bayswater Road.

'... then I didn't want to leave him for so long. I put the advertisement in. You were my only pupil.'

Of all budding violinists in London, I.

'Last night he died. That was his favourite concerto. I've taken your money under false pretences.'

Her secret was out. Mine, fortunately, she seemed not to have heard.

We live in Sussex now, in a little house from the back of which you have a clear view of the Downs.

In our sitting room there are real chairs and rugs, books and busts: Bach, the master of counterpoint; Chopin, who knew the precise meaning of the piano; Beethoven with his prodigal architectural sense; Wagner with his genius for orchestration.

They have mellowed with the years. I, too, though not my love for Hermione.

We do not talk of music much, nor of the Bayswater Road, but sometimes, usually on summer nights, Hermione takes out her violin, the only child she has, and plays.

She looks at me and we do not know whether to laugh or cry.

Sleeping Beauty

1968

Because it was almost September, the wind, temperate though it was, started drifting in from the Adriatic each evening towards six o'clock. The first tendrils of its soft embrace sent Franco, steel-muscled in his white shorts, to his sunset task of lowering and securing the umbrellas of those who had left the beach, shaking and stacking mattresses and retrieving forsaken pages of *Die Welt*, *Corriere della Sera*, and the *New York Times*.

San Rimano, exceedingly chic without being exclusively so, catered to every nationality. The Excelsior Hotel, for whose wide white beach, cabins, and comfort Franco and his wife, Rosetta, were personally responsible, was of the very highest order.

Already, most of the Italians had taken their high spirits and their ball games and departed in their Alfas and Lamborghinis for Genoa, Florence and Rome. A clutch of middle-aged, panama-hatted Americans waded knee-deep into the water daily, discussed 'back home', and waited for their coronary thromboses to overtake them. The Dutch and the Germans were still at large, and a few English littered their cabanas with a variety of ill-assorted gear more suited to a safari than to the daily fifty-yard traverse from hotel to shore. The French, with their infinitesimal bikinis and bottles of suntan oil, travelled lightest of all. Only one, at this evaporating end of the season, remained at the Excelsior.

She was very tall, very slim and very beautiful, no longer in the first flush of youth. Leaning a little backwards, as if once she had been a model, she had sauntered down to the beach at the beginning of the previous week, dressed in tan linen slacks and clinging black silk shirt; around her head she wore a canary-yellow scarf. She had smiled at Rosetta but had not asked for a cabana. She had merely arranged with Franco for a mattress, and to this she made her way at exactly the same hour each morning, dressed in precisely the same clothes. Her hair was touched with grey. Prematurely, Rosetta conjectured. Her figure was that of a woman no more than thirty.

Each morning, she followed the same routine. Having greeted Rosetta and Franco, she ignored everyone else, stepped out of the slim pants, which she folded with expertise, whipped the black top over her head, and hung them both neatly over the spokes of the umbrella. This procedure left her in an apology for a yellow bikini, which matched exactly the scarf about her head and which drew, not in the least surreptitiously, some dozen pairs of eyes. Her last chore was the removal of the scarf itself, which was tossed into the wicker basket beside her mattress.

Running pink-painted fingernails through the greying hair, she would walk unhurriedly and elegantly into the sparkling sea and, when she could no longer stand, swim in a leisurely, effortless crawl until she seemed almost to disappear. As languidly as she had gone, she would return, materialising from the water unconcerned about the two sagging strips of her bikini and seemingly unperturbed by the rows of eyes now firmly fixed upon her. Back at her mattress, she would stand, legs slightly apart, comb the hair back from her face, retie the yellow scarf, rub oil into every particle of flesh uncovered by the two strips of canary cotton, apply a dash of scarlet lipstick to her wide, beautiful mouth, and when all was ready, spread a black towel on her mattress and lie down to sleep. By the time she awoke, the sun was usually high in the sky. The colour of her skin had metamorphosed over the days from honey blond to golden cognac.

It was Jasper who christened her the 'Sleeping Beauty', but Stephanie who fell in love. Theirs was the umbrella next to hers. Neither of them wearied of watching her turn from time to time from back to front, like some tender roll baking in the oven, without so much as opening her eyes. Occasionally, in her sleep she smiled with the wide scarlet mouth.

On the day of the disturbance, for which Stephanie blamed Jasper and Jasper blamed Stephanie, it was suffocatingly hot. By ten in the morning, the rays of the sun were pitiless.

The trouble began over the comic paper that had arrived that day from England. It belonged, by rights, to Stephanie, whom, at twelve, it intrigued immeasurably; it had been appropriated by Jasper, who, at fourteen, was not above enjoying it when none of his friends was in sight. Stephanie was bored; she was also hot. Tiny drops of perspiration beaded her upper lip. She did not feel very well in the region of her stomach; also, she wanted to read her comic. She reached across to where Jasper lay idly happy on his mattress and grabbed at the paper.

Jasper tightened his hold.

'Give it to me.' Stephanie was whispering, anxious not to waken the Sleeping Beauty.

'I'm not finished.'

'It's mine!'

'You can have it in a minute.'

'I want it now!'

'Shut up.'

Stephanie made another grab. There were tears in her eyes.

'Give it to me.'

Jasper folded one knee over the other indolently and continued reading.

The temperature, the tedium, and the unpleasant sensation in her stomach were too much for Stephanie. With one hand she pulled Jasper's nose good and hard and with the other she snatched the comic.

Jasper howled with pain and rage; he also aimed a kick at his sister, which landed, unfortunately, in the already tender region of her navel. Stephanie lay face down on her mattress and howled.

Jasper saw that he had gone too far.

'Look, I didn't mean to kick you.'

The howling did not diminish.

'I said I didn't mean to kick you.' Jasper looked around, embarrassed at the rumpus his sister was creating on the torpid beach.

'You've woken the Sleeping Beauty,' he whispered. 'Can't you belt up a bit? I've said I'm sorry.'

It was like talking to the shimmering air.

The Sleeping Beauty was now awake. She was also sitting up. She looked at Jasper and at Stephanie, still on her stomach, sobbing as if her heart would break.

'Where is your mother?' the Sleeping Beauty said.

'We have lost her,' Jasper said.

'*Mon dieu*!' The Sleeping Beauty leaped to her feet. 'Franco! Franco!'

'I mean,' Jasper said, 'she is dead.'

The Sleeping Beauty sat down again on the edge of her mattress and faced Jasper. 'Who is looking after you, then?'

'Our father.'

She looked vaguely about her. 'And where is your father?'

'In Basle.'

The Sleeping Beauty sighed.

'He will be here at the end of the week,' Jasper said helpfully.

'But it is only Monday!'

'We are quite capable of looking after ourselves for a few days,' Jasper said with dignity. He followed the glance of the Sleeping Beauty towards the shaking form of his sister, who still whimpered into the mattress.

The Sleeping Beauty turned her over gently. 'Something hurts you?' she said.

'She's just mad because I swiped her comic paper,' Jasper said. 'I said I was sorry.'

Stephanie gave him a scathing look and wiped her tears on her beach towel. 'I have a stomach ache,' she said to the Sleeping Beauty, who was now sitting beside her.

'You eat last night the zucchini?' the Sleeping Beauty asked. 'I have something for you in my room.'

They left Jasper on the beach, with sole access to the comic, which he no longer wanted to read. He had promised his father to look after Stephanie. He had failed.

When the Sleeping Beauty returned, she was alone. 'Your sister is sleeping in my suite,' she said to Jasper. 'Too much sun and zucchini. When she wakes up, she will feel better.'

Jasper, looking glumly out to sea, did not answer.

'You also have the stomach ache?' the Sleeping Beauty said.

'No.'

'What have you?'

'Nothing. I shouldn't have teased her. I promised to look after her.'

The Sleeping Beauty told him that it was not his fault at all, but a combination of the heat and the strange food that was responsible for upsetting his sister. 'Tell me about your mother,' she said, wishing to distract him.

'I told you. She is dead. She was very beautiful and always laughing.' He looked sideways, making a mental comparison, which did not escape unnoticed. 'Then she became very ugly and did not laugh at all.'

'It must have been sad for you.'

Jasper shrugged. 'I was at school.' It was Mrs Giddins, their housekeeper, who now packed his suitcase; sometimes half the things were missing or unmarked. 'It's different for Steph.'

The eyebrows went up questioningly.

'She's a girl.'

'And your father?'

'He's the worst of the lot. He sometimes goes to the city in a blue suit with a brown tie; he's colourblind, you see.'

'I see.'

All that day, Stephanie slept. The next, she remained in the Sleeping Beauty's suite, fed on bread sticks and frequent small drinks of Fiuggi water. By Wednesday, she was quite cured and appeared her normal self, although a trifle pale, on the beach.

During the time that his sister had been indisposed, Jasper had struck up a friendship with the Sleeping Beauty. She was not prepared to lose very much sleep in pursuit of their intimacy, but in her waking moments they discovered a mutual interest in cars, of which she had two, a Buick Riviera and a Ferrari Spyder, and an appreciation of Mario Mariotti, who was to sing in the hotel that weekend. She did not talk much about herself, except to say that her business was with clothes and that each summer she took two weeks off to lie in the sun like a sand lizard and do absolutely nothing.

'Then I am sorry Stephanie has disturbed you,' Jasper said, when she revealed this indulgence.

'It is nothing. I adore children. And I have none of my own.'

It was at that moment that Jasper conceived his plan. He

hugged it to himself all day and didn't reveal it to Stephanie until that evening after they left the beach.

While the Sleeping Beauty slept on, they packed their belongings and exchanged a few friendly remarks with Franco, who always smiled with Rosetta over the bearing and poise of the fourteen-year-old Englishman.

'I think a little drink before we change,' Jasper said as they reached the hotel. 'Don't you agree, Steph?'

'I'm gasping.' She sat down in the shade on one of the white wrought-iron chairs on the wide terrace, where the band played beneath the stars nightly.

Dominic, white-coated, tray in hand, bowed low before them.

'Good evening, Dominic,' Jasper said. 'I'll have a Negroni.'

Dominic winked. 'Certainly, sir. And for the young lady?'

'I'll stick to Fiuggi,' Stephanie said.

'Steph,' Jasper said, when Dominic had come and gone with his alcohol-less Negroni and Stephanie's mineral water, 'I have an idea.'

'I've already had it.'

'You can't have.'

'You aren't the only one allowed to have ideas.'

'But I've only just had this one.'

'Well, I had it yesterday.'

'Perhaps it isn't the same.'

'It's the same.'

'How do you know?'

Stephanie looked at him. 'Is it about the Sleeping Beauty?'

Jasper looked at her in amazement.

Stephanie said, 'I think she's absolutely divine. But that's not to say that Father will.'

'Father and I,' Jasper said, 'have similar tastes in women.' With that, he called for another Negroni.

On Thursday and Friday, they scarcely took their eyes off her; it was as if, like the fairy godmother, they were afraid she would disappear. She remained very much in evidence, however, her golden-cognac tan deepening nicely into tawny port.

When their father arrived from Basle on Friday night, they had decided to play it cool. They told him of Stephanie's malaise and how a kind Frenchwoman on the beach had looked after her with such solicitude. They phrased it in such a way that he imagined her, as they had intended him to, as a motherly figure with flabby arms and a moustache, surrounded by a brood of children. They were glad the Sleeping Beauty did not appear in the dining room that night and their father's first sight of her was on the beach.

They were established with their extra mattress well before the customary time of the Sleeping Beauty's arrival.

'I hope we have no one noisy next to us,' their father said, unfolding the *Financial Times*. 'I'm looking forward to a little peace and quiet.'

'No, only the woman who looked after Stephanie,' Jasper said and, before his father could say a word, asked, 'What is the price of gold?'

When she arrived and stood beside them, hanging up her neatly folded clothes, Jasper whispered to his father, behind the newspaper, 'I think we had better introduce you. After all, she was terribly good to Steph.'

His father growled. 'If you insist. One has, I suppose, to be polite.' He lowered his newspaper, and the pink pages fluttered unheeded to the soft white sand.

Jasper closed one eye at Stephanie.

They watched them, the ebony reed in the two strips of yellow cotton and the upright figure of their not undistinguished-looking father, walk down the beach and out into the gentle sea.

When they returned, the Sleeping Beauty was invited to join them for lunch, but did not accept, preferring to sleep; it was as if she hoped to digest the sun.

Their father's mind was on neither the prosciutto nor the lasagne on which they lunched. Usually he took a nap in his room. Today, for some unfathomable reason, he opted for the beach.

'You will burn,' Jasper warned.

'I shall ask Franco to shift the umbrella.'

Saturday night at the Excelsior was gala night. In addition to the residents of the hotel, the elite of the surrounding district put on their finery and dined there or came later to dance and enjoy the cabaret on the fairyland of a terrace.

At first, Jasper and Stephanie were afraid she would not appear.

'You two are exceptionally quiet,' their father said, suffering just a little from prolonged exposure to the sun. 'Is something troubling you?'

'Not in the least,' Jasper said.

'We feel remarkably fit,' Stephanie added.

'I was not enquiring after your health,' their father said. 'Something is up. I feel it in my bones.'

They were seated at a table on the terrace, not too far from the band, when she appeared. Exquisite women at the Excelsior, in particular on gala nights, were like so many grains of sand. The Sleeping Beauty was the jewel of them all. She was dressed in pale-blue satin, the sleeveless top cut plain like a shirt and edged with amber, the floor-length skirt divided into wide pyjamas; her waist was very, very small. Followed by all eyes, she came to join them. She was the most splendid sight Jasper and Stephanie had seen.

'Our favourite singer,' she said to Jasper, as Mario Mariotti took the mike.

'Shall we dance?' their father said.

She was very tall indeed, but their father was taller. They moved over the smooth marble floor as if they had been dancing together all their lives. Now and again she leaned back her head and laughed. They seemed to be very happy.

At midnight, Stephanie and Jasper were sent to bed. Their father took the Sleeping Beauty to the discothèque, where it was very dark, very crowded and exceedingly noisy.

Although they had said goodnight, Jasper and Stephanie stayed talking to Dominic for a while alone in his deserted bar, then decided they had better go up.

'Let's just go and have a peep,' Stephanie said.

'What for?'

'You know perfectly well,' Stephanie said, 'I want to see how things are going.'

The music assaulted their eardrums; their eyes were scarcely able to pierce the gloom. It was some moments before, on the packed floor, they were able to distinguish their father and the Sleeping Beauty.

They needed no more than a peep. Head and shoulders above the rest of the crowd, they were rocking to and fro in each other's arms, close together from head to foot, their eyes tightly shut.

Well satisfied, Stephanie and Jasper went upstairs.

Considerately, they did not wake their father on Sunday morning. Imagining him to have danced away the night, they scarcely expected him on the beach before lunch. They were a little surprised, however, that the Sleeping Beauty's mattress remained empty, too. They had somehow expected her to be made of sterner stuff.

Weary themselves, they dozed off in the sun, which seemed for the first time to be losing some of its intensity. When they awoke, their father, surrounded by Sunday newspapers, was lying beside them.

'Good morning, chickens,' he said. 'I thought we might go water-skiing. The sea looks as smooth as a millpond.'

Jasper looked at Stephanie, both looked at the still-empty mattress beside them. Their father followed their gaze. They looked up and down the beach, sure that somewhere they would see the scarlet mouth, the yellow scarf.

'Gone home,' their father said. 'Her husband is meeting her in Milan.' He hid himself behind the business section.

For a long moment, his children were speechless. Then Jasper whispered indignantly, 'She wasn't wearing a wedding ring.'

'Wanted to get her fingers brown,' Stephanie whispered back, with a sudden flash of that feminine intuition which is the higher form of logic.

'Oh, well,' Jasper said, with a certain philosophical melancholy. 'It isn't long until Christmas. Perhaps we shall do better at Gstaad.'

A Day for Roses

1970

Katie mentally subdivided the men who came out of the station into the 'peckers' and the 'huggers'. The majority fell into category number one.

She remembered laughing – what seemed like a hundred years ago, but could not in fact have been more than four or five – at stories of dutiful American wives in their nightdresses who ferried their husbands to the station in the mornings and equally dutifully collected them at night. Never at any point in her cogitations had she dreamed that she would evolve into an English counterpart.

In those days home had been a minuscule flat in Earls Court, which had nothing in its favour save that it was centrally situated and no one had to be ferried anywhere. They did not in fact own a car, which perhaps was just as well as there was no space to park within half a mile. She could not now remember when exactly they had decided to make the break. Certainly not when the flat had become too small.

That had been a gradual and insidious process, starting with the three children in one bedroom and ending with ironing in the sitting room, books in the kitchen, everything in the bathroom, and no corner that any one of them could call his own. She supposed there must have been a time of optimum strain when carrying shopping and babies up and rubbish and babies down three flights had taken its maximum toll; when the dirt and the noise and the traffic haze, which never quite cleared even in summer, had become unbearable, but she could recall no precise moment at which Richard had said, 'Let's go.'

When visiting friends who lived 'out' in their neat little semis or 'ranch-style' moderns, they had caught the last train back to town muttering never, not even for the dubious pleasure of park and patio and somewhere to hang the washing. 'I should turn into a cabbage,' she remembered saying once to Richard. 'London is where things happen.'

'They do come up to town,' Richard said. 'It doesn't take long in a car.'

'But the effort! I'm quite sure that after a while you'd simply vegetate, the high spot being meeting your husband at the station and taking him home to something that had taken hours to prepare and which he'd be far too tired to eat!'

Yet here she was in the station wagon with Flip, secure in the canine knowledge that the train was not yet due, asleep on the back seat, dinner in the oven, the three children in their own rooms settled down (she hoped) to homework, and Nicolette applying her false eyelashes when she should have been laying the table.

In Earls Court she might have spent the afternoon in the British Museum or the National Gallery, or upstairs talking to Paul who came from Guadeloupe and painted, or downstairs with Madeleine who had five children and was a researcher and still found time to teach an evening class twice a week. Today she had come from the Wednesday Club where young wives like herself from the right little tight little community met suitably clad and coiffed to gossip and, when they could remember, to raise money for worthy causes.

And yet and yet and yet ... from the vast windows of their split-level open-plan house with its laundry room and shower room and place for the wellingtons, you could watch the changing of the seasons no matter where you looked: from the bare branches to buds and blossom that left you breathless, then overpowering verdure sheltering a long hot summer, to brown and gold and russet and the inevitable regrets. In Earls Court there had been only chimneypots with no life cycle and, outside, the multiracial occupants of bedsitter land, treading the pavements with layabouts and artists and typists and down-at-heel ladies who had known better times trailing shopping baskets on wheels. Now, like the Wednesday Club, her milieu was homogenised. The children could mix with anyone they were likely to meet; their mothers, although they picked and chose, arrived with the same selection of items at the supermarket checkout each week, and even the dogs knew each other from walking on the common.

At first Richard and she had gone no less to the theatre. After a while it had become a chore. They had the car, it was true, but she disliked meeting Richard in town, feeling an outsider, she disliked the long drive back, and it was simpler to sit down comfortably and watch television and read the reviews in the Sunday papers so that she could hold her own at the Wednesday Club. For the children, as Richard had promised, it was bliss. There was skating on the ponds in winter, tobogganing on the common, picnics in summer, blackberries far into the autumn. For herself too: everything stayed clean and fresh, and there was pleasure in opening the windows.

She found, however, that she read and listened to records less and was surprised to catch herself gossiping for hours on the telephone, tearing to shreds reputations about which she couldn't care a hang in the first place, or hadn't. Now they had become her world – Pat and Wendy and Marcia and Lola – until there were times when she could recall only with difficulty spaghetti hoops from a tin with Paul and trailing to the launderette where conversation was far more stimulating than at the Wednesday Club, although no one gave you home-made chocolate cake for tea.

It was all right for Richard. He had the garden and golf on Saturdays, though she had not yet brought herself to be one of the wives who went too, and each day he made the exciting voyage into the big City, hating it, he said, leaving her with the trees and the open spaces. In imagination she followed him to the dirt and the noise and the crowded streets and comfortable discomfort of the lovely convoys of large red buses.

She did not complain. First because she felt it to be unjustified. She had wanted to be married and to have a family, and why should she deny them the opportunity to be reared in beautiful surroundings? And, second, she knew that she was not the only one to have made a sacrifice, only what it was exactly that she had sacrificed she was not quite sure.

Each evening found Richard, the latest copy of *The Motor* on his lap, examining the specifications of Maseratis and Lamborghinis, while outside in the double garage stood a perfectly serviceable station wagon absolutely ideal for the life they led and going on holiday with the children and the dog. Lamborghini might be written on the page but Katie was well aware that all Richard saw was the mortgage and S.E.T. and income tax and Joanna's dancing classes and the central heating oil and Simon's extra French.

Richard worked hard and had a flourishing legal practice; had he remained single, the Lamborghini could well have metamorphosed from fantasy to reality. As it was, he bore the burdens of a wife and children and an au pair and a split-level house and a large garden and a dog and lessons for this and lessons for that, repairs to this and repairs to that and the fares that went up and up while his fees did not.

Most of the misgivings concerning their removal to the pseudo-country Katie had kept within herself, realising that it was the best for the most. It was necessary almost to admit now that she positively enjoyed the life and even the Wednesday Club had a certain conviviality and was not so crashing and ludicrous a bore as at first it had seemed. It was more than pleasant on sunny days to sit on the terrace with neither haze nor smog, watching the children screaming with enjoyment under the hose, which played upon the lawn. It was good to spend the afternoon in the hairdresser's knowing that it was Wendy's turn or Lola's to pick up the children from school or take everyone to dancing class. If she had missed out, she wasn't sure on what. She had never really given room to her thoughts or vague misgivings, which were all they were, until today. But today they had come rushing to the fore like flood-waters, previously dammed, swamping her brain and giving rise to bitterness and recrimination.

It was their wedding anniversary and Richard had forgotten. Last night he had sat till late, *The Motor* before him, dreaming of Lamborghinis. This morning, as on any other, she had driven him to his train, he had pecked her cheek like all the other 'peckers' and disappeared into the station. It was the first time he'd forgotten, and she scarcely believed it possible.

In London they had celebrated, in the early days, at a Chinese or Indian restaurant, seedy but romantic, later graduating to French and Italian places with strung-up fishing nets and Chianti bottles. Since they had moved it had been the Bell or the Orchard or the Old Oak Manor, to which people came from far and wide, even from town, and there was dancing. Never, ever, since the very first had he forgotten and never, ever, had there not been roses. It was early for roses and he always apologised laughingly for the small buds that withered and died, or those that had drooping heads, but would not yield them to any other more easily obtained yet less romantic flower. In Earls Court he used to bring them in person, taking the three flights two stairs at a time in his haste to present them, to take her in his arms ... Since they moved they had been delivered, decorously, from the local florist, wrapped hygienically in cellophane, the card with its message of love meticulously attached with an outsize pin.

All day she had waited for the bell. There had been the fishmonger, the dog's-meat man, a parcel from Harrods that looked hopeful but which had turned out to be hockey socks she had ordered for Jennifer, a telegram for Nicolette to say that her mother was ill (unlikely) and would she return home forthwith, and, finally, silence. She could not believe it. Fourteen years was a long, long time, it was true, but it was unlike Richard to forget and beneath her pride to remind him. She blamed it somehow on the split-level and the trees and the laundry room. It was all mixed up in her mind and she felt, unrealistically, that in Earls Court it could never have happened. They could not have stayed there; that she knew. Could not possibly have afforded anything larger or more suitable in town. Perhaps he no longer cared; perhaps there was somebody else while she occupied herself with the hairdresser and the Wednesday Club; perhaps he had a little love nest in town? It was not unheard of. One or two husbands of the Club members had gone off the rails at one point or another, on their own admission; others, according to gossip, were highly suspect. Not Richard though. It was her imagination taking wing. He would step briskly out of the station in the forefront of the next little exodus bearing red roses.

She never minded waiting at the station. It was nice to sit

down and it was a chore that always amused her. From six o'clock onwards the courtyard was a kaleidoscope of movement, Minis vying with staid saloons and saloons with station wagons for position. Clashing with each little posse of tired businessmen returning to their homes, and heading in the opposite direction, were the wives, fastidiously groomed, going up for an evening in town. They always looked incongruous, Katie felt – although she had been often in the same situation – in their patent shoes and their clean white gloves going through to the grimy trains. What else could they do? Once at the theatre or San Frediano's or L'Epée d'Or they would be congruous again.

Another train came in and Flip awoke; it must be getting near time. She switched on the ignition as the woman in the Mini in front received her evening peck upon the cheek and drove away. Katie eased up to take her place, and Flip, having stretched, put a paw upon her shoulder and hung his head out of the window so that he could watch the entrance to the station. The newspaper woman was busy, not so much selling papers to the wives going up to town – they did not want to dirty their white gloves on newsprint – but giving messages that had been left with her during the day to schoolchildren that their mothers might be late, or to husbands that the car wouldn't start and would they walk or queue up for the bus.

As each man came out he looked with some anxiety left and right for the familiar car, the familiar wife, though each, Katie thought, with her deep freeze at home and identical report of the day's events, was somehow interchangeable.

She felt Flip become agitated. Bemused by her thoughts, she had neglected to keep vigil. There on the pavement, looking to right and left, was Richard. There were no roses.

He said good evening first to Flip, then to her. He took his place beside her in the car.

Don't you know what day it is?

'What's for dinner?' he asked. 'I'm starving. All day in court. Didn't stop for lunch.'

I did not, would not, she thought, put candles on the table, serve dinner *à deux*, your favourite moules; there is cottage pie.

'Children all right?'

Children? What about me? Flip and the children and the dinner and I the producer, the *metteuse en scène* who made it all happen but remained in the background.

He greeted Nicolette, the children, helped Jennifer with her chemistry, had a second helping of cottage pie.

I shall not cry.

There was a television programme he wanted to watch; they watched it, endlessly. She had no idea what it was about. I shall not cry.

Nicolette went out. The children one by one to bed. Flip to his basket.

This is our day.

He held out his hand. She realised there was something in it: a box, a small box. Taking it from him, she opened it.

A rose, but made of diamonds: perfect; exquisite; costly to excess.

'For all the roses that have died,' he said.

Now she cried, and he could not understand, because men never did, that in women it could be a sign of happiness.

Do You Remember?

1974

They had not gone out after the wedding; John had not suggested it. He had not thought of a very special table for two at any eating place familiar or surprise. Thus it was after a day of action, reaction and mixed emotions that Helen found herself, with a blue and white butcher's apron over her rose wild silk, standing in the kitchen, champagne corks littered like the confetti there had not been, poring over the magazine article 'Cooking for two: that first dinner'.

The illustration showed a polished wood table complete with flowers and candles.

The dining room table, at present groaning under its load of French casseroles with cast-iron bottoms, fancy chopping boards, and multifarious fondue sets, was out for a start. That left the kitchen, at whose counter top with its remains of tired smoked salmon sandwiches she looked wearily, or a tray in the sitting room in front of the television. The article permitted no compromise: best china, best silver, prettiest mats.

She cleared a space on the Formica counter top, noting with distaste distinct evidence that the bride, at the last moment, had trimmed the bridegroom's hair using the kitchen scissors so to do, and applied herself to the next paragraph headed 'Food. Not the time to experiment'. She had never felt less like experimenting and decided without difficulty on fresh grapefruit in deference to John's waistline. Right. Next? 'Give garlic a miss, although a well-seasoned but simple dish is suggested.' Medallions de boeuf, beans and duchesse potatoes; breaded lamb chops (with little frills on their tails); escalopes of veal, depicted with a yellow-eyed fried egg atop. Sighing, she closed the magazine and went to the larder. The top shelf held huge chip pans, giant casseroles neither French nor cast-iron bottomed, a fish kettle of truly noble proportions. She was not used to cooking for two. She decided it was an occasion for a hideously expensive can of chicken in aspic, followed by the peaches in brandy she always kept on the shelf but never felt justified in using on an ordinary day.

Dinner for two it certainly was. Using the tin opener, she wondered how it would be alone with her man. It would not, of course, be the first occasion by any stretch of the imagination, but this time it was for keeps. The feelings that the situation evoked were, to say the least of it, mixed. What would they talk about? Thank heavens for television, although that was a disgraceful admission to have to make. What plans would they discuss? What decisions were there to take? Just herself and John. Such a frighteningly small unit, a unit that had today given away its final chance to enlarge its potential.

Why Jane of all people, Jane who would never leave home, Mummy's baby, Jane, had had to fall in love with and marry a New Zealander was one of fate's unkinder cuts, on which Helen did not care to dwell. Not if they were to get any dinner at all, that was. It was different with the boys. One half expected it in a way, although not one of her friends could match one son in Nova Scotia and another in Nepal. But Jane! Little, fond, loving Jane. Had they been such frightful parents? John's friend in psychiatry said, on the contrary, the children were so well adjusted they were able happily and confidently to cut the apron strings, which was the best for everybody. Thinking of the upstairs flat, which once had been the nursery floor and which Helen had always secretly hoped might house the newly married Jane, she wished perhaps they might have been a shade less understanding, a fragment perhaps more cruel.

Of course, the world had shrunk, yet you could not exactly, with impunity, pop over to, or telephone too frequently, New Zealand or Nepal. She hated her friends, most of them at any rate, in particular Iris, with her four children living within spitting distance, and Geraldine who dragged a steadily increasing bevy of grandchildren through the toy departments at Christmas. She imagined herself trying to buy holly-sprigged wrapping paper in August, or something equally ridiculous (she wasn't quite sure how long parcels took, but she knew the time to be outrageous), and remembered the radio's yearly admonitions about final dates for posting overseas mail. One could of course keep in contact but where was the substitute for the smiles or tears on a dear face, the feel of a small, warm, confidently clutching hand?

Feeling herself becoming maudlin, she picked up the peaches in brandy, wondering how best to attack the lid, and thought of the wedding. Wedding! Well, the most weddingly thing about it had been her own outfit. Not that it hadn't been a jolly affair. Jolly to the point of being bizarre. But not a wedding such as one was accustomed to.

The register office ceremony had been over in the wink of an eye. Lucky actually that Jane had made it at all. She was blow-drying her hair until half an hour before. The bridegroom, all husky six-foot-plus of him, had not aspired to a tie and at the reception, by request of the indubitably happy couple, there had not been one speech.

Times, one could not say otherwise, had changed. New Zealand, Nova Scotia. When she and John had got married, you were considered lucky if you got so far as your own shores. There was none of this trekking to French valleys and Greek mountains with not a worry and scarcely a change of clothes. The whole ethos had changed, come to think of it. In her day if you went to a party you stayed at it. You also knew the name of the host and afterwards wrote a polite thank-you note. When you danced you made physical contact with your partner and when the music stopped you clapped. Today the music never seemed to stop at all, if you could call it music, that was, that dreadful noise that shattered the eardrums every time you turned on the radio.

'Dinner ready?' John said.

'I didn't hear you come in.'

'You were lost in thought. Penny for them?' He picked up the tray she had prepared and carried it into the sitting room.

When they were comfortable, she said: 'I was thinking how times have changed. I mean, in our day the only things that were "switched on" were lights. Do you realise that whole breeds are dead or dying – maternity nurses, maiden aunts, sewing ladies, companions – and au pairs, babysitters, home helps, and flatmates have been born?'

'Coal was delivered by horse and cart,' John said, warming to the game, 'and chicken was for Sundays.'

'We had trams, silk stockings, and lace mats under glass.'

'Milkmen had horses, tobacconists sold tobacco, and when you went to the barber you knew you were going to get short back and sides.'

'It is beyond their comprehension,' Helen said, 'the children's, I mean, that we had no boutiques, heated rollers, tights, astronauts, supermarkets, or disposable nappies and dishcloths. That we existed without washing machines, and waste grinders. That "engagements" meant just that and that "diamonds were for ever".'

'Can you imagine me,' John said, 'having my hair set?'

'Or me wearing patched blue jeans and plimsolls?'

'Pets were fed on household scraps, nothing drip-dried ...'

'One had neither ballpoint pens and aerosols, nor polythene bags ...'

'... Parking meters, Sellotape, fish fingers ...'

'... Launderettes, instant puddings, the Pill ...'

'They do not realise,' Helen said, finishing up the last of the peaches in brandy, 'quite how fortunate they are.' She listened. 'Was that the bell?'

'I don't think so.' John stood up. 'Yes, it was. Who the devil could it be?'

'If you answer it you'll find out,' Helen said, as she had been doing for the past twenty-six years. He was the same with letters, never opening one until he'd turned it this way and that, examined the stamp, held it to the light and speculated who it could be from. She heard voices in the hall and piled the remains of supper on to the tray.

'Guess who?' a familiar voice said from the door, before she had time to make it to the kitchen with the tray.

'Jane!'

She sat down, overcome with weakness. What was the trouble? Surely they hadn't decided on divorce after two hours! Had Nick walked out? Jane changed her mind? In the blink of an eye she saw herself pushing her grandchildren triumphantly down the high street, nodding patronisingly to Iris on the other side of the road; in the stores at Christmas time buying dolls with interchangeable wardrobes.

'It's all right, Mother,' Jane said.

'Is Nick with you?' Helen asked suspiciously.

'Of course. He's talking to Dad.'

'Then I don't understand.'

'It's quite simple,' Jane said. 'We guessed the two of you would be sitting here in this huge house, supper on a tray ...'

Helen pulled it towards her defensively.

'... playing games.'

'Games!' Helen said incredulously, wondering what had come over her daughter. 'When did you last see your dad and me playing games? Any sort of games. He can't play bridge, never did have a head for cards of any description ...'

'I didn't mean that kind of game.'

'What on earth did you mean, then?' Helen asked.

'"Do You Remember?"' Jane said gently. 'I bet – well, Nick and I both bet, actually – that you'd be sitting here, the two of you, recalling how it cost a penny on the tram from Gran's to the Town Hall ...'

'Tuppence!' Helen said.

'... hair was permanently waved, and the only sort of wedding was white, usually floral, and preferably choral.'

'What utter rubbish!' Helen said. 'We weren't doing any such thing.'

'So we decided, Nick and I,' Jane said, ignoring her, 'that since it might be an awfully long while before we see you again, and since we don't have to be at the airport until five in the morning, which means leaving at three, that we'd like to take you out. We've got tickets and it's a good play, so get your skates on, there's a darling.'

Helen said dazedly: 'A theatre! But don't you want to ... I mean you and Nick ... the wedding ...?'

'Mother!' Jane was laughing.

'I'd forgotten,' Helen said, picking up the tray once more, primly, 'times have changed.'

At Jane's insistence she left the supper plates and the chaos in the kitchen, which she protested half-heartedly would not clear itself away, and put on her rose silk coat again.

The play, a comedy from Broadway, had Helen laughing until the new mascara she had invested in for her 'mother-of-the-bride' role was running down her face.

After the theatre, dismissing the tinned chicken and peaches in brandy, which Helen had to admit to herself had been some time ago, Nick insisted on taking them to dinner at a cellar restaurant, open all night, where the food was super and Helen felt frightfully old. By the end of dinner, however, the dolly birds did not seem quite so young, or the music quite so loud, and John was laughing as she hadn't seen him do in months, and before they realised it was one in the morning.

'We must take you home now,' Nick said, 'or we shall miss our plane.'

At home, the curled-up sandwiches in the kitchen did not seem so sad.

'We will go out more,' John said in the bedroom.

'There are loads of new places to eat we don't even know about,' Helen said, reaching for a hanger.

'We will sell this house!' John said decisively.

Helen stared at him. They had lived in it since they were married and John had always declared that there he would die.

Now he was saying: 'We'll buy a flat, a small flat ...'

'But the garden?' She always teased that he loved her less than his roses.

'We shall go abroad, travel ...'

'The business?'

'There are younger men.'

'Where would we go?'

'Does it matter?' John said. 'Do you realise that after twenty-six years of hard labour we are free? Free!'

Helen pitied Iris with the heavy brood of grandchildren she pushed daily down the high street, and Geraldine ploughing hotly round the shops. She saw vividly the Parthenon, the Taj Mahal, the Leaning Tower of Pisa … they might pop in to New Zealand on the way.

In bed, John said: 'In our day, when you waved people off on their honeymoon that was that!'

'Yes,' said Helen contentedly, making herself comfortable. 'Do you remember?'

The Pink Case

1975

I travel for my magazine – one of the better-known fashion glossies. I suppose you would call it a job in a million: Kenya, Canada, Finland, Lapland, Argentina, Japan ... you never know from one moment to the next where the Fashion Editor's fancy will take her, and you have to be ready to pack your bags and go at a moment's notice; footloose and fancy-free.

You must know the sort of thing. A black wrap-around (cotton for coolness) against the wide blue yonder of the Persian Gulf. Click. White ankle-length in Waikiki. Click. Sables on the Ponte Vecchio. Click.

We might spend days in Bahrain and finally get one picture so that all the chicks would rush like lemmings to the classy boutiques for the cheesecloth shift or the espadrilles, or whatever it was we were plugging.

No matter that our model was covered with bites and had been up all night with the trots and that the espadrilles fitted nowhere. It was my job to get it together so that she looked suitably happy, that the photographer was sober enough to do his stuff, the hairdresser and the make-up girl in the right place at the right time and not scuba diving or chatting up the locals with a view to business, amorous or otherwise.

It isn't easy, believe me. I earn my money. You could arrive in Bangkok without one vital piece of a two-piece ensemble; in Detroit, on a hair-fine schedule, the thousands of cars all nicely aligned, and the cameraman still arguing with Narcotics over what they swore was dope but which in actual fact were pills prescribed by his doctor for hay fever.

I was good, you see, about dealing with people. I could wheedle my way round obstreperous Customs Officials; produce rooms in hotels that were fully booked; think ahead, so that the whole team with all its paraphernalia remained together in good health and with their wits about them, to all intents and purposes at any rate.

It was one of fate's odder quirks that the first time in over twelve years I slipped up seriously was in regard to myself.

Of course, it had to be Jamaica! The land of 'soon come' and tropical torpor. In Paris or New York the action might have been somewhat faster.

When I first got the job – the promotion, I mean – and the travelling started, my father bought me a Louis Vuitton travelling kit, brown canvas with the squiggles which were actually the designer's initials interwoven into the dark-brown leather trim. I know it set him back quite a bit. I was thrilled at the time; jetting round the world with my classy luggage. It took me a while to realise that about two-thirds of the travelling population seemed to have identical suitcases.

Whether imitation, plastic trim instead of leather, and not quite the right initials, it didn't matter. I'd stand next to the porter in Sydney where it all got shunted round and round on a playground merry-go-round, yelling, 'That's it! No, hang on, it looks like it but it isn't ... That one! No, mine has a strap ...'

It was a sudden decision. The week before I had walked into the travel department of a well-known store and bought one large, roomy, lightweight case in what I can call hideous, shrieking pink. All I had to do was learn the word for pink in a million different languages and – bingo! I'd be away while the others were still searching for the word for porter.

We left Sydney in 12 degrees, raining. I had my fur coat over the blue jeans in which I always travelled – I liked to be comfortable – and a T-shirt topped by various sweaters that I could peel off to suit the climate.

We travelled on a 747; our little team of six with enough temperament between us for a football side, a lot of Chinamen making a lot of Chinese noise, and a random selection of others. Roughly seventy of us on a plane capable of carrying almost four hundred. Not bad! It mitigated the tedium of the film, the plastic food, the baby, belonging to an American couple, who didn't stop crying all the way to JFK.

We had five hours to spend at Kennedy. Being in transit, there was nothing we could do but eat and sleep and cuss out the first-class passengers who until then had been segregated from us mere mortals in another part of the plane; splendid isolation from the proles, with their own little upstairs bar.

I was halfway through my pastrami on rye – two inches thick with pickles and French fries on the side – when I caught sight of him. He was the sole only likely-looking man in the whole crowd.

Although I was pushing thirty next birthday, you see, I hadn't given up, the only trouble being that the older you got the narrower the field seemed to become. I had no intention, however, of spending the rest of my life either alone or embroiled in the trauma of some impermanent liaison.

He was tall and dark and as impeccable, even after eight hours, as only an Italian can be: biscuit suit, black shoes, crisp white shirt, dark tie with a pearl pin. Boy, oh boy! I looked around for a companion but he seemed to be alone.

Sara, our model, interrupted my daydreams to say she had a headache and a sore throat and thought she was sickening for something; she threatened chickenpox, as it was around in her kid sister's school. By the time I had calmed her down and dosed her up it was time to transfer to the DC9 and the last leg of the flight to Montego Bay.

At Montego the heat hit you like the steam from a kettle. The natives, standing around in bright coloured shirts and pants, chewing indolently on toothpicks, watched us in silence. There was no trouble with Customs and a taxi driver had been sent to meet us. He carried my new pink case.

The manager of the hotel, a harassed fellow Australian,

escorted us to our various bungalows. I helped myself to iced water from the vacuum flask on the bureau, took my nightie from my holdall, switched on the air conditioning, flung myself into one of the trim beds and fell fast asleep.

I slept like the dead, as I always do after travelling, and woke at seven to hear the maid pottering around in the kitchen.

The table was laid on the terrace. Orange juice and butter and coffee and jam and hot toast and hot buns and a wooden bowl of pineapple, bananas and hazeberries artistically arranged.

I lingered as long as I could over breakfast, knowing that as soon as I made a move all hell would be let loose. We did not have too long for each assignment and most of the time it was all go. My first job would be to rouse the others, who would be full of complaints and not at all anxious to get to work.

I decided to give them another half hour, while I bathed and dressed, before I woke them.

The towel was large, white and fluffy, just as I, sybarite that I am, liked them. I swathed myself in it and rummaged in my handbag for the keys of the new case. A swimsuit and a cover-up were all that would be necessary.

The zipper worked smoothly. I turned back the lid and – wow! Where were my cotton shifts, my voile shirts, my cute little numbers for the evening?

The case was packed beautifully and pristinely with trousers and shirts, some of them embroidered, but all of them utterly and unequivocally male. I sat there on the floor, utterly and completely stunned. It was shrieking pink, it appeared to

be new but, quite simply, it was not my case. I had a vision
of myself swimming, dining, dancing, in my pale-blue nightie
which was, to say the least, transparent.

Stupidly, I suppose because I thought it unique, I had not
thought to transfer the leather label bearing my name and
address from my old case of blessed memory. All that there
was, both on my own and on the one before me, was the flight
number – to Montego Bay!

And then I thought, he must be somewhere on the island,
in the area really if not actually in the hotel, or he would have
made straight for Kingston.

Feeling like a criminal I looked vaguely through the garments for clues and felt a surge of embarrassment as I imagined someone searching my own carelessly packed bag in
similar fashion. There was no form of identification that I
could see, only that the owner was meticulous in his dress and
had someone absolutely super to iron his shirts. The only lead
I got was that his initials were FC.

Stirring myself to action, I decided that there was nothing
for it but to put on the crumpled jeans and the none-too-clean
T-shirt I had worn on the flight and call the manager.

Shock number two: before going to bed I had slung my
travel-weary garments in the corner by the second of the twin
beds. They were no longer there. I closed my eyes and remembered with horror that this was Jamaica.

In the tiny kitchen the maid, whose name I later discovered
was Mercedes, was singing to herself.

'Yes, ma'am,' she said with a wide smile, 'I don taken yo clo's and washed him. Reckon you don' need dem blue jeans no mo'. Look, de sun shinin'."

'When will they be back?' I asked.

'Don't you worry 'bout nothin', ma'am,' she said. 'Soon come!'

It was a phrase to cover hours, days, weeks, years. This was the land where the Caribbean tongued the silver sand to reach the coconut palms and the red-leaved almonds; the land of corato, hibiscus, frangipani, oleander, jasmine and jacaranda, whose fragrance was unforgettable at night; the land where no one ever hurried.

The manager was sympathetic, concerned. He came at once. Mike and the others were horrified at my plight. Sara, who had recovered from her indisposition, offered me her clothes. Would that I had been 32–22–33 and ten years younger; I might have been modelling swimsuits too!

Mike, who was the nearest in size, lent me his jeans, which were rough and hard, and Sara a peasant top which did nothing for me except to make me look pregnant.

The manager said to leave it to him. He would contact the airport, instigate enquiries, track down the missing case. Of one thing he was sure. No one had arrived at our hotel with the wrong suitcase in screaming pink. I had to leave it to him. Our schedule was too tight and it was too hot to go tearing round the countryside arguing with officials for whom time had no meaning.

We took off for the first session on the beach at Negril. It was breathtaking and for a while I forgot my dilemma.

Sara did her stuff against the background of mile after mile of deserted white sands fringed by almonds, oranges and coconuts whose leaves fell to the ground like dead sighs. Mike was in terrific form and Sara had never looked better. She wore the blue bikini, which was little more than two pieces of string and matched the sky, the black one-piece and shook her raven hair in the breeze, the brilliant orange kaftan into the back of which I had to stick a clothes-peg to hide the fact that it was not really her size, and the demure white smock, her hair like a schoolgirl's in pigtails.

After two hours we were all pretty flaked out. We packed our things into the jeep and everyone except me flung himself into the water. I felt like I took my harp to a party and nobody asked me to play.

Back on our own beach we sat at the straw-thatched bar, lapping up banana daiquiris and Planter's Punch, which did little to improve my mood.

Before lunch, I excused myself, leaving the others to their curried goat and kebabs, and shut myself in my bungalow with a club sandwich.

On my bed Mercedes had laid my own jeans and shirt, clean and dry; it helped a little. I would give it one day, I decided, before collapsing again on the bed, then equip myself at the hotel boutique at the expense of the magazine. I could not work up any enthusiasm for the idea. I liked my own wardrobe.

I slept until Mike called me to say it was six o'clock and the manager was having a party on his lawn to which we were all invited. There had been no progress with my belongings.

Mercedes, who came to tidy up, smiled her happy smile and said, 'Soon come.' I assumed she was referring to the missing case, and dressed once more in my jeans.

It was quite something. Or at least would have been. The cottage was high up on the hillside where a breeze cooled the milky warmth of the tropical night. The swimming pool was floodlit, peacock-green, the lawn illuminated with flares, and the air filled with the rhythmic beat of a Calypso band.

Boys in white jackets circulated with whisky sours and lobster dip and sausage rolls. Tanned American beauties, all of whom seemed to me at least six foot tall, wore flowers in their hair and were totally captivating with their beautiful bodies in beautiful dresses and their slow-sexy drawls.

I decided that the only thing to do was to drink myself into oblivion.

I can't tell you how long we stayed, remembering only that at some point, which seemed hours later, we drifted down the hill, Mike supporting me, into the black night.

None of us wanted dinner. Time was catching up with us and we had had quite a day. I fell asleep without bothering to undress and when someone banged at the shutters I looked at my watch and it was one o'clock. I had no idea if it was night or day. A quick glance in the mirror jogged my memory. My clothes were rumpled, my hair like the wild woman of Borneo, and I had mascara running down my face.

I opened the door, assuming it was Mercedes.

It was my pink case and next to it, in the biscuit-coloured suit and pearl tiepin from first-class, was my Italian from JFK.

It was still night, the terrace lit by spots, the cicadas singing. We looked at each other – he so smooth, I so wild I must have looked crazy – then at the pink case. Then we laughed.

How can I describe the next few days? Paradise Lost became Paradise Regained, with no apologies to anyone.

The mornings were for work and the rest of the day for Fabrice – my new love's name. He had been visiting a friend in Runaway Bay, before coming to the hotel.

He took me to the Great House, Rose Hall and Cinnamon Hill, where we rode through the plantations on beat-up horses, picking peppers from the trees and drinking coconut milk. We swam in the tepid water, lay on the hot sands, sheltered from the rains. At night we watched the limbo dancers, the fire-eaters, and crab races, and danced to the haunting native band.

His father was Italian but his mother Australian. He had been educated in England but now spent his time between his house in Belgravia and his mother's flat in Sydney; that was when he wasn't in Rome or Barbados or St Moritz.

I was too old to believe in fairy stories; actually believe. I was content to enjoy the best time I had ever had in my life, knowing that it could only endure for a week.

We lay on mattresses in the private pool of his cottage, drinks in our hands, sunhats over our eyes. Some days we hardly moved, except to call room service when we were hungry. While I worked in the morning Fabrice played tennis or golf, snorkelled or water-skied. We didn't bother with the Mannheimers or the Joneses. I scarcely had time for Sara and

Mike, who in any case were doing their own thing. I was only aware of the passing, too quickly, of the days.

When it was over, I packed my pink case, laying on top as if it were porcelain the Calypso record he had bought me, *This is My Island in the Sun*, and the sad story of Annie Palmer, the White Witch of Rose Hall. It would pass many Sydney evenings and enable me to recall in a flash the cups of gold, and almonds freshly picked, the starry sky and the symphony of the night.

To look at us you would have thought us a happy throng. Sara with her tan, and Mike with his cameras, saying goodbye to the soursops and the gentle tamarinds, the giant flame trees, and Mercedes in her blue-and-white-striped dress waving happily from the door of the cottage.

I had said goodbye to Fabrice the night before. I could not recall it without distress, so busied myself with the luggage and my myriad responsibilities.

I spent most of the journey sleeping. All of us did, exhausted by the events of the week and the steam heat of the island. I was dreaming of the vultures, or buzzards, I never knew quite which, swooping and rising again over the coral reef, when Mike shook me to say we had landed. I looked out unenthusiastically into the grey bleakness of the Sydney winter and wondered whether it was only the vultures that had been the dream. There was nothing to reassure me that not twelve hours ago I had embraced Fabrice in an agony of farewells.

I took no pleasure in the fact that of all of us I was the first to spot my pink case doing its circular tour on the baggage rack, so triumphantly visible.

I waited only a few moments. A half-dozen cases came tumbling down to be heaved on to the bench in front of me by the familiar Aussie porter.

I spotted mine, which he put down in front of me, then to my utter amazement another, identical – pink twins!

I stood stock-still.

Fabrice was by my side. I thought I would faint with happiness. He picked up the cases, one in each hand, looking at them fondly.

'One of yours, one of mine,' he said, then smiled his fabulous smile. 'Next year when we go back,' he said, 'who knows, one of ours?'

I'll Pay Half

1975

Whenever my mother came shopping with me, when I was very much younger, of course, she would clinch the argument over a dress she considered eminently suitable and I did not by taking the pin from her emotional hand grenade and slinging it casually in my direction: 'Take it, darling, I'll pay half!'

You must have seen us in the shops. Possibly not in the early days when you struggled in and out of dresses in tiny, over-heated cubicles where there was no room to hang a thing, let alone swing the proverbial cat. Later, I mean, when the changing rooms became communal, a kind of free girlie show run on a tight budget where they couldn't afford merchandise from the top drawer. It might have been funny had it not been so pathetic: the laddered tights, the grubby smalls, the braless types who seemed generally the very ones who were most in need of them. Fat behinds attempting desperately to squeeze into size 10 jeans, spotty shoulders in backless dresses, bean-poles in loose-covers.

I often had the desire to cry in anguish, 'No!' as some Boa-
dicea admired herself in pink chiffon but knew very well that
the image she saw, twisting and turning in the mirror, was not
what she was but what she wanted to be, her fantasy self. We
all had them. I was no exception. Perhaps that was why there
were always the scenes with Mother.

There was, of course, nowhere for her to sit while I went
through my own private little dress show or what Mother was
wont to call a 'mannequin parade'. They planned it that way,
the shops, I mean. She wasn't supposed to be in the changing
room anyway. There was a notice outside: 'Customers Trying On Only'. We always worked it though, like some sort of
practised shoplifting team. Another warning read: 'Three garments only to be taken into changing room'. It was simple; I
would take three and Mother another three.

I often wondered if the gum-chewing salesgirl who sat on
a high stool issuing discs, red, yellow, or green according to
the number of items you had, really thought that Mother was
going to buy a bikini that was no more than two pieces of
string, trousers that left no room for the imagination, an evening number in which underpinnings were not only unsuitable
but impossible. I don't suppose they really cared. They were
only there to prevent looting, which, in common parlance,
was known as 'shrinkage' and waited for the hours to pass so
that they could escape from the Hades of sweaty female flesh
into the fading sunlight of the King's Road.

She was very patient. Mother, I mean. It wasn't too bad,
either, in the morning when we were fresh. About midday the

snapping began and we both recognised the need for refreshment. We talked politely over a wilted salad or a greasy hamburger until it was time once more for seconds out of the ring and the next round.

She would, of course, have liked to get me into one of her sort of shops where the madam would be unequivocally on her side and where the clothes cost a bomb, but that was a battle we had resolved long ago. War was now waged on my own ground. I say war. It was, I suppose, more a cold one, if you can call it that in a temperature of around 80 degrees and what seemed to be a total lack of breathable air. Out of – from her point of view – a pretty unlikely conglomeration Mother would select an armful of what she considered the most 'suitable' things. They were generally 'constructed' rather than 'made' out of some serviceable material and their chief assets seemed to be one, that they would 'last', and two, that they would take me anywhere. Anywhere, I knew well enough, meant a family occasion, wedding or funeral, although there never seemed to be any in the offing, when I might have to be seen with her. They might take me anywhere, granted, but as far as I was concerned I wouldn't be seen dead in them.

It was just the beginning, at that time, of the ethnic look, and Mother simply couldn't see how one might either wear or pay good money for a few yards of fraying cheese-cloth, a navvy's vest, or a row of beads. At the end of the day, by which time we could cheerfully have murdered one another, she would still be clinging tenaciously to her sensible garment in a colour that 'matched my eyes' which would hang in my wardrobe till kingdom come, suitable for everything and wearable for nothing. Invariably, taking advantage of the fact that I was out for the count although trying the Grecian peasant smock I knew would go a bomb on any summer occasion for the hundred-and-fourth time (and which she said would fall to pieces in the wash), she would clinch the deal by declaring that the blue gabardine suit, or whatever it was she was clutching, would 'come out every year' and that if I took it she would 'pay half'! It invariably worked.

I would return the peasant smock with a last lingering look to the bored salesgirl who was dying to go home, and watch Mother write her cheque for half the gabardine suit which, carrier-bagged, she would thrust into my unenthusiastic hand.

At home I would rush round to Fleur, my best friend, who would say 'Very nice', while her eyes shrieked 'My God!' then hang it in my wardrobe where it would stay until too short, too tight, or merely too old, and be sent on its way to the 'Home for Handicapped Horses' or whatever Mother's pet charity of the time happened to be.

Those times, of course, had long passed. There came a point where she could no longer stand the hissed arguments in the changing rooms, the sulks and tantrums, the endurance tests of those shopping days. She simply capitulated, not understanding how anyone could survive without a single pair of 'court' shoes, a leather handbag, or a 'best coat'. I'm not sure whether it was 'the age' or 'her age' that had finally caught up with her but she suffered the faded jeans, the tie-and-dye, the thonged sandals worn with moth-eaten furs from Portobello

Road, generally in silence. When I started paying good money for dresses the like of which she had given away gladly after the war she nearly did her nut, but by then she had something else to think of, more important than the comparative merits of cheesecloth and gabardine.

The something else was me 'settling down'. She had, I suppose, according to her lights, been remarkably patient. I had been through the motions of a red-brick university, emerging with a mediocre degree of not the slightest practical use, done the Greece and India bit, starry-eyed and knapsacked, started and abandoned a million different jobs. The fact that I was a product of my environment and a million light years away from an unmarried girl of twenty-four in the immediate post-war years did not impress. It was not that she was without understanding. She did her best, along with the rest of her generation, to go along with our *modus vivendi*, our morals, or lack of them, our casual approach to things that to her were of fundamental importance.

Looking at it her way, since leaving school I had had my freedom. I had studied, travelled, sought gainful employment, formed relationships; she had not interfered, until lately.

It was very subtle. I was between flats and had been living at home for a bit when she suddenly sprouted little dinner parties. Not for me, understand, but for friends of hers she might not have seen in years but who just happened to have eligible sons.

She started dragging me to drinks. '... the So-and-Sos said to be sure to bring you along ...' as Tom or Dick or Harry was down from college or back from France or whatever. I'd stand there sipping dutifully and eating little damp things made by waitresses or by the more capable hostesses six months before and consigned to the deep-freeze. Tom or Dick or Harry and I would invariably hate each other on principle and could hardly wait till the politeness was over and we could each get back to our own particular crowd.

Sometimes we had them to dinner. These occasions were worst of all because Mother became arch. 'I'll leave you two to clear the table for me while I make some coffee. I believe you were both in Corfu last summer so you must have lots to talk about.' Or, 'Jane has a degree in Politics and Economics she's probably much too shy to talk about, and Christopher came top of his year at Sydney Sussex ... Why don't the two of you take a walk in the park ...?'

You may ask why I submitted. I suppose I didn't see it as submitting; merely being amenable to their well-laid, if abortive, plans for me while leading my own life. It was a not too painful form of saying thank you for all they had done for me over the years. I did not want them to think me either unappreciative or ungrateful for the sacrifices they had made and the heartache I had caused them, wittingly or unwittingly, over the almost quarter of a century I had been around.

The pièce de résistance of Mother's scheming on my behalf came about at the same time as I met Clive. Her protégé's name was Wallace. Wallace! I ask you! Although not actually an 'Honourable' himself, his father was and if he survived long enough to outlive his father and his uncle, who was the present holder of the title and who had produced only daughters, he would ultimately become the viscount.

So Wallace was the feather in Mother's cap, the diadem in the tiara of her vicarious ambition. She found him through the work she did, and she worked very hard, for the Red Cross. In the year when she, fortuitously as she thought, was deep into her machinations vis-à-vis me, she found herself co-chairman of the local group with Wallace's mama. Papa was a Lloyd's underwriter when he wasn't hunting, shooting, or fishing, and Wallace himself seemed to do nothing more testing than hang around in his wake. Rumour had it that if Papa hadn't been who he was there wouldn't have been any wake anywhere for him to hang around in. Eligible and handsome he might have been, but he wasn't exactly what you'd call fireworks as far as the top storey was concerned.

For Mother's sake I tried, genuinely. Shutting my eyes to the fact that he wore baggy corduroys and short back and sides, I attempted to remember – for Mother's sake – that given luck I might one day be a viscountess and, my hand in his invariably cold limp one, suffered Henley, Ascot and Wimbledon. I spent two whole ghastly weekends at his 'place' in the country where his mother seemed continuously to be piercing me with her chill blue eyes and his father was not aware of my presence at all.

I made an ass of myself in Scotland where I didn't know one end of either a gun or a horse from the other and made numerous social gaffes upon which they were far too polite to comment. Over dinner at the Ritz, which was typical, Wallace asked me to marry him.

Mother was cock-a-hoop, but then she chose not to recognise Clive. As far as she was concerned he did not exist. She was very smart at not seeing when she wanted. Poor Clive, the cards were stacked against him. Every one, that was, except the fact that I was gloriously, hopelessly in love with him and knew that there was nobody else with whom I would rather spend what remained of my life.

To begin with he had been married before. To my way of thinking this meant that he now knew exactly what he wanted but to Mother he was 'no good'. He was ten years older than I whereas Wallace was three months younger. He was one half of a successful song-writing team, which to me was exciting, to Mother precarious. He wore shirts open to the waist so that you could see his nut-brown chest and was obviously what Mother called rather quaintly a 'lady-killer'. He was the kindest, most generous, easy-going man I had ever met. There were neither tensions nor pretensions. When we were together I had to be nothing except myself. I could air my innermost thoughts and he his. We accepted each other totally and absolutely. To my mind that was what marriage was, or should be, all about.

Mother was horrified. Not least, I think, because when he wasn't wearing his open-chested shirt he came to collect me in a polo-necked sweater or a safari suit. It wasn't that she was unaware of current fashions but thought him too 'old' for young men's gear; that through me he was seeking to recapture his lost or misspent youth. Wrapped up with the ideas – swollen to goodness knows what unknown grandeur – in her head of me and Wallace, she treated Clive as something of a joke, when she wasn't dismissing him altogether.

The crunch came, if you can call it that, when they were both away for a few days leaving me a breathing space: Wallace in the country, Clive in St Trop.

Mother had asked me to come with her to choose a hat for an important luncheon at which she was to be the guest of honour and at which she had to make a speech. For the past twenty-four years, to my certain knowledge, she had managed very nicely choosing her hats without me. When she insisted that my advice was essential I realised that there was something more to the expedition than met the hat, so to speak.

It came over lunch, which we had, quietly and calmly, not like the old days, at Simpson's restaurant. She had even gone so far as to reserve a table. It did not take too many brains to foresee what was coming. Why we couldn't have talked at home I didn't know, at least I did know, because Father wasn't utterly and completely in her camp. He was always able to see both sides of every question and to this there was, as far as she was concerned, only one.

We talked of this and that over the pâté, and that and this over the canard à l'orange. You would never think we were both dieting and used to nothing more at midday than a lettuce leaf.

She waited – very subtle, Mother – until we had chosen from the trolley with its silent crème brûlée, its pyramid of profiteroles weeping chocolate tears. The waiter had come and gone before she said: 'You are going to marry Wallace?'

I really didn't want to upset her. I knew that it hadn't been intentional that I was an only child, but then it really wasn't my fault either that she pinned all her too-high hopes on me. I could not complain. She had reared me splendidly and unstintingly, then given me my head from the age of eighteen. She did, she really did, what she thought was her very best not to interfere in my life.

'I'm in love with Clive,' I said. Just to say it brought back the warmth, the tenderness, the feel of him, and made me grow weak at the knees.

'He's very charming,' she said, sure she was playing her cards right. To condemn outright would be foolish. 'But he's years older than you, and besides, he's been married before.'

She made him sound shop-soiled, which I presume in her eyes he was. 'Besides, it's a very up and down way to earn a living.'

There was nothing I wanted more than to go up and down with Clive.

'With Wallace,' she said, 'you wouldn't have to worry. There's the house in Chester Square and the place in the coun-try ... Chester Square is perfect, his mother tells me, furnished to the last teaspoon. You wouldn't have to have one of those ghastly wedding lists ...'

I dug my fork into the profiteroles as I listened to her sing-ing the praises of Wallace, who was as utterly suitable as the blue, structured gabardine suits of the old days that I never, but never, wore. She was carrying on about Scotland and win-ter sports while I thought of Clive and St Trop. Wallace never went to the sun at all as it brought him out in prickly heat.

I pushed my plate away and decided it was time to make my position absolutely clear. That I was no longer sixteen or eighteen and quite capable of making up my own mind.

'I'm going to marry Clive,' I said in a voice that could be heard six tables away.

She put down her spoon on the crème brûlée and looked at me as if she hadn't really heard aright.

'But Wallace ...' she said.

I had to remind myself that the days of the old dressing-room struggles, the shopping expeditions, were well and truly over. There were no more arrows in her quiver, no more tiny persuasive darts in her armoury.

I looked at her and realised she was biting back not only the tears but the desire to get her way at all costs as she had in the old days. Poor Mother; I took her hand, as the realisation finally dawned that a husband was not something you could select, just like that, and wrap up in a paper bag. There was no salesgirl she could appeal to, no instinct of appeasement in myself. It was no longer a question of cheesecloth versus gabardine and not the slightest use her offering to pay half.

The Man Who Understood Women

1976

He stood on the platform at Victoria inhaling its particular
and unmistakable smell, indistinguishable to the outside eye
from a hundred other commuters. He was not even remarkable by the fact that he was wearing odd socks, one grey, one
almost grey but actually slate-blue. It was, after all, Monday,
not the best of days and the mornings still exceedingly dark;
there was not one of them on which he did not regret the
economy he had practised in neglecting to have a light that
would come on as you opened the door inside his custom-
built wardrobe. At the time it had seemed the very epitome
of extravagance – he liked comfort but not ostentation – but
each winter morning as he selected socks and shirt and tie
and pants and tried to distinguish dark-navy from light-navy
he cursed himself for his short-sightedness. A considerate
man, he did not like to put the main light on in the bedroom
for fear of waking Veronica, who was not at her best in the
early hours. He would rather rummage and peer, attempting

to distinguish blue from green, and curse inwardly, as he equipped himself each morning fittingly for the City. Some men he knew, several in fact, expected their wives to be up at the same time as they, to awaken them even with tea, and to prepare breakfast before they left. He did not consider this fair. Just because he had to get out of bed at a quarter to seven Monday to Friday he did not see why Veronica should. True, he would have liked her company in the mornings before he left but he was perfectly capable of squeezing an orange and boiling an egg and he could see no reason why she should be deprived of her sleep. Each morning, therefore, he bathed and dressed with the very minimum of noise, glancing occasion-ally at the familiar sleeping figure, beneath the duvet in which they had recently invested, on the right-hand side of the bed.

It was damp but not cold. 'Temperatures higher than nor-mal' the forecast had said as he waited for his egg to boil. For once they were right. The platform gleamed with surface mois-ture but there was none of the foot-stamping, arm-swinging bitterness that came with the icy weather and brought with it the annual desire to move further into town.

He glanced at the headlines in the evening paper allowing his eyes to wander no further. If he gobbled up the nightly ration of news now, on the platform, there would be nothing left to nourish him on the train, to while away the minutes from Victoria to Haywards Heath. As it was, there was only one paper instead of two. The economy had been brought about by the recent inflation, the mess into which the country was getting itself, and the need for everyone to tighten his belt.

It was not easy. Having established standards, one was bound to keep them up even though it appeared to get daily more and more difficult. With the purchase of one evening paper only Brian Kingsley felt that he was doing his bit, particularly since the paper he chose was not the one he preferred for its presentation of the news but the one in which Veronica liked to attempt the crossword puzzle. The balance of current affairs could, he felt, be put right in front of the twenty-two-inch colour television set at nine o'clock. It was not a large sacrifice.

'Evening, Brian.'

'Evening, Eric.'

Eric, he knew without looking, would not be wearing odd socks, not indeed because he had an interior light in his cupboard but because he was married to Helen who was a paragon of all the virtues but whom Eric, as everyone agreed, treated abominably.

For Eric there was no do-it-yourself morning egg, no teak-Formica breakfast bar on which to rest his elbows.

Eric breakfasted in the dining room, sugared his grapefruit from an antique silver caster, one of a pair, and had his coffee, first and second cups, poured into the Minton cup by Helen, already made-up. Never, he boasted, had he so much as opened the fridge, unless of course to get at the ice, which reproduced itself endlessly in a special compartment at the top. No wonder, Brian thought, Helen always looked so miserable. By 6 a.m. she had laid out Eric's tie and suit and shirt, together with his clean underwear and matching socks and, suitably house-gowned, was prepared to sit at the breakfast table with him, making scintillating conversation. He was not surprised that, as rumour in Haywards Heath had it, she had a lover in Brighton from which she was no more than a short ride on the train on which she was frequently seen. What a pig. What a male chauvinist pig, as the current phrase had it, to expect his wife to rise at an unearthly hour, winter and summer, just because *he* had to, seemed utterly unreasonable. He was living in the past, Eric was, when there had been maids and cooks and other hired help for people in his position. He seemed unaware that these had given way to automatic juicers and electric toasters and coffee pots and that it was no great chore to throw a few switches in the mornings. Brian would not have been at all surprised to discover that he even expected the long-suffering Helen to polish his shoes.

On the 7.05 a.m. to Victoria and the 6 p.m. to Haywards Heath they often discussed their wives. Usually, wary of what they might reveal, in jocular fashion. It was surprising how many men expected their womenfolk to be rays of sunshine, pillars of support, each and every day. They seemed not to be aware, as Brian was, of the very nature of the species; that life these days was hard for women, a continuing hassle with bills and supermarkets and accumulations of tiny frustrations to do with children and plumbers and truculent machinery which a sympathetic ear could do much to mitigate. Brian did not expect, as many of the others did when he came home in the evenings, for the outpourings of the day's events over the Martinis to be one-sided. Unlike Eric, who considered happenings outside the Stock Exchange to 'be of little importance', Brian was aware that within the three-quarter-acre boundaries of The Oaks there could be sufficient happenings in minuscule during the course of a day to cause alarm and despondency, and to require both understanding and sympathy. He saw his home as a business in miniature with Veronica as Managing Director; Eric, he was sure, if he gave any thought whatever to Helen, considered her as some kind of unpaid, unvalued servant, and as such expected her to have neither feelings nor problems.

It was not only his wife whom Brian understood. His powers of empathy extended to his office and its employees. In particular to one Lavinia March for whom he was planning to leave Veronica, his children – now old enough, he felt, to stand on their own feet – and The Oaks and all it entailed.

It was two years now since Lavinia had walked into his office in reply to the advertisement he had placed in *The Times* after his secretary for the last ten years had retired to care for her old mother in Worthing. Accustomed to being cosseted by a woman of middle age he had been unprepared for a dolly-bird, although it did not come as an altogether unpleasant surprise. Lavinia, although she had legs that went on for ever, hair to her bottom, and translucent green eyes, appeared to have all the necessary business qualifications. With the proviso of a month's trial Brian decided to give her a chance. He learned gradually that she came from a good but impoverished army family with a place in the country, that she 'shared' with two other dollies in Sydney Street, and was engaged to an airline pilot of whom as time went by Brian became more and more jealous. When he was away Brian did his best to sympathise and keep her spirits up. When he came home Brian expressed approval of the new sweater or shoes she generally bought with which to greet him, and let her off early. He did not complain when she arrived late for work after dancing the night away, or on Mondays not at all after a riotous weekend in Paris or Bruges. The airline pilot was more than generous and Lavinia had more bits and baubles to hang round her neck, more handbags and perfume and crocodile notecases than anyone he knew. He considered, however, that she was treated extremely unfairly. It was obvious to anyone that she was crazy about the man whose twisted heart she wore on the fourth finger of her left hand but that he did not treat her well. That he left her for weeks at a time he realised was due to the exigencies of his occupation, but for weeks he did not write or call, left her on tenterhooks as to when he was next going to reappear. It was no way to treat a woman, not, in particular, one so desirable as Lavinia.

He took her out to lunch and encouraged her to discuss her problems. Over caviar or smoked salmon, which she adored, she admitted to him that she hated being left at home for weeks at a time while her fiancé flitted from capital to capital round the world. That she hoped by the time they got married he would have got flying out of his system and settle to a nice job in insurance. That it really was very lonely at times in the shared flat in Sydney Street.

After six months of lunches and drinks after office hours and heart-to-heart talks Brian felt so sorry for her that he decided, on his next business trip, to take her to New York. She agreed with alacrity. He discovered that she liked champagne at mid-morning, to dance all night, and that she was quite remarkable in bed. He bought her a ruby pendant, which buried itself in her cleavage, to commemorate the trip and reminded himself that he was old enough to be her father.

It became a habit. He took her to Amsterdam and Stockholm, to Brussels and Copenhagen. When he did not need her she made herself useful getting the shopping on the list Veronica invariably gave him for each city.

After a year in his employ she gave the airline pilot back his ring and allowed Brian to buy her a tiny flat in World's End, convenient for Victoria, and a Mini to enable her more quickly to get down to visit her people.

After two years he realised that he could not live without her. He discussed it with Lavinia and discovered that the feeling was mutual, Veronica, of course, was aware of her existence. When she came to the office she made polite conversation with Miss March, whom privately she considered a bit dumb, and on each of the two Christmases she had been working for Brian Veronica selected for her a suitable present. She knew nothing, of course, of the fact that she accompanied Brian on his business trips nor about the flat at World's End. Only that on two nights a week, and occasionally three, Brian arrived home late and exhausted from clients whom he had to entertain.

Admirable character that she was, Brian knew that she would not take too badly, once the first shock had passed, his decision to leave her. There had been no crisis, during the twenty-five years of their marriage, which she had failed to face up to. Birth, illness, death, four moves of house, impossible stages of the children's development, there had been nothing that had not only left her undaunted but with enough courage and wisdom to help him too. It had been a partnership in which she had been strong; unlike his impending one with Lavinia who relied on him for every little thing. He had arranged, of course, to leave his wife well provided for. She could remain at The Oaks, which he had put in her name, and she would not have one single financial worry. On that point his conscience was clear. It was clear also on the point that apart from being a good manager as far as the house and children were concerned she did not depend on him in the physical sense. Both before and after the time that he had formed a relationship with Lavinia their sex life had been on the perfunctory side. There was always so much to do in the house and garden and the children wanting this that and the other, that at night time they were both tired and had rather allowed it to lapse.

There would, he felt, be no hardship there, and in time she would most likely marry again.

All in all, he had, he felt, sorted everything out nicely, and was looking forward to his new life. He was selling everything, except for one of the cars, which he would leave for Veronica, and abandoning the rat race.

He had bought a tiny cottage in the country where he and Lavinia would bury themselves. From this love nest he would emerge once a week only to keep an eye on his business, which would run very well without him. Besides, his future needs would be simple. They would grow their own vegetables (not that he knew much about it, it was Veronica who saw to the garden), eat simple, wholesome meals cooked by Lavinia who was learning from a book he had bought her, and travel – if at all – by bicycle, horse-drawn caravan, or canal boat. There would be need for no sophistications such as dishwashers, rotisseries, and waste grinders, which brought their own counter-irritations, and they could live very nicely without the pseudo-pleasures of theatre, restaurant and cinema. In this idyllic milieu he and Lavinia (hair washed in rainwater collected in a butt) would live out the rest of their days. He looked up and down the platform at the rolled umbrellas and bowler hats and felt pity for his fellow-commuters trapped in the nasty mess of their own civilisation.

The customary gang had collected around Eric and himself by the time the train arrived.

They clambered into their usual carriage and put their newspapers on their laps. It was talk till Croydon and after that the newspapers like so many shields up before the eyes until two minutes before Haywards Heath when they were smartly folded and put into identical briefcases.

'What did you think of the meeting last night?' Brian asked when the noise of the train pulling out had settled to a steady rhythm.

It was another role he would have to give up. For two years now he had been chairman of the Woody Dene Residents

Association to which most of them belonged. Its business was to deal with such matters as the private road in which most of them lived with its inevitable trespassers, unlawful parkers and speed fiends; Mrs Reed-Roberts's frightful habit of chewing up everyone's grass verge with her abysmal driving; noise after midnight; and the latest and most urgent problem: squirrels.

At the meeting of the previous night a motion had been passed to engage one Mr Nokes, at the cost of several pounds per resident, to eliminate the pests, with which they were all troubled. Regardless of the exclusive nature of Woody Dene itself, or the illustriousness of its inhabitants, they destroyed daffodils and crocuses, lovingly planted, before they saw the light of day, and in summer gobbled up lettuces, beans, and strawberries with reckless abandon. Previously they had all dealt individually with the invaders with their own shot-guns but the problem had become worse. There was now no moment when you could look into the garden and fail to see them hopping nimbly up the trees or gambolling playfully on the lawns preparatory to bringing the fruits of weeks of hard labour in the gardens to naught.

'What about my dogs?' Eric asked. 'Wouldn't like old Nokes taking a pot shot at them.'

'He has strict instructions,' Brian said, 'to ring the bell before entering the gardens and advise the owners to keep their pets inside.'

'I hope you've told him not to call on me,' Nigel Avery said. 'Melanie would have a fit.'

'I can understand her not wanting to have them shot,' Brian

said. 'Although I consider it selfish and misguided I respect her views. But to actually feed them! Have you explained to her that they're vermin and the damage they do?'

'Melanie thinks they're rather sweet,' Nigel said. 'She wouldn't hurt a fly.'

'Rats!' Eric said. 'That's all they are. Just happen to have bushy tails.'

'As far as Melanie's concerned she'd rather shoot Mr Nokes,' Nigel said.

Seeing that they were about to get into deep water over Melanie and the squirrels, Brian decided to change the subject to that of the gate at the end of the road, which had by law to be kept closed for twenty-four hours annually in order to preserve the estate's private status.

'Gate-duty,' he said. 'We didn't exactly get many volunteers.'

At the station Helen with the Rover was very much in evidence. Come hell or high water, Eric was met nightly with a wifely peck and a clean car and, Brian suspected, with the chilled Martinis waiting in his impeccable home. Some of the other wives came too, but not with the regularity of Helen. She had become part of the landscape and had she not been there they would have been excused for thinking that they had left the train at the wrong station.

Brian did not expect Veronica to meet him. He did not expect her to cook the dinner and interrupt it in all weathers to get the car out and drive the two and a half miles to the station after a long day. It simply wasn't fair. Although it entailed a short walk for himself, unpleasant in cold weather and positively muddy in wet, he drove himself to the station in the mornings, left the car in the station car park, and in the evenings drove himself home.

At The Oaks he shut and locked the garage and took out his front-door key, never so inconsiderate as to bring Veronica unnecessarily to the door. He smelled disaster as he opened it. It was apples, Veronica explained, burned instead of baked. She had put them into the oven before slipping down to the shops and forgotten to put water into the bottom of the dish. Not to worry, she had taken something from the freezer. Unflappable Veronica. He looked at her in her well-cut pants and smock top. She had kept her figure; looked after herself. You would not think she had borne three children, one of whom was now old enough to get married himself. There would certainly be no trouble if she wanted to get married again, she'd probably enjoy it really. She had often said lately she was bored and wished she had a career. Now that the children needed her less she had time on her hands despite the three days a week she spent at the Citizens Advice Bureau. He wondered when he should break the news to her and decided after dinner.

It was a good dinner: consommé, veal escalopes in an orange sauce, with tiny new Italian potatoes, and a home-made blackcurrant sorbet with fruit from last summer's crop. To complement it, and perhaps to boost his courage, he had opened an Haut Marbuzet, of which he drank two-thirds and Veronica one.

He blotted out the polished refectory table with its Harrods table mats and silver wine coaster and wondered how it would be with Lavinia in the cottage. The dinner – well, the dinner he was not so sure about. She was studying the cookery book he had bought her but at the moment elected not to be able to boil the proverbial egg. His imagination baulked. The dinner didn't really matter anyway. It wasn't good for one to eat so richly and so well; afterwards though ... afterwards! Love in a cottage; how many dreamed of it and how many had the courage of their convictions?

He glanced at Veronica doing complicated things with the Cona. If there was one thing he enjoyed it was his after dinner coffee. That moment of peace when he felt the day was really over. They had the coffee beans sent especially from South Molton Street each week and Veronica ground them in the electric grinder.

'Paul phoned,' she said. 'He's coming down this weekend. There're a couple of parties he wants to go to.'

'Didn't think he was coming to see *us*,' Brian said.

'Oh, I don't know. I think he appreciates the home comforts. I thought we might ask the Prices for a drink on Saturday. Claire has turned out to be absolutely stunning. I met them in Sloane Street. It would make a change from some of those frightful girls he brings home, Afro and reeking of smoke.'

He realised suddenly that he might never see his grandchildren – then, of course, that he would; Veronica was not one to be unreasonable and the children were sufficiently progressive these days to accept anything.

'Whom should we ask with them?'

'With whom?'

'The Prices. You can't just have George and Myra and Claire. It looks so obvious ...'

She was lighting the small lamp beneath the coffee. He wondered if this was the moment to tell her.

'... I thought perhaps Eric and Melanie. We haven't seen them for ages. Charles and Phillipa might be down.'

'I see Eric on the train twice a day.'

'I meant socially. You know we were thinking about Spetsai for the summer. They can tell us about it. They seemed to have had a wonderful time. Only if we want to we shall have to call the villa people soon. I believe the best ones go quite early in the year. It would be nice if the children would join us but I don't suppose they will.'

He wondered if she would go to Spetsai on her own. Probably a hotel, more likely, where she could meet people.

She gave him his coffee, black as night, as he liked it. He knew it would taste as good as it smelled.

'Come and sit down. There's something I have to tell you.'

'When I've finished.' She was clearing the table. 'Just get this lot into the dishwasher. Once I've sat down I never want to get up again.'

Orderly, methodical; with Lavinia it would be different. They might not clear the table ever. At least not until they'd made love. On the table perhaps, under the table.

'If it's about having the outside painted I thought we should stick to the same colour. Iris has this marvellous new man,

Italian, doesn't speak a word of English but frightfully cheap. He did their kitchen and utility room. He does odd jobs, too, like putting up things so I thought biscuit again …?'

'No, not about the house.'

'Shan't be long then.'

He didn't hurry her. She'd had a busy day and liked to relax at the end of it. He understood how it was with women. He listened to the small familiar sounds coming from the kitchen. The clunk of the fridge as leftover food was stored away. The fierce, noisy motor of the waste grinder, the chink of china, the rattle of cutlery. Like the captain of a ship Veronica kept everything in its place. She was a good girl, good wife, in fact. Probably if Lavinia hadn't come along …

She came in, running her fingers through her hair, which, unlike Lavinia's, was short. She had the roots tinted every three weeks and the whole lot every six, making jokes about the increasing encroachment of the grey. It was a soft auburn; if one did not know, one would not know. It was amazing what could be done these days.

She sat down. There was something in her hand. She held it out.

'These are the new colours. But I still think biscuit has a warmth, a mellowness about it.'

'It wasn't about the house.'

'What then? More coffee?'

'No. No more coffee. I don't know quite how to put this.'

'Put what? You think Paul should change his course? You never did think History frightfully important but—'

'It's not about Paul. It's about me.'

'You're not well?'

'Quite well. I meant you and me.' He took a deep breath. 'You remember Lavinia? Lavinia March who works for me?'

'What are you talking about? Of course I know Lavinia.'

'We're going away together. I'm going to leave you.'

Veronica had been sitting still but somehow sat stiller.

'It's been going on for some time. Quite a long time now really. I'd better tell you the whole story.'

He told her about the trips abroad, the business trips, about the two or three nights a week he came home late, about the cottage in the country, about how much they loved each other.

When he had finished she was still sitting in exactly the same position, except that she was twining and intertwining her hands as she did when she was anxious.

He looked at her kindly.

'You won't have to worry about a thing. I've put the house in your name and you'll have more than enough to live on, I think you'll find I've been particularly generous. The children are provided for too. Until they get married, that is.'

Having got it all off his chest he felt better. He looked at Veronica.

'Lavinia March?' she said.

'Yes.'

'And it's been going on for some time'?'

'Yes.'

'I've been rather stupid, haven't I?'

'I did my best to keep it from you. I didn't want to worry

you. When there really wasn't anything to be worried about, I mean.'

'That was very considerate.'

'I do try.'

'When will you be going?'

'I thought quite soon. I thought it better than ... prolonging things ... tomorrow or the next day.'

'What about the Prices?'

'I'm sorry. I didn't know you'd asked them. I could stay till after the weekend if you like.'

'No. I'll make some excuse. They'll have to know sooner or later anyway. You'll want your suitcases from the loft.'

He smiled. 'You're always so practical.'

'You can't go away without suitcases.'

'Indeed. '

'There's just one thing.'

'Yes?'

'Those presents. The pearls from Hong Kong, the candlesticks from Copenhagen. Did she choose them?'

He understood how important these small things were to women.

'Of course not,' he lied, managing to get some indignation in his voice.

'You're old enough to be her father. She's only a year or two older than Jennifer.'

'We love each other. I'm sorry.'

She didn't shout or scream. He hadn't expected her to. He knew they could sort the whole thing out amicably.

She stood up.

'Where are you going?'

'Upstairs.'

'Want me to come with you?'

'No. I'd rather be alone for a while.'

He understood.

'I'll take a walk. Stretch my legs. Shan't be long.'

He shut the front door quietly and walked down the drive into the dark road.

Some men would have followed her upstairs. Made a nuisance of themselves.

He was congratulating himself on his understanding of women and their need to be alone when he heard the shot ring out.

Soufflé à L'orange

1976

My mother had always told me I should learn to cook. So of course I did everything but. By the time I was eighteen I could ride, skate, play the violin (a bit), water-ski, and do batik, but I couldn't make gravy.

'You'll settle down one day, I suppose,' Mother said. 'And then what will you do? All the violin-playing in the world won't fill his stomach.'

'I'll get by,' I said, and at first it seemed that I would.

At twenty-one I was engaged to Charles who could afford to employ a hundred cooks, and preferred eating in restaurants anyway.

At dinner time I nibbled exotic delicacies at the Connaught or the Mirabelle. No anxiously stirring sauces over a hot stove for me!

Unfortunately, the more I liked his way of life, the less I liked Charles. I had already made up my mind to stop seeing him when I met Alexis and Mother was at last able to say 'I told you so'.

Alexis had been married before. His wife had been French and a paragon of all the wifely virtues (except fidelity). She was an accomplished needlewoman and every night she whipped up meals fit for a king. According to Alexis her most unforgettable dish was soufflé à l'orange, a heavenly concoction the like of which he'd never tasted before and was not likely to again since she was settled cosily and permanently in Peru with a tin millionaire Alexis had once regarded as his best friend.

Alexis's flat was a testament to his ex-wife's capabilities. If you sat, it was on petit-point cushions she had worked; if you stood, a watercolour she had painted stared you delicately in the eye; in the bathroom you dried your hands on a linen towel she had embroidered. I could see there was to be no restaurant circuit with Alexis. The Connaught and the Mirabelle once in a while, but he was patently a man who loved his home. I loved him. This man I knew was for me. Oh yes: when you find it you know what it is you have been looking for. I thought he would not be unduly impressed with the riding, the violin and the batik. I purported not to understand the look in my mother's eye. What she did not know was that along with the skating and the skiing I had acquired a not unnatural cunning. It had always stood me in good stead.

He did all the right things, Alexis – wooed me, courted me, showered me with gifts – in the best trad manner.

Of course I knew the kissing had to stop some time but I put that time off as long as I could.

At the time I was sharing a flat with Diane. I invented a passionate and ubiquitous lover for her so that when Alexis finally said the words I'd been expecting I was one jump ahead.

'Why don't we just have a quiet dinner at home?' he said one night. I wasn't sure whether he meant his or mine but I was ready with the answer.

'I'll come over to you,' I said, my heart thumping. 'I don't want to jeopardise this big thing of Diane's. I'll bring dinner with me.'

I didn't say 'cook', note.

Next morning, I paid a visit to Luigi who kept the delicatessen underneath the block of flats where I lived. He sold every sort of pasta you could imagine and the finest olive oil and black and green olives and exotic things in bottles. Luigi also made luscious takeaways. Pizzas and quiches, lasagnes, portions of duck with oranges in foil dishes ready to heat, terrines and pâtés.

I think he was a little in love with me, you couldn't tell with those eloquent Sicilian eyes, but anyhow, we came to an arrangement! Together we would plan a menu. Luigi would cook it and deliver it to my flat. I would transfer it to my own dishes, pop it in the car, and away to Alexis. It worked brilliantly.

One, and sometimes two, nights a week I sat at Alexis's dining table and served him tempting morsels of Italian masterpieces. We had soup of two colours, capelletti (as made in Rome), red mullets a la Livorna, mussels fried in oil; we had liver in the style of Venice, cutlets in the style of Milan, and 'intoxicated pork'. We had gnocchi and torta, pastry with honey and nuts, rice fritters, and Bolognese bread. One day, when Luigi was in a particularly creative mood, I surpassed myself with partridges, with zabaglione, small pastry rissoles with anchovies in brine, and cenci to follow.

Replete, I looked at Alexis from beneath my lashes. He was putting on weight. He lit a cigar and examined its glowing end in the serious manner of cigar smokers.

'I have found myself a paragon,' he said, indicating the scraped clean dishes that littered the table. 'I don't know how you do it.'

I collected the casseroles. 'It's just a question of organisation.'

The cigar was going well now. He settled down contentedly. 'I must be the luckiest man in the world.'

Lucky he may have been, but as the winter passed and Luigi sent delicious salads of pimentos, tomatoes and chicory to mark its demise he seemed no nearer to making our liaison a permanent one. He was the gentlest, kindest, most considerate man I had ever met, with his full share of passion when necessary. I loved him madly and I didn't know what to do about it.

It was Diane, my flatmate, who came up with the soufflé à l'orange.

'You said that was her speciality,' she said. 'Why don't you try it too?'

Excited that it might just sway the balance, I put on my coat and went straight down to Luigi.

'The problem is the soufflé must be served immediately. The customer must wait for the soufflé. The soufflé don't wait for the customer,' he told me.

'I could drive very fast,' I said.

'*Mamma mia*!' His face was ashen. He leant forward. 'Open the door, close the door, open the door, close the door, the soufflé ...' he gesticulated violently, '... pouff!'

'Pouff!' I said, 'Forget it.'

'No!' The Sicilian eyes flashed. He stood up. 'I'll do it.'

I waited for a propitious evening. We had a week with no quarrels. Alexis seemed particularly sweet. 'OK,' I told Luigi. 'Wednesday.' On Wednesday I rang the office to say I would not be in and booked myself in at my favourite beauty place. I had the whole bit, massage, sauna, facial, manicure, pedicure, hair. When I came out I hoped I looked like a million dollars; it had certainly cost me that.

At five-thirty it began to rain. I watched it out of the window, not appreciating its significance.

By seven-thirty it was not only raining heavily but blowing half a gale.

Excited as a child, I laid Luigi's offering in its cardboard hatbox on the back seat of the car. I had collected the cold collation early in the morning, so I was free to concentrate on the soufflé now.

I switched on the ignition. Nothing. Not a murmur, not a whirr. A dull click; nothing. I could not believe it. Not tonight. I looked at the hatbox and wondered what was going on inside while various alternatives slid through my mind. The breakdown service? Too long. Diane? No car. A passer-by hopefully mechanically minded? I did not want to stand there out in the wind and the weather with my head beneath the bonnet pretending it all meant something. A taxi? At this time of the evening, in this weather! It seemed the only way.

I stood on the pavement, the hatbox clutched to my bosom. My hairdo flagged, my make-up ran, I could feel the mascara in my eyes. I did not really care, not even when my skirt stuck wetly to my legs and my shoes filled with water. I was concerned only for the soufflé.

It must have been twenty minutes, although it seemed like more, before a taxi dropped someone off at the flats.

Alexis, when he saw me, clucked with sympathy and suggested whisky and a hot bath. I babbled on about my cardboard box and needing to get to the kitchen. I think I was quite demented.

So far, so good. I popped the soufflé into the oven and, stopping only to dab at myself ineffectively with a tea towel, I insisted that we eat.

I had laid the table earlier. You must have guessed by now that I was not one to miss a trick. We had almond-green candles to match the almond-green carpet and the almond-green mats (embroidered, of course, by Madame, but I let that go) and the best translucent white china. I had set a posy of freesias in the centre of the table.

Throughout the cold collation (veal with tunny fish sauce and tarragon salad) I sat in agony of excitement. This, I felt, was to be the night. Alexis looked at his most desirable but he seemed to take an age over the veal, helping himself to more and more salad while I imagined dreadful things taking place within the oven.

At last he was finished.

I cleared the plates and told him I would not be a moment but that I had something special for dessert. I wanted to build up the atmosphere, you see.

I took as long as I dared, then opened the oven. There it sat, perfect, tall as a chef's hat and leaning slightly to one side, puffed and lightly browned.

I picked it up tenderly and carried it through.

'Soufflé à l'orange,' I said triumphantly and set it down in front of Alexis.

He looked from me to the soufflé and then to me again. His eyes widened. 'I don't believe it!'

I handed him the serving spoon and set the plates before him. 'Quick, before it collapses.'

We ate the lot. It was a dream; the sunlight sweetness of Valencia oranges laced with Cointreau.

'Scrape the dish,' I said. 'I'm full.'

Alexis did so. Every last scrape, enjoying every bit. At least I thought so. I suddenly noticed his face.

'Is anything the matter?'

He was staring into the soufflé dish. He looked quite pale. I snatched it from him. I realised suddenly that I had forgotten, in my hurry, to put the dessert into one of my own containers. Inside this dish, in large letters was written 'LUIGI'S TAKE-AWAY'. And the telephone number.

I could not look. I dared not. Not until I heard him laugh. I wanted to cry, run, hide. I could stand anything but the laughter. It was to have been my night of nights, my zenith. It was more than anyone could bear. Blast the skating and the riding, the water-skiing and the batik. I should have taken my mother's advice.

It seemed hours before Alexis led met gently to the sofa, before I realised that he was caressing me, talking, that he was not angry.

'I've deceived you,' I said, not caring about the tears. I could not look more of a mess if I tried.

'Thank goodness!'

I sat up. 'You don't mind?'

'I was beginning to lose hope.'

'Of what?'

He pulled me round to look at him. I almost fainted with happiness and disbelief at the look on his face.

'I didn't want another paragon,' he said. 'I couldn't live up to it. Far too much of a strain. You always looked so perfect, and then the cooking … it was all too much.'

'You like me …?'

'As you are,' he said. 'Soft from the rain.' He touched my skin. 'Mascara running down your face …'

'I can't even cook,' I said, 'not an egg! I thought you wanted … you were used to … "Let's eat at home," you said. I distinctly remember.'

'I was going to make us an omelette,' he said, 'and play you my new LP.'

I started to cry. It was all too much: the deception, my guilt. I let it all come out.

'I thought you wanted a soufflé,' I sobbed. 'I wanted to make you a soufflé à l'orange!'

He dried my tears and took me in his arms.

'But I really can skate, and ski, and play the violin,' I said into his shoulder. 'And do batik. Honestly!'

The Moules Factory

1994

Ever since, as an adolescent, Maisie had watched Jean Gabin in *Le jour se lève* (with subtitles), she had wanted to learn French. Now that Marvin had sold the business she had time on her hands, so with a desire to get out of the house as much as anything else, she implemented her wish. She took to the French course like a duck to water. The teacher told her that she had an ear for language. She had also enrolled in a literature class.

On Mondays and Thursdays, while Marvin watched *his* TV programmes (as if the producer and the director had created them especially for him), Maisie lost herself in Bellow and Faulkner, Flaubert and Henry James, and it was as if a window had opened in her soul. It was clear to her that days of domestic servitude passed in a bungalow in Burlington, Massachusetts, interspersed with holidays in Florida, hardly amounted to a full life. Her problem, she concluded, was Marvin.

Her husband had not only been told of the unhealthy state

of his coronary arteries by his cardiovascular specialist, who had cautioned him to pay more attention to his diet, but he was not keen on travelling and would, if he could, have lain on a sofa and had the landscape carried past him.

When, inspired by thoughts of Paris, of the valley of the Loire, of terraced Bordeaux vineyards and the sweet smells of Provence, Maisie interrupted his chat show to suggest going to Europe, Marvin looked at her as if she had proposed that they volunteer for the space shuttle.

It was Marvin's mother who provided the solution to her problem. Not directly, for in the New Jersey Home where she was cared for by a dedicated staff, old Mrs Burgess was aware of neither time nor place. It was while she was dunking a chocolate-chip cookie into her cup of Earl Grey tea, that Marvin's mother looked directly at Marvin and said clearly, 'You'd always do anything, Marvin, for one of my chocolate-chip cookies.' Maisie could not imagine why she had not thought of it before. She had tried unsuccessfully to seduce Marvin with the Paris of Napoleon, of Zola, and Degas and Proust. Now she changed tack. Dismissing the fact that he had been cautioned about his cholesterol, she tempted him with soups and sauces, pâtés and pancakes, frogs' legs and fritters, bisque and bourrides. It was Marvin who called the travel agent. Marvin who started a regular exercise programme in anticipation of a gastronomic dream.

By mid-morning, on the transatlantic flight to Paris, the trolley had begun its halting progression down the aisle.

'I like my lunch early,' Marvin said with satisfaction, the

moment he heard the rattle of the wheels. Level with his seat, the stewardess held a foil-wrapped dish in either hand.

'Beef or chicken?' The turquoise eyeshadow shimmered.

Marvin thought for a moment then turned to Maisie. 'Which do I like?'

The crimson nails tightened around both of the containers.

'Chicken,' Maisie said.

'We had chicken last night.'

'Take the beef then.'

'Is it baked or broiled?' Marvin enquired.

'The beef?' The girl looked as if her arms were getting tired. Maisie was aware of a frisson of impatience from the hungry passenger in the seat beside her.

'The chicken,' Marvin said.

'Baked ...' the stewardess aimed the chicken in Marvin's direction, '... with rice.'

'I don't touch rice.' Marvin recoiled as the container made a perfect landing on his table. 'What's with the beef?'

'Noodles.'

Maisie smiled apologetically as Marvin picked up his dish and thrust it into the outstretched talons.

'I'll take the beef.'

It was Maisie's French teacher who had told her about the hotel on the Left Bank. Awakened by the sound of mechanical brushes as they sluiced the early-morning gutters, Maisie had to pinch herself as she looked out of the window, in her night-dress, on to the street of old stone town houses that described a straight line to the Seine.

Across the river she could pick out the Sacré-Coeur. To her left, Les Invalides. To her right, the Quai d'Orsay.

'What time did you tell them to bring the breakfast?' Marvin asked from beneath the bed covers.

It was past eleven when they emerged into the Rue du Bac.

Maisie had prepared herself for this moment. She had mastered the street plan, pored over the Métro map, memorised the promenades. She was determined not to hurry over this city. Not to be an American tourist darting from one monument to the next. Was not Paris, with its quays and its courtyards, its Gothic railway stations and equestrian statues, itself a work of art?

She was pointing out the green dome of the Grand Palais above the chestnut trees of the Champs-Elysées, when she realised she had lost Marvin. He had taken off his distance glasses to read a menu displayed on a lectern in the street.

'Four courses,' he said, 'and a half-bottle of wine. Only twenty dollars!'

Maisie pulled him towards the Arc de Triomphe. 'You've just had breakfast.'

'A couple of croissants! I'm starving.'

Maisie was so intoxicated with the jostle and commotion of Paris, with the magnetic exuberance of the metropolis, that she neglected to remind Marvin that not only were croissants made with butter, but that he had put butter on them. As far as she was concerned she could not have cared less had she never eaten again.

Struggling to retain her composure (had not Marvin, after

all, both countenanced and financed this trip?) she took two steps forward and one step back as she paused every few yards – at Marvin's insistence – to translate the bills of fare. They had lunch at a restaurant that boasted a rosette for its food. Maisie would sooner have gone to a café. By the time they had finished it was already four. Marvin was just as disinclined to get up from the table as he had been to choose a restaurant.

'Come on,' Maisie said, 'the museums will be closed.'

That night Maisie could not sleep. She lay next to Marvin in the sagging bed thinking about the *Coronation of Napoleon* on the vast canvas in the Louvre.

'Maybe I should have ordered the cold lobster,' said Marvin. 'The thermidor was very rich.'

For Maisie, the next few days were like a dream come true. The city with its palaces and its gardens, offered up an infinitesimal part of its treasures, and the names of artists and emperors, poets and politicians took on new meaning. While her cup was filled with 'renaissance' and 'revolution', Marvin revelled in soups and sauces, ballottines and blanquettes, the likes of which he had never encountered before. Maisie was far too busy to nag him about his cholesterol.

They left Paris and, with Maisie at the wheel of the hire car, headed for the Loire valley. Marvin had his head in the guide-book. Maisie waited for him to read out a description of their first chateau.

'Crevettes with sorrel ... fricasséed sweetbreads ... Eels simmered in old wine ...' Marvin intoned. 'I can't wait.'

As she stood on battlements or traversed a formal garden,

imagining that she was Joan of Arc beleaguering Orléans, Diane de Poitiers or Catherine de' Medici, Marvin's voice would break into her dreams: 'Green cabbage with butter', 'stuffed mushrooms with cream'. It was not that Maisie was indifferent to the gastronomy of the region, simply that thoughts of it did not engage her every waking moment as they did Marvin's. Marvin had difficulty in fastening his pants. He had gas. And acid indigestion.

They continued their perambulations, staying at hotels that had been specially selected by Marvin more for the quality of the boudin than the beds. Last thing at night he spoke of breakfast, first thing in the morning it was lunch. By the time they left Bordeaux for the coast, a strange glint had made its way into Maisie's eyes.

Arcachon, renowned for its shellfish, was the apotheosis of Marvin's trip. As they strolled along the promenade, between the quaint hotels and the broad expanse of smooth sand edged by the Atlantic waves with a brodérie of foam, they were stopped every few yards by white-aproned waiters offering free tastings of oysters. Marvin was in his element.

The sight of her husband as he threw back his head to slurp the slithery molluscs from their shells revolted Maisie. She tried to suppress her disgust. Enticed into a restaurant, he ordered bouillabaisse (for two) and demolished the steaming tureen with its floating coquillages and menacing rascasses all by himself. The bouillabaisse was preceded by several visits to the buffet table, at which he piled his plate. Maisie watched silently as he consumed a double portion of dessert.

They decided to spend a few days in St Jean de Luz. The weather was perfect; warm sun fanned by a light breeze. Maisie sat in a deckchair and read her book. They had picnics on the beach. Marvin spent his mornings carefully choosing them.

When they were rested, Maisie refuelled the Peugeot. High on the rubbish-strewn cliffs she stopped the car to look at the view. Not waiting for Marvin, she ran among the white daisies, among the tangled grasses and the yellow and purple flowers, over the remains of bonfires and discarded wine bottles, until she could see the cream-flecked breakers as they hurled themselves on to the curiously striated rocks far, far below. Watched by a solitary dog, its head on one side, she opened her arms to the morning sun and allowed the sea breeze to caress her cheeks, making her feel like a young girl.

'Marvin!' she called, her voice carried by the wind. 'Marvin!'

Marvin, carrying his camera, got out of the car. A smile illuminated his face as he pointed into the distance where Maisie, who had come to meet him, could just make out a low white building with a sign on its red roof.

'Now, would you believe it,' Marvin said with sheer joy. 'It's a moules factory!'

Followed by the dog with its black and white patches, they walked together over the potholes and the wild flowers. Taking Marvin's hand, Maisie told him all about the lighthouse they had come to visit, about the ancient fort built by Henry IV. She quoted a passage from the guidebook about the premature death of Queen Marie-Thérèse.

Marvin opened his mouth. Maisie thought he was about to make a comment on the stirring history.

'There's an auberge near the lighthouse ...' Marvin said, and Maisie's heart sank, '... that specialises in moules.'

They walked as far as the signpost, which pointed towards the Spanish border.

'I'm just going to get a picture,' Marvin said, letting go of Maisie's hand, 'then we can have lunch.'

Maisie watched with the dog as Marvin, flattening the singing grass, made his way to the cliff edge. She felt as if she were on top of the world. There was no one as far as the eye could see and the silence was disturbed only by the occasional zoom of a passing car. If life could always be like this, she thought, if only man would not seek to penetrate the measureless sky, displace the sea, harness the wind, pollute the good earth.

Holding on to his camera, Marvin inched his way to the edge of the cliff.

'Take care!' Maisie called.

At the sound of her voice, the dog cocked its head on one side. They had never kept an animal. Not even when the children had been small. Marvin didn't like animals in the house. Looking into the brown eyes, liquid with understanding, Maisie had a sudden sense of déjà vu. The dog kept close to her side as she watched her husband, silhouetted against the skyline.

Treading gingerly, Marvin stood poised, his finger on the shutter release of his camera. Then he leaned over until he had a clear view of the rocks.

It was as he put his eye to the viewfinder and inclined from the waist as far forward as he dared that Maisie saw Marvin put a sudden hand to his chest. It was like watching a film projected in slow motion. Joan of Arc, Diane de Poitiers, Catherine de' Medici ... Dropping her handbag, twisting her ankle, followed by the dog, she felt herself run towards him as if the distance were measured in miles rather than in yards. There was a cry, as if Marvin were being strangled, a sound so blood-curdling it was as if it had come out of a nightmare. As in a nightmare, the harder Maisie ran, the less ground she seemed to cover. She knew that she had her hand out, that she called Marvin's name, although no sound emerged from her throat, that Marvin twisted and turned, his face distorted grotesquely until, tipped over by the weight of the huge belly that flopped over his trousers, he seemed to fly like a seagull over the cliff, followed by his camera and her horrified gaze.

Throwing herself on the rough ground, the dog by her side, Maisie edged forward, the earth crumbling beneath her. She could see the granite rocks at the base of the cliff, which had seduced Marvin with their formation.

By craning her neck, and holding on to a bunch of thistles, she was just in time to see the merciless waves swallow up her husband's Crimplene-shirted body, just like an abandoned stick, and draw it effortlessly out into the boundless sea in whose bosom lay his lobsters and his crayfish, his oysters and his clams.

All that Maisie could think of, to her eternal horror, to her eternal shame, was that at last Marvin would be happy. At last he had got his moules.

Southern Comfort

1998

I am well-travelled in all senses of the word. Five continents and four husbands. I don't make a big issue of either. I can go down with cramps, rashes, fevers, gnat bites, snake bites, stomach acid – anything that doesn't require major surgery – anywhere in the world and be my own physician. In my drugs bag I carry every pill known to man and then some, yet I haven't slept in twenty years. Twenty years is a long time.

I know you have panaceas. Hot milk. Cold milk. Hypnotism. Relaxation tapes. Sleep clinics. This therapy. That therapy. Leave me alone. I've swallowed the pharmacopoeia. I've heard your theories. I've tried them all. Twenty years is long enough. I get into bed. Or not. I fix my pillows. Goose-down, duck-down, feather, fibre, rubber, synthetic, non-allergic, orthopaedic, square, oblong, crib, air-filled, water-filled. Even hops. Hops! Sometimes I pick up a book. Then the whole damned pantomime begins. A blue pill, then a yellow, then a white. like candies all night long. I drop off for an hour, two maybe, till my whole body shrieks out 'pill' and I fumble like a drunkard for the water carafe. Those to whom sleep is no problem, 'balm of hurt minds', 'sweet nature's second course' and all that garbage, cannot hope to understand. They will never know how long are the small hours or how empty though peopled with forgotten voices, fragmented places, familiar and recurring anxieties. They will never know the blind panic that comes with the first tongue of light as it identifies like an aching tooth the hairline cracks in the dense drapes, with the first note of the earliest bird signalling the utter desolation of yet another *nuit blanche*. They will not have yearned, prayed, wept for oblivion that will not, no matter what the pill nor the strength of it, descend. They will not know what it means to be more vigilant, more alert, than in the day, wide-eyed, the senses painfully aware, while the old snore and the young coil innocently like snakes round sleeping partners, and golden babes with flickering eyelids quietly breathe away the night plucking at the blankets with scaly fingers like those who are about to die.

At such times death would be welcome. Don't think I haven't considered it. Unconsciousness at any price. Anaesthesia, concussion, it doesn't need to be natural.

It comes, of course, sleep. If you can call it that. Ten minutes, twenty, before it's time to rise. Although there's nothing to rise for, 6.45 a.m. is my wake-up time and that's when I wake up. Wake! Well, I open my eyes from the few minutes' respite that was the night and wonder whether with my arid mouth, my reverberating head, the raw orbs that pass for eyes, my snarled-up nerves, it is possible to make it through another day. One way it is possible. Only one. Across the room is my lifeline, my life. Appraising the shape of the familiar bottle with its reassuring label, I know that only with its help will I manage to traverse that no man's land of time that lies between now and the next confrontation with the enemy.

There are doctors, you say. Doctors bore me. They agree I am an interesting case, although it's my money that interests them. Who can blame them? A wealthy widow with an art collection worth tens of millions of dollars (husband number four) and as much again in the bank. Old money.

Milward brought me to Jamaica the last Christmas before he passed away at the wheel of the Merc. An insulin-dependent diabetic, he succumbed to a coronary infarct. It was on the cards. Macabre as it may seem, Jamaica is the only place in the world to which I have remained faithful.

Jamaica, with its Blue Mountains and undulating fields of sugar cane, where the lukewarm waters of the Caribbean lick the white sands to reach the coconut palms and red-leaved almond trees. Jamaica, land of cloves, of cinnamon, of spice, with its yellow corato and hibiscus, its oleander and its jasmine and its fragrant jacaranda. It is for none of these that I return, as faithfully as the humming bird, the moment the Christmas trees appear in the windows of Park Avenue. It is not for my cottage where the bougainvillea and thunbergia hang sweetly from the pergola and tiny lizards drop on to my breakfast table with its moist bowl of papaya and watermelon. It is not for Agatha my maid, dark as night and golden of heart, who will be there waiting, nor for the daytime song of the blackbird, the chorus of the evening crickets with the solo call of the bullfrogs. It is neither the ever-changing colours of the mountains nor the rainbow curtain of the falls that brings me back to the island year after year. It is for oblivion. It does not come cheap.

The cottage Milward rented, and which I ultimately bought, was in a complex of privately owned hillside properties not too far from the facilities of the main hotel. It has no name. Only a number.

That first Christmas, the last we were to spend together (if you can call it that), there was an urgent message from New York waiting for us on our arrival. Milward said it was a crisis, but I guessed it was nothing more urgent than the charms of his latest PA – a raven-haired girl young enough to be his granddaughter – and without waiting to unpack, he headed straight back to JFK, saying he'd be back in a few days and leaving me in the care of Agatha.

I never take more than a cup of clear soup and a little cold chicken or beef at lunch. Agatha told me that if I was tired from the journey she would call room service and have it brought to the cottage. I wanted to take a look at the place, however, and find out who was staying there – we never did the circuit without bumping into someone we knew – so I showered and changed and took the cinder path in my gold mules, through the soursops with their heavy prickly fruits and the giant flame trees towards the restaurant, which was set on stilts and open on all sides.

There was the usual mix of well-heeled travellers in exotic leisurewear lifted straight from the winter holiday pages of the women's magazines. It was the year of the sarong, which, cunningly tied and in bright colours, looked, according to the fashion gurus, particularly alluring in the crystalline light of the tropics. I recognised poor blank-eyed Poppy Wilmington whose elevator no longer quite reached the top storey, and the Hailey-Whites, my neighbours in the Hamptons, and waggled a couple of fingers in greeting as I was ushered by the Captain to a prime table overlooking the ocean with its coral reef.

I sat, gold linen napkin in my lap, fortified by the Southern Comfort I had imbibed before leaving the cottage, feeling only moderately self-conscious at my unaccompanied state, when a soft voice said, 'Good morning, Madame. My name is Carstairs. I'm the maître d'. Today I can recommend the lobster and the red snapper papillot or you are welcome to help yourself from our luncheon buffet.'

I looked up.

Six foot three and dark as velvet. Bamboo slim with an exquisite head, flat ears, moist eyes, and a slow smile, which revealed impeccable teeth, only one of which was gold. He stood motionless, his pale-blue tuxedo elegantly draped round his spare frame, his notebook poised, ready to take my order. He did not stir, yet I knew that when he did his movements would be fluid, effortless.

'Carstairs,' I said, as much to test the name out on my tongue as anything else.

'Madame?'

'You can bring me a little bouillon and some beef. Rare. I seldom take anything more at midday. And Carstairs ...'

'Madame?'

'After lunch I should like to discuss my menu for tonight.'

Throughout lunch he did not come near me. Lithe, boneless, his lapis studs winking from his frilled shirt-front, he attended to his duties, conducted his orchestra, the darting eyes missing nothing, the commanding presence everywhere, gliding smoothly between the tables, greeting, directing with the merest wave of the menu. Coordination itself. And so beautiful.

Over the bouillon on which floated a green julienne of scallions, I laid my plans. I always got what I wanted. My four husbands had seen to that. There was nothing that did not have its price.

I only played with the beef, realising that it was not going to be easy. I knew what I was up against in this part of the world where the white man no longer ruled and the destiny of the country had long been in the hands of the native population. I guessed how it would be with Carstairs, but I was not accustomed to being thwarted.

I refused coffee and dessert, and waited until he came soft-footed to my side. I kept him waiting.

'Carstairs,' I said when I was ready. 'Tonight I should like to have a lamb cutlet and a little green salad. French dressing. I am not a big eater. I don't care for fancy food.'

He inclined his head and made a note on his pad, the pale undersides of his hands gleaming.

'I shall have it in my cottage. Number fourteen. My husband is away on business.'

'No problem.'

'I would like you to bring it yourself.'

The pencil stopped and I could hear the clatter and chatter of the restaurant.

'That will not be possible, Madame.'

I placed my used napkin on my plate.

'Carstairs, in this world everything is possible. What time do you close the restaurant?'

'After the last guest has gone.'

'That will do very nicely.'

Signing the bill for my meagre lunch, and without looking at him, I returned to my cottage.

I suppose he checked me out. Mrs Milward Sandilands Burrows who could feed his entire family for a year on what she spent each week at the beauty parlour. Mrs Milward Sandilands Burrows to whom to say no was to risk losing a job for which the fight had been long and hard, and which could never be regained.

I have said enough for you to have cottoned on to my secret. There had been men before (apart from my husbands), rough trade I suppose you'd call it, and there would be men again. It was part of my sickness and I could no more live without them than I could contemplate a day without my Southern Comfort. You would be surprised if I told you how many men are available to a pampered, bloated and grossly overweight 'blonde' crossing the frontiers of old age, even if they are not available.

Back in the cottage Agatha had unpacked. I passed the afternoon between the percale sheets of the cool bed to dispel the fatigue of the long journey.

At six o'clock I went over to the hotel where a boy from Italy, who wasn't at all bad-looking, fixed my hair. I had my nails done too, mainly to pass the time.

Agatha helped me dress in a pale-blue peignoir with a matching Alice-band. She tidied the cottage and left a thermos of ice-water and some fruit and cookies in the icebox. She changed from her pink-checked overall into a cotton dress and armed with the inevitable umbrella against the tropical rains that came without warning, she bade me goodnight, telling me that she would see me in the morning.

It was nine o'clock and the steam heat of the evening swallowed every particle of air. I sat fanning myself on the lamp-lit patio and watched the limos ferrying the guests from the cottages to the restaurant. I thought of them at table, Carstairs waiting upon them. After a while I grew tired of looking at the dark palms and starry sky, and listening to the cacophony of the night. I went inside and closed the shades and switched on the air-conditioning. I didn't much like the noise of that either.

The black-and-white ceramic tiled floor of the sitting room was strewn with cane mats woven in the intricate circular pattern indigenous to the island. On every table there were bowls of flowers – orchids, cups of gold, allamanda – freshly picked. They complemented the tones of the loose covers and the conch shells, open, obscenely pink, on the shelves.

I sat on the sofa holding an ancient copy of *Stories from the*

New Yorker, which someone had left behind, and settled down to wait.

It was not five minutes before there was a discreet knock on the door.

'Room service.'

It was not Carstairs.

Four boys carried in a round table, covered with a gold cloth, on which, beneath a silver dome, sat my solitary cutlet.

I ate slowly. Very slowly. I don't think anyone could have made a lamb cutlet last longer. After a while they knocked again to clear away. 'Was there anything else, Mrs Burrows?' No, there was nothing else.

It was ten forty-five. I eyed the Southern Comfort and it looked me straight back in the eye. Although there was ice in the icebox I had no mind to struggle with it. I took it straight.

The light in the bathroom was fluorescent strip. I looked a hundred. I went back to the sitting room and the rapidly diminishing bottle.

Towards midnight I began to hear the cars returning along the roads and over the 'sleeping policemen', taking the first guests back to their cottages.

At 1 a.m. there was a knock at the shutters. More of a tap really.

'Who is it?'

I opened, knowing.

He wore a white tuxedo, black satin revers, onyx studs and links. He had to incline his head to step inside. I noticed the gold signet ring on his finger, matching the gold tooth.

'I came to see if you enjoyed your dinner, Mrs Burrows.'

'The cutlet was very good.'

I had turned down the lamps and hoped I didn't look too bad.

'Is there anything else I can get you?'

I looked at him, tall, thin, handsome. I looked at him directly and noticed that the lashes curled upwards over the gazelle-like eyes.

'Yes, Carstairs,' I said softly, 'as a matter of fact there is something else.'

I led the way unsteadily into the bedroom, where Agatha had prepared only one of the twin beds. He hesitated for only a second, wondering about his job, no doubt, although he had had plenty of time to think about it. For one dreadful moment I thought he was not going to follow me, then I heard the soft fall of his feet.

Carstairs, Carstairs. In the limpid mirror of your eyes I was young, beautiful, desirable, needed, loved, possessed. The vaulted ceiling with its fan turning like a huge propeller over our sweating bodies was lovelier than the velvet night, stars thrown in for good measure.

He did not speak, did not lose his dignity, but was aware of my needs as he was instantly aware of the needs of every diner in his restaurant. Carstairs the virtuoso, I his violin.

Milward was away three days. For three nights I had Carstairs. For three nights I slept. No pills, no potions, no alcohol. Slept like a log, a baby. Slept like I was comatose. Slept till Agatha woke me gently opening the blinds.

When Milward came back bright and breezy with dark rings beneath his eyes, he took one look at me and commented that the rest had done me good. Yes, Milward, I said, I like it here. Jamaica has done me good.

That night we ate in the restaurant. Milward gave Carstairs fifty dollars to look after us. He slipped it into his pocket. I did not raise my eyes above the wine-red tuxedo that skimmed the mobile hips.

It's five years now since Milward died. At Christmas time his wealthy widow can be found at her hillside cottage in Jamaica where, in the afternoons, she disappears, alone, and in a taxi, often for several hours. Although the other guests assume that she is visiting the Craft Market, they find it curious that she returns empty-handed, with neither the ubiquitous straw hat nor souvenirs of hand-dyed batik.

In between times she is to be found in her Park Avenue apartment where sometimes, in the small hours, she puts on a CD and with a far away look in her eyes moves rhythmically to the beat of a Calypso: 'Annie Palmer' (she was a wicked witch), 'Tak' Him to Jamaica' (where the rum come from), 'Yellow Bird' and 'Island in the Sun'. Like many women of her size she is surprisingly light on her feet.

She knows that some day she will become old – old old – and that Carstairs will move on. Until then, as soon as the first flakes of snow fall on Park Avenue, she picks up the telephone and books her flight to Jamaica. It's a long way to go for a good night's sleep.

Moving

1999

'They've arrived,' Belle said from the window where she was watching, 'in a Cadillac.'

'What do you expect?' Mrs Menzies selected a strand of apricot wool.

'Mother!' Belle warned. 'You promised.'

Mrs Menzies threaded her tapestry needle with the aid of the 'D' section of her bifocals. 'I promised not to say anything in front of them.'

'Don't you think, then, that you should get yourself in the mood?'

'I shall never be in the mood.'

Belle sighed.

'Don't worry. I shan't let you down. What do they look like?'

'Smart. Very smart. I'm surprised she's able to hold her head up. So many gold chains. He must jog. At least five miles a day. Youngish.'

'*La jeunesse dorée*,' Mrs Menzies said. 'They are the ones with the money.'

'They are indeed,' Belle said. 'Are you going to let them in?'

'Where's Grace?'

'Tidying the spare bedroom. He's looking at the roof very professionally.'

'There's nothing the matter with the roof. Your father had it completely retiled before ...'

'Look, it's no use being touchy.'

'I am not being touchy. All I said was there's nothing the matter with the roof. Of course, if you'd rather I kept out of the way. You and Grace ...'

'Mother, don't take it out on us. He's finished with the roof. They're coming up the drive.'

Mrs Menzies put down her canvas. It was the last of the dozen seat covers she had embroidered along the years for the William and Mary chairs. She would not be needing them. Doubted if anyone would need them now that dining rooms had fallen into desuetude.

She stood by the front door to compose herself.

'Reeded glass would improve it no end,' she heard a firm female voice say. 'I would imagine the hallway's dark as night.'

The bell rang.

Mrs Menzies, her face threatening, opened the heavy oak door. At the last moment she caught Belle's eye, remembered her promise, and fixed a ghastly smile around her mouth.

'From Town and Country Properties,' the man in the cashmere sports coat said, waving the duplicated details with the coloured reproduction of the house.

'You are expected. Please come in.'

They stood on the nineteenth-century rug, unique in composition and palette, with its filigree Herati border, which Mrs Menzies had brought personally from Iran in the days when it was still Persia.

'I told you it would be dark!' the woman said triumphantly.

Her husband shot her a glance. 'My apologies for invading your privacy on a Sunday but it's the only day ...'

'It has to be sold,' Mrs Menzies said, as if by rote.

'... and at lunchtime.'

'Just a snack,' Mrs Menzies said. 'Of course at one time when my husband ...'

'We're Howard and Lois Cobb. Mrs Menzies?'

'It's pronounced ...' Mrs Menzies felt a presence behind her. 'Oh, this is my daughter, Belle.'

'What a pretty name!'

'Short for Anabelle after ...'

'Aren't you going to show the house?' Belle said.

'I am, aren't I, showing it? This is the hall,' Mrs Menzies said superfluously, waving a vague hand, and wondering why women of Lois Cobb's configuration insisted on wearing trousers.

She was running a red-tipped hand over the oak balustrade. 'I guess it could be stripped and painted.'

Mrs Menzies's mouth dropped open.

'If there's one thing I can't stand it's a dark hallway.' Lois Cobb crossed it and stumbled. Her husband caught her. She looked round. 'Take care, Howie, That old mat ...'

'There is parquet flooring throughout the ground floor,' Mrs Menzies said. 'It takes a bit of polishing but it pays. You don't see floors like that today.'

'We would have wall-to-wall,' Lois Cobb said. 'Shag-pile.'

'You mean you'd cover ...?'

'Why don't you start in the drawing room,' Belle suggested. 'Then they can see the garden while the sun's out. The weather forecast said rain, but it's held off so far. You never can tell with the weather forecast ... Are you interested in gardens, Mr Cobb? My mother grows the best roses for miles around – of course, we have the soil for it – but then you must be if you're considering a house out here.'

Howard Cobb followed his wife into the drawing room which was bathed in yellow light.

'As long as there's room for a pool and a handsome terrace. We have a gas barbecue. Two dozen steaks at one time.' He looked through the leaded lights at the lawn, surrounded by roses and hollyhocks, lovingly tended. 'Might even manage a tennis court as well. What do you think, Lois?'

She was looking at the fireplace, which to Belle meant hot-buttered toast and chestnuts.

'This would have to go for a start. I wonder about the chimneybreast?'

'No problem. Picture windows, floor to ceiling. Patio doors; let some light into the place.'

'We used to have dances for the girls,' Mrs Menzies said. 'More than fifty young people ...'

'We could extend another twelve, thirteen feet ...'

Mrs Menzies wondered if they were considering moving in with a regiment.

'It certainly has potential.'

'Would you like to see the garden?' Belle asked, opening the French windows.

Outside there was a garden room, brick on three sides, in which they kept the faded wooden deckchairs, the canvas rotting. Even on showery days in summer you could sit just inside it, waiting for the clouds to pass.

'It's very useful,' Belle said, remembering all the homework she had done there as a child. 'When it rains, suddenly, you know, as it does.'

Mrs Cobb clapped her hands with delight. 'It's quite charming, Howie. A perfect changing room.' She turned to Belle. 'Of course, there'd have to be a bathroom.'

'Bathroom?' Belle said.

'Serving the pool area.'

Mrs Menzies was looking at the lime tree, majestic and glorious, hundreds of years old, in full leaf. She could see it from her bedroom when she lay in bed and had often fantasised her own death – peaceful of course – with the tree in full view.

Mr Cobb followed her gaze.

'Take some getting out.' He scratched his head. 'Roots might even go under the house.'

'Getting out?' Mrs Menzies said faintly.

'To make room for the pool.'

'I expect you'd like to see the kitchen,' Belle said, leading the way round the side of the house.

It was almost a year since her father had died, leaving her mother alone in the big house. They had decided it would be for the best. At least she and Timothy and Grace had. Embroiled in their lives, none of them could visit more than infrequently. They had worked on their mother both singly and conjointly. It wasn't that they didn't understand about the house; it was the total impracticality of its upkeep. They appreciated that it had been their mother's first proper home as a young bride, that she had kept it all through the war, turning it into a convalescent home for servicemen. They knew that she loved every stick and stone of the place, as they did themselves, and were aware how she felt about leaving it, and that the rambling dwelling with its gabled roof was more than a sum of its parts. It was roses plucked still wet with dew, purple beads of blood drawn by the thorns; huge Christmases when the grandparents were alive; Grace falling from the garden swing the three of them took it in turns to paint; Timothy on the doorstep with his first girlfriend; Mr Harper who had grown old tending the garden each Wednesday.

There was no other way. Apart from the work entailed there was the expense. The garden couldn't be managed without Mr Harper and the heating still ran on anthracite. The outside of the house had to be painted every few years and ... there was no end. Between them the decision had to be made.

Just within the side door – which Belle could not bring herself to say had always been known as the 'welly' room, because of the boots and raincoats and plimsolls and hockey sticks and ice skates and cricket bats it had housed over the years – they huddled together, an awkward foursome.

'I'll lead the way,' Belle said. 'This is the kitchen.' Mr and Mrs Cobb stared at the scrubbed wooden table and the glazed cupboards through which you could see the china with its familiar willow pattern, at the Welsh dresser, the Aga cooker, and the worn lino on the floor.

My father was ill for so long, Belle wanted to say in its defence, there simply wasn't the money.

She intercepted their glance. It said: how on earth can people live like this?

'It's a very roomy kitchen,' Belle said weakly. The Cobbs looked up as if to assess its spaciousness and saw the paint flaking from the ceiling, above which a bath had overflowed. There was no more to be said.

They passed on into the hall again. It was the moment Belle had been dreading. 'Upstairs next, Mother?' she said. 'I should think Grace has had time to tidy up.'

'What about the dining room?' Mrs Cobb said. You do have a dining room?'

'Yes,' Belle said. She looked at her mother who was removing some imaginary fluff from her cardigan and refused to meet her eye.

Her father had first been taken ill ten years ago. A day Belle would not forget. It was Sunday and he had been mowing the lawn, his relaxation after a week in the city. Her mother had been preparing lunch for the visiting family. A Sunday like any other. Timothy had seen to the drinks and Belle was taking hers out to the garden when the mower stopped. She remembered thinking, how odd, in the midst of a row, like knitting, but had thought it was only to empty the grass box. Her father had just stood there, transfixed. A cerebral embolus, out of the blue, had paralysed one side of his body. It happened so quickly. One moment of disbelief, then she must have shouted because her mother and Grace and Timothy came running out of the house and all at once there were doctors and ambulances and confusion disturbing the peace of the Sunday morning. The beef was charred to a cinder and they had to throw it away.

Her father had recovered, partially and painfully, from that first stroke. A man wont to boast that he had never had a day's illness in his life, reduced to a pitiful slowness of speech, a shuffling of step, a need to move his left arm, obstinately useless, with his right. The second episode, affecting the other side of his brain, had come three years later, like a thief in the night. It has robbed him of all movement, all speech, and had left him a human vegetable, with eyes.

The dining room had seemed the best place. Her mother and the nurses who came and went could more easily keep an eye on the invalid and it was less tiring. Belle could scarcely remember when it had not been a sickroom with the high bed and the paraphernalia attendant upon one unable to do a single thing for himself.

Afterwards the bed had remained. They had no desire to use the room. Not one of them could have eaten a bite in a place so full of memories.

Last week the Church Army had come to take the bed away. It

was at the suggestion of Town and Country Properties. The table was now back in position with its William and Mary chairs.

'In here,' Belle said, opening the door.

The Cobbs, both Howard and Lois, were silent. Either they could not believe their eyes – the room was, Belle supposed, rather shabby – or they felt, as she did, the presence of the wasted body by the wall, the comings and goings of the white-capped nurses, the watching hours. No, that was absurd.

Mrs Cobb was tugging at the twin doors of the serving hatch that led to the kitchen.

'Don't you ever use this?' she asked. 'I always think a hatch is so practical.'

'Not very often,' Belle said.

Mr Cobb tugged. 'Warped,' he said. 'The whole thing would have to come out anyway.'

'You need some imagination,' Mrs Cobb said, half-closing her eyes. 'A black-glass-topped table and some decent chairs.'

Mrs Menzies, who had been standing in the doorway pulling at her handkerchief, looked at the much-loved furniture and wondered who could possibly love a table with a black glass top. 'Decent chairs?' she said weakly.

'Leather and chrome. Get rid of that old cornice and the overmantel, lower the ceiling ... a sort of grotto with concealed lighting ...'

'Grotto!' Mrs Menzies could not believe that she had heard aright.

'Room doesn't look as if it's ever used,' Mr Cobb said, 'it has a sort of odd ...'

'Mother eats in the kitchen,' Belle said quickly. 'It's cosier.' She felt rather than saw her mother glance at the wall against which the bed had stood for so many years.

'We'll go upstairs now,' Belle said firmly, holding open the door.

Upstairs the Cobbs decided to turn the old nursery into a guest bathroom, Timothy's bedroom into a sauna ... unless, of course, they had it by the pool.

They discussed under-floor heating.

'It's a very warm house,' Mrs Menzies said. 'Most of the rooms face south and get every bit of sun.'

'Double glazing,' Mr Cobb said, making notes on the particulars from Town and Country. 'Essential.'

His wife was shaking her head at the 'dreadful leaded lights' and 'not a single closet you could really call a closet'. Had it not been for Belle, Mrs Menzies would have asked what you could call them and how it was they had all managed to keep their clothes quite satisfactorily in them for so many years.

Mr Cobb stood on the ladder Belle held and peered into the loft.

'How is it, Howie?'

Full of memories.

'Black as hell. Runs the length of the house, as far as I can tell. A stairway, a window, a decent floor, and you might do something with it.'

Belle assumed that the note he made was 'Loft. Potential'. At the front door Belle said, 'Would you like to see the garage?'

'I glanced at it as I came in,' Mr Cobb said. 'I guess something could be done.'

'Two cars easily,' Belle said, 'and the bikes.'

'Up-and-over doors,' Mr Cobb said.

More beautiful oak destroyed.

'Remote control. Intruder alarm,' Mr Cobb added to the notes which by now covered most of the two sheets of paper.

When they had gone Belle considered it politic not to look at her mother, but to say brightly: 'How about some lunch – I'm starving.'

Grace came down the stairs. 'Have they gone? Didn't you even offer them a drink?'

'Drink!' Mrs Menzies said. 'We haven't any polystyrene cups! They probably wouldn't know what to do with crystal.'

'It's not our business,' Belle said. 'You want to sell the house, don't you?'

'Not to them,' Mrs Menzies said. 'Glass and chrome, and what about my roses and my tree? Over my dead body!'

But when the offer came for a sum larger than they had anticipated, even she knew that the battle had been lost.

'You will like it in Fulham,' Belle said. 'Near the shops.'

'In that horrid little town house ...'

'You wouldn't consider a flat.'

'... full of those screaming infants.'

'It won't be full of screaming infants. You have plenty of imagination. You can do it up as you like.'

'There's a split-level cooker,' Mrs Menzies said. 'It will be nice not to have to bend. Belle?'

'Mmm?'

'Do you think I could dig up that horrid patio with the multi-coloured random paving and have just a tiny lawn and a few roses?'

'I don't see why not.'

'And that downstairs room, with the bunks and the blackboard and the electric trains ... it could, I suppose, make a sewing room. The sitting room isn't really a bad size. Once they remove the convertible sofa and the haircord carpet and the rubber plants and all that horrible hi-fi. I could have a pretty little cornice. Some watered-silk wallpaper ...'

'There's no end,' Belle said, 'to what you can do with a house.'

À la Carte

2010

It was Gail who suggested that her mother try Internet dating. She had persuaded Stephanie, who taught English in a deprived school in North London, into believing (almost) that fifty-three was the new thirty and that going online was a great way to get back into the game.

'Give it a go,' Gail had said, not once but many times until, in an idle moment between marking sadly illiterate essays and eating her solitary dinner, Stephanie had logged on to U-Date and, in the boxes indicated, described her personality type, revealed her interests (listening to music and belly-dancing), outlined her perception of an ideal relationship and pressed the 'search' key.

There were not many people, according to her daughter, who hit the jackpot first time. Scrolling through the dozens of thumbnail images of men looking for women who were 'gentle and caring' or 'fun-loving, confident and smart', Stephanie had clicked on Dominic, a substantial, chess-playing, widowed solicitor who liked reading, travel and listening to music.

It was five years now since Robert, who taught history in an upmarket boys' school, had sneaked off with a fluffy supply teacher, five years since Stephanie had been on her own. Once she had got over the shock of her ex-husband's betrayal, and to fill the gap which the absence of what she had imagined was an entirely satisfactory marriage had created, she had sought out a new interest and found it in a twice-weekly belly-dancing class that got her out of the house. Between her full-time job, caring for her affectionate King Charles spaniel with whom she carried on a one-sided conversation, and practising her new hobby, her time was fully occupied.

Having at first approached each other tentatively in a local wine bar, she and Dominic had got on like a house on fire. Any initial shyness on her part – it was a long time since she had dated – had been dispelled by Dominic's kindness and his warm personality. It was a level playing field and together they went to concerts and restaurants, walked on the Heath near which Dominic lived, and discovered, among other things, that they shared similar birthdays and that each of them had a daughter. He would not let her pay for anything. It was not until Stephanie began to feel, much to Gail's delight, not only safe, but that there could indeed be life after Robert, that she invited Dominic home to dinner.

Although she had never been a great cook and since she had been on her own didn't bother too much, picking up something from the supermarket on the way home from school, the menu she decided upon was ambitious. Individual cheese soufflés would precede the crown roast of lamb with a herb crust and would be followed by raspberry pavlova. Her heart, for some reason, fluttering like a young girl's, she spring-cleaned the terraced house left to her (together with the mortgage) by Robert, got out her recipe books and, admonishing herself to 'act her age', put a couple of candles on the kitchen table.

When Dominic arrived, his face almost hidden by yard-long red roses for which she did not have a tall enough vase, he kissed her firmly on the mouth, arousing sensations that over the past five years had become alien. Leaving him in the living room, where he made himself comfortable in the armchair and switched on the TV, she went into the kitchen where she put the flowers in a plastic bucket, struggled with a bottle of Côtes du Rhône and, as the recipe dictated, set the soufflés in their ramekin dishes in a bain-marie and slid them gently into the oven. When they were risen to perfection and would, like time, wait for no man, she announced, her voice urgent, that dinner was ready.

'Hang on,' his eyes were fixed on the screen. 'Arsenal have given away a free kick!'

By the time he took his seat at the kitchen table, the cheese soufflés had collapsed. Singing her culinary praises Dominic seemed not to notice. The crown roast of lamb had been cooked to perfection, although it was not for her to say so. While he ate it, leaving a clean plate, he reminisced about his late wife, a keen horticulturalist who was never happier than when she was pottering about the large garden or bottling and preserving the fruits of her labours.

When Stephanie enquired could he manage a little more of the lamb, Dominic consulted his Rolex before stroking her bare arm warmly and looking steadfastly into her eyes. She thought he was about to say something.

'What's for pudding?' Something in his voice triggered alarm bells in her head as he handed her his empty plate. 'Just going to check the score.'

Stephanie thought about the pavlova with its chantilly cream and its egg whites whisked laboriously by hand. She opened the fridge where the pale cloud of meringue reposed in its raspberry splendour then shut it again firmly. Picking up the fruit bowl she set it before Dominic on the table and watched as an expression of disappointment, like that of a thwarted child, scudded briefly over his face.

He selected an apple. 'Do you mind if I take this inside?'

Clearing the remains of the dinner which, if you counted the planning and the shopping, it had taken her almost two days to make, she saw herself, in a moment of clarity, dreaming up puddings and listening to the disembodied voice of the football commentator ad infinitum. Dismissing the idea from her head, she thought what a good life she had made for herself since Robert had walked out of it, with her circle of like-minded friends, her rewarding job, her cosy house and her dog. Belly-dancing over to the dresser, she picked up her mobile and, with a smile of relief on her face, telephoned Gail.

O Sole Mio

2013

William Lightfoot sat at the table for one overlooking the lake, which he had occupied for the first two weeks in June for the past five years. Since Helen had died, leaving him on his own, it was simpler to contact the Hotel Bella Vista as soon as his fork was out of the Christmas pudding than it was to wade through the sea of unsolicited offers of tours and sea voyages to exotic destinations that came through the letterbox of his Sussex cottage, a five-minute walk from the bank that he had managed for almost fifteen years.

Snapping open the napkin he had earlier fashioned into a crisp white fan, Alfredo, the waiter, laid it reverently across William's well-pressed chinos, and unconsciously humming a few bars of the popular Italian love song, 'O Sole Mio', handed him the menu.

'*Carrots cream soup* ...' '*Grilled sliced sodfish* ...' '*Goffredo potatoes* ...'

Looking round the familiar dining room as Alfredo went in

search of the wine into which he had made inroads the previous evening, William took surreptitious stock of his dining companions. The table next to his was usually occupied by two English women, a frail mother and her suntanned, widowed (according to Alfredo) daughter of indeterminate age who had been visiting the Hotel Bella Vista for at least as long as he. Tonight, to his surprise, the younger woman was on her own. Acknowledging her presence with a courteous nod – William considered cross-table gossip to be ill mannered – he wondered whether, dinner being over and in the absence of her mother who usually accompanied her, she would make her way to the nightly *passeggiata*, joining the strolling crowds to gaze in the windows of the silver shops with their enticing trinkets.

Pouring the purple Bardolino into his glass with as much panache as if it had been a vintage claret, Alfredo, with whom William had become friendly over the years, followed his glance to the vacant place at the adjacent table.

'The signora is sick,' he confided.

Averting his gaze hurriedly and looking out at the limpid lake, at the sailboats and the car ferry, which plied its regular way to the terracotta roofs, the steeple and the gentle cypresses of the opposite shore, William ordered the 'carrots cream soup' followed by the 'sodfish' and reviewed his existence, which once had been suffused not so much with the precious metals of the beguiling silver shops, but with the golden aura of love. After five years, while still unable to come to terms with the fact that no one, not even his children who led their own frenetic lives, really needed him, he had learned to live with it.

His annual two weeks in Bellagio, where the tranquillity was food for the soul, and the beauty of the surroundings a panacea for the heartache that had become part and parcel of his existence, were a godsend. All winter, as the white aconites were replaced by sweet-smelling jonquils and finally by the roses that bloomed around their cottage and which Helen had loved to dead-head – he could see her now with her Sussex trug – he looked forward to the simple comforts of the white bedroom, with its diaphanous curtains and faded watercolours of the lake, from the window of which he could see the landing stage with its curved awning and its glass visitor information booth with its timetables and its clock. The mornings, after a leisurely breakfast, taken on his minuscule balcony amid the familiar noises of slammed doors, running taps and laughter provoked by shared intimacies from which he was excluded, were reserved for sightseeing. They were the forerunners, the *antipasti*, of his day.

Taking the ferry with the sturdy backpackers, the families with young children and the oblivious lovers, he allowed himself to be transported to ancient islands with their monasteries, their classical gardens and spectacular parks which – although there was no longer anyone to share them with – never failed to delight. While the nearby attractions disposed of the morning hours, each one to be dissipated, the magic of the sights and sounds, the natural splendour of the surroundings, were decimated by the dull ache of his isolation.

'How was the fish, signore?'

Dragged back from his daydreams, William regarded his empty plate. 'Excellent! The fish was excellent.'

Smiling as happily as if he had caught the 'sodfish' himself, Alfredo removed his plate and brushed the tablecloth, as if his life depended upon the removal of every last crumb, before setting before him the hotel's signature dish of home-made pannacotta topped with a giant strawberry.

On his way out of the dining room William intercepted with a pang an unmistakably passionate glance that passed between a honeymoon couple in the centre of the room. Remembering things past, he tried not to dwell too closely on the innuendoes implicit in the look. It was too painful. Averting his gaze, he stared straight ahead to where Alfredo stood to attention at the door of the dining room.

'*Buona notte,* signore,' there were beads of perspiration from his evening exertions on Alfredo's forehead.

'*Buona notte,* signora.'

Glancing round, William saw that the widow from the next table who had finished her dinner at the same time as he, was covering her bare shoulders with a gossamer stole and making for the street and the *passeggiata.*

'*Buona notte,* Alfredo.'

Hesitating only for a moment, William realised that although Alfredo had gone into his familiar rendering of 'O Sole Mio', the words that he put urgently to the tune were Elvis Presley's: '*It's now or never ... Come hold me tight ... Kiss me my darling ... Be mine tonight ...*'

Their eyes met only for a moment as William, straightening his shoulders and summoning up his resolve, followed the bobbing blond ponytail and the clacking heels of the widow from the next table through the glass doors of the Hotel Bella Vista and out into the street.